ADDITIONAL PRAISE FOR
Demon Spirit, Devil Sea

Jam-packed with fascinating science, this suspenseful novel delivers as an entertaining and enlightening read. Our endangered earth is in good hands with Charlene D'Avanzo.

—MEG LITTLE REILLY, author of *We Are Unprepared*

Oceanographer Mara Tusconi takes you into the rough waters of Haida Gwaii where the turbulence on the water isn't the only challenge she faces.

—EMILY JACKSON, cofounder of Jackson Kayaks, two-time world champion freestyle kayaker

⋙ Also by Charlene D'Avanzo ⋘

Cold Blood, Hot Sea | A Mara Tusconi Mystery
(Foreword INDIES 2016 Finalist)

PRAISE FOR
Cold Blood, Hot Sea

Sleuths will have to figure out who done it, but the real crime is the backdrop here: the endless heating of a fragile planet.
—BILL McKIBBEN, author of *Eaarth*

Artfully mixing scientific detail with her characters' personal struggles, D'Avanzo creates a tense story that makes it clear: When profits are favored over the health of the planet, we are all at risk.
—JOEANN HART, author of *Float*

…an intriguing whodunit, plenty of tension, and a compelling story that kept me glued to the book for two evenings…I especially loved some of her real Maine characters.
—GEORGE SMITH, author of *A Life Lived Outdoors*
and *George's Outdoor News*

A great read that gives us more to think about than just the plot twists.
—GARY LAWLESS, co-owner of Gulf of Maine Books

A page-turner set in Maine's picturesque working waterfront where lobsters aren't the only ones feeling the heat.
—KAY HENRY, cofounder, Northern Forest Canoe Trail
and Mad River Canoe

Paddlers will love this book's hero—an oceanographer who uses her kayak to thwart climate change deniers.
—LEE BUMSTED, registered Maine Sea Kayak Guide and author
of *Hot Showers! Maine Coast Lodging for Sea Kayakers and Sailors*

DEMON SPIRIT
DEVIL SEA

Charlene D'Avanzo
A MARA TUSCONI MYSTERY

Demon Spirit, Devil Sea

©2017 Charlene D'Avanzo

ISBN: 978-1-63381-109-6

front cover and map design by
Rick Whipple, Sky Island Studio

designed and produced by
Maine Authors Publishing
Rockland, Maine
www.maineauthorspublishing.com

Printed in the United States of America

This series is dedicated to scientists struggling to understand the extraordinary complex phenomena associated with climate change.

AUTHOR'S NOTE

THIS FICTIONAL STORY IS BASED ON AN ACTUAL EVENT. With the Haida Nation's consent, in 2012 U.S. entrepreneur Russ George dumped a hundred tons of iron sulfate into waters off the Haida Gwaii archipelago fifty miles west of British Columbia. George promised that resulting plankton blooms would enhance salmon numbers and provide money from carbon credits. Neither happened. While many oceanographers decried George's experiment as a violation of international treaties on ocean pollution and a moratorium on geoengineering, no United Nations science team from Maine visited the Haida Nation to investigate the event.

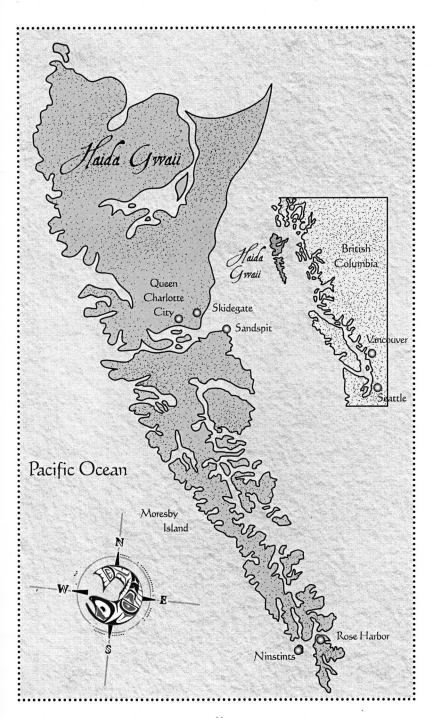

Haida Gwaii

Haida Gwaii

British Columbia

Queen Charlotte City

Skidegate

Sandspit

Vancouver

Seattle

Pacific Ocean

Moresby Island

N

W E

S

Ninstints

Rose Harbor

DEMON SPIRIT
DEVIL SEA

1

A COCKTAIL OF FEAR AND FURY BUBBLED UP FROM MY belly and coated my tongue—taste of cold metal. I slammed a neoprene-gloved hand against the jammed lever at my hip. Did it again. Glanced back.

The offending rudder sat limp and useless on top of the kayak's stern.

"Worthless piece of *junk!*"

Like a racehorse, the kayak found the riptide and leapt ahead. My head snapped back, ponytail whacked my neck. I jerked to attention, gasped as icy wind fingers grazed windblown cheeks. Ahead and sixty degrees off starboard on Augustine Island's tip, waves smashed into boulders, spray leapt skyward.

Augustine, our campsite for the night. I could not—absolutely would not—fly right by.

The situation was dire. Without a working rudder on a long, skinny kayak, I was helpless against Haida Gwaii's relentless current and wind. At lightning speed, the angry, unfeeling sea would sweep me from safety and away from any living soul.

I am a woman alone in a cockpit inches from deadly cold water three thousand feet below.

North Pacific Ocean. Vast. Frigid. Deep.

I'd kayaked Maine's coast for years, but New England offshore didn't hold a paddle to the misleadingly named Pacific.

The boat hit an eddy, wobbled, and slowed. I patted the deck like it was a horse and whooshed out the breath I'd been holding. Vigilant about tipping over, I used the paddle as an outrigger to position the boat sideways to the current, and squinted at the backs of five kayakers. Bouncing on waves, paddles seesawing from side to side, they were tiny against the blue-black sea. Harvey Allison was easy to spot in her banana-yellow boat. *I* should be right there—stroking alongside my fellow oceanographer and best friend. I'd worry about the ton of fieldwork we faced. She'd joke about my lists and schedules. I'd pretend to be indignant.

But the Haida watchman we'd hired to motor us from Kinuk Island to Augustine had gotten stuck god knew where with a broken outboard. Pacing Kinuk's beach, I'd jumped on plan number two. We'd join a couple of women on their Kinuk-to-Augustine kayak tour. Easy two-mile paddle, I said. We'd have plenty of time to sample fish in Augustine's Eagle River.

A runaway kayak fifty miles off the coast of British Columbia was categorically not part of my plan.

I willed Harvey to look at me. She twisted in my direction. Her kayak jiggled. She flapped her paddle.

"Sorry, girl," I said.

Like mamma duck, the kayak guide led his little pod away from me. I glared at his back and tried the turnaround ploy on him.

It didn't work. The metal taste in my mouth turned hot. A half-hour into our expedition, this Bart character guide leaves me—in *his* piece-of-junk defective kayak? Harvey must have pleaded with him to get me. But he couldn't leave four novice kayakers scared and paddling poorly. Maybe he figured I was an experienced kayaker who wanted to go off on her own.

If he did, it was Davy Jones' locker for me.

My kayak hit a row of waves and nearly threw me over. I leaned toward them and slapped the paddle flat on the sea surface to brace. In forty-five-degree water, hypothermia could paralyze me in minutes. In the too-big outfitter's wetsuit, I'd be dead in fifteen.

Drowned.

Suddenly, I could not breathe. Lungs on fire, bands tight-ened around my chest. Drowning, my greatest terror. I shook my head, grunted like a wrestler, sucked in air, willed fear away.

Squaring my body against the foot supports, I dipped the paddle into the water. Hard right, *pull*. Left, keep 'er stable.

Hit Augustine Island. My god, just hit the blessed island.

Hard right, *pull*.

Augustine's tip was still ahead on my starboard side, but the speeding kayak would come up on it fast.

I clawed at the water. "Right. Come *on*. Right, *right*."

No good. At high tide, the current carried me at racing speed—in the wrong direction. Worse, the kayak banged up and down against building waves, making rudderless steering a joke.

Fear bubbled up again like vomit. I spat it out.

"Get a grip, Tusconi," I said. "Figure out how to fix the friggin' rudder."

I pictured the mechanism. Stainless steel cable ran from the rudder to foot braces inside the cockpit. The lift-line cable at my hip allowed paddlers to raise and lower the rudder. What could go wrong?

Lots. Lift lines jammed. Cables broke. Rudder brackets twisted. Things I could repair on dry land. But out here in the cockpit there was absolutely nothing to do but try like hell to reach that island.

Hard right, *pull*. Left, keep 'er stable.

At five knots, the kayak surged straight ahead—not one bit to starboard. And I knew why.

Back at the Maine Oceanographic Institute, I'd studied Haida Gwaii's currents. Longer than wide, Augustine Island protected Kinuk's inner bay from the Pacific's ravages. The outer bay, where I happened to be seated, was a very different story. A paddler dumb enough to venture out there'd be trapped in current that raced past the island's tip.

If I zipped past Augustine, the jig would be up. The big ocean's crashing waves twice the length of my boat, icy water, sharks—I'd be at the mercy of all of it.

What suddenly lay ahead erased all thoughts of currents and sharks. I squinted, squeezed my eyes shut, popped them open. The Maine kayaker's nightmare.

Fog.

The clammy murk smothered me in an instant. Splashing waves, sky, light. Vanished. Replaced by a wet, woolly gray. My heart beat fast against layers of fleece, paddling jacket, and life vest. Breathing fast and hard, I swiveled and squinted in every direction. The vapor was so dense there was no telling where miasma ended and sea began. Waves booming against rocks said the island was tantalizingly close, but dead blind in fog, I couldn't see a thing.

The scientist in me kicked in again. Water and air warmed by July's sun met frigid open ocean. That meant fog. But for once, science couldn't help me at all.

The kayak raced on through the gloom. Too soon, the booms were muted. I'd just slipped past my refuge. My fate was certain—I *would* drift out onto vast ocean in a seventeen-by-two foot boat.

Panicked, I hyperventilated. My gasps echoed back in the murk.

I shoved the useless paddle into deck bungees, closed my eyes, and tried to slow my breath. In. This could *not* happen. Out. I would *not* drowned in the element I devoted my life to and loved. In. There'd be *no* headline—"Maine scientist dead in sea kayak off Haida Gwaii, the Queen Charlotte Islands"—in my hometown's *Spruce Harbor Gazette*. Out. I'd *never* leave Angelo, my godfather and only family, alone.

I blinked and frowned at a bizarre notion. Did this occur for a reason? Had the Raven—the native Haida's trickster—set me up to drown? I shook my head. Spiteful spirits did not exist. If someone wanted me dead, the trickster had to be human.

A half-mile behind my stern at Augustine Island's tip, ghosts of boulders emerged through wispy fog. I faced my ocean fate, raised my paddle overhead, and shrieked at the Haida spirits, Jesus, any damn thing that might hear me.

2

THE CALL, HIGH AND PIERCING, ANSWERED FROM BEHIND. I twisted toward the screech and nearly fell out of my boat. Close on my port side, a streak—long, sleek, and blood-red—flew by. Behind it an oval eye, black as liquid night, stared and morphed into a glowing sphere. The rest was a black blur longer than my kayak. Stranger still, the thing radiated a warm glow that evaporated an envelope of fog around it.

In an instant, it was gone. I blinked. Only fog to port. I craned my neck to starboard and behind as far as I dared. Nothing.

Fog and fear had messed with my mind. Red and black fog-zapping creatures decidedly did not exist except in fairy tales.

Using my paddle as an outrigger again, I struggled against waves that smacked the boat, the impossible I'd witnessed, fear racing through my veins. A distant sound wormed its way into my consciousness. I jerked to attention and strained to hear it over sloshes and smacks.

The friendly drone of a motor.

Any Maine boater knows that fog amplified sound—especially low-frequency, long-wavelength tones like foghorns.

And boat motors.

I closed my eyes, slowed my breathing, and focused every synapse on the possibility of a distant low rumble. Nothing but the slap of my damn boat against the water.

Heard it again.

An unmistakable drone grew louder. I tried to turn toward it and came close to tipping the boat. The beat-up dinghy pushed through the fog and slid alongside, motor sputtering. A strapping man, hair blue-black as a raven's—but very much human—sat in the stern, one hand on the outboard's handle. With the other, he swung a paint-chipped oar over his gunwale. I grabbed my end and our boats touched.

From peril to human contact in a flash—that was fast, even for me.

I gasped and managed, "Goddamn."

Silent, my rescuer studied my face.

"Who *are* you?"

His voice, deep and deliberate, carried a Canadian lilt. "William. Kinuk Island Watchman. I was supposed to motor you to Augustine." He tipped his head toward his stern. "Got stuck in Rose Harbor with a dead outboard. I'm *so* very sorry."

The young man's dark, gentle eyes searched mine. Warmth flowed through me.

"Um, ah…hey, marine motors take a beating. Thank god you're here now."

Grayish bilge water sloshed over William's cracked rubber boots. Generations of peeling paint colored the dinghy's interior green, white, and blue. Of course, my tub was no prize either. I pointed a thumb over my shoulder. "Rudder's jammed."

William pushed my boat forward. The kayak wobbled as he fiddled with the rudder. From the mumbles, I guessed the thing was good and jammed. Finally, he called out "beauty!" as he yanked the offending appendage down into the water, and let go. I positioned my left foot on the brace, swept my paddle across the water's surface, and grinned as the kayak swung to the right and faced him.

"I'm Mara. You saved my life, um…"

William held up his hand—and as if he rescued floating maidens every day—acknowledged my gratitude with a slight nod. "Mara, head back to the bay. I'll follow 'til you're out of the fog and on your way to the campsite."

In front of the puttering dinghy, I paddled hard and plowed through three-footers with ease. When we reached the calmer waters of Kinuk Bay, William motored alongside.

"You okay now?"

I grinned and hand-pumped my paddle overhead.

"Great. See you on Augustine. I'm helping Bart with the kayak group." William cranked his motor. The dingy wallowed. He sped off with a roar.

I followed his wake. Alive, in control, and feeling strong, I drank in the seascape as the kayak slid through blue-green ripples tipped in silver that reached the western horizon. I let loose my hair and whooped as the salty breeze whipped it behind. To glide through this maze of islands and bays completely beyond the reach of man-made noise like traffic or neon, halogen, and every other kind of artificial light—this was a sea kayaker's dream.

I could turn my back, for now, on the dangerous, indifferent sea.

To port, a flank of moss-draped cedars hid the rest of Augustine's dripping rainforest. Gusts of wind bathed me in rich, earthy perfume. I stopped paddling, closed my eyes, and filled my lungs with the manna of life and time.

My kayak slid up the rocky shingle beside the other boats. Harvey ran over, grabbed the forward loop, pulled me higher onto dry land, and sat on the bow to steady the boat. I climbed out.

Harvey scaled the cobbles in two strides. I pulled her tight into a bear hug, inhaled her favorite shampoo. Maine's Burt's Bees, of course.

I'm not the bear-hug type. Harvey stepped back and scanned to check for damaged body parts. Satisfied, she placed her hands on my shoulders. Her gray eyes searched mine. "Mara. You vanished. I was *so* worried. What—?"

I gestured toward William's dinghy. He'd dragged it above the waterline. "William. Saved my butt."

Harvey glanced at the banged-up dinghy, back at me. She tipped her head. "Striking guy."

"Come on. He's twenty years younger than you."

Even though she looked my age, Harvey had just celebrated her fortieth birthday.

She tossed her expertly shaped bob. "Thanks for the reminder. I'll remember it when you blow out nine more candles."

"Seriously, Harve, really, really sorry to worry you." I walked to my kayak's stern. "Rudder got stuck." On both knees, I moved the thing up and down. "Don't see what's wrong." I opened my mouth to tell Harvey about the mirage, but closed it. The time wasn't right.

Harvey jiggled my kayak with her foot. "Your rudder didn't work. So, *what* happened?"

The aroma of grilled fish wafted our way. Down the beach, a little clutch of women stood around a campfire, sandwiches in hand. My stomach reminded me it was lunchtime.

"Remember the current we talked about where Kinuk Bay meets the Pacific? Twenty-plus knots? I got caught in it." I stood and wiped gritty hands on my thighs. "The tide raced out. Took my rudderless kayak with it."

Harvey's eyebrows shot up. "What—"

"Tell you more later. Okay? We've got to figure out what we're doing, and I need something warm to eat."

We picked our way across smooth cobbles that covered the shingle beach. Harvey rested her hand on my shoulder like she was worried she'd lose me again.

"Same plan?" I asked

"Yes. I was worried—besides about you, of course—because Bart knows slightly more than zero about counting fish, even though he said he did. Incredible. How can people exaggerate like that? So I cornered William right after he pulled up. Thank God he's done salmon counts and can explain the Haida's methods. Now you're here, we can motor around to the river, review their techniques, look at data. Get this show on the road."

Harvey was a get-the-show-on-the-road kind of gal.

"Point number two for William," I said.

We reached the campfire. Three women introduced themselves to me.

One of them, Gwen, licked her fingers before she spoke. "Sounds like you folks have work to do. Bart's taking us for a hike."

William handed me a plate. "Have a salmon burger. Are you all right now, Mara?"

His dark eyes locked with mine for an instant.

"Um, terrific. Thanks to you, of course."

"Good. When you're finished, we'll take the boat around to Eagle River. There's a hut where we store everything. You can see our equipment, go over our methods, whatever you want."

Harvey handed me a bag of chips. "Sounds perfect, William. And from what I hear, you're hero for the day."

A huge smile made crinkles around his eyes. "Never been called a hero before."

William held the dinghy while we stepped in. Given the grungy bilge water, I was happy to be wearing paddling wet shoes. From the way Harvey tiptoed to the stern, I was sure she thought the same thing.

We sped along Augustine's eastern shore. Above the motor's drone William yelled, "Eagle flows west, into the Pacific.

Ancestors named it "the river that never sleeps" because salmon run pretty much year 'round."

I called out, "What's running now?"

"Coho. That's what we're counting."

We rounded the point where I'd screamed like a crazy woman and witnessed the bizarre vision only an hour earlier. It seemed like a scene from a bad movie. I shook my head to erase the image.

William beached the boat at the mouth of Eagle River. I hopped out, looked upstream, out at the Pacific, back upstream.

"I've never seen a trout or salmon stream like this," I said.

William tipped his head to the side. "What do you mean?"

"In Maine, rivers and streams that carry salmon are rocky and run fast. This looks like a wide, slow-moving, meandering river with a pebbly bottom."

"Eagle flows fast after a rainstorm, then it slows down."

"Makes sense. Augustine's watershed's small."

Harvey interrupted the geology lesson "William, why don't you give us a quick overview of the iron, ah, experiment."

William clapped his hands together. He spoke quickly. "Sure. We chartered a ship and added the iron about twenty-five kilometers out there." He gestured toward the Pacific. "Last week was the third time."

"Iron slurry, right? How much?" I asked.

"Yes. Two hundred tons."

I'd read the number. But standing on the beach, it was hard to imagine *anyone* dumping that volume of cherry-red slurry into the stunning archipelago's water. I tried not to show my disbelief. "My goodness. That's a lot."

"Mr. Grant said we needed that much."

Roger Grant, in my opinion, was a slimy businessman who'd conned the Haida into giving him a load of money for a bogus scheme. I'd have to figure out a polite way to voice my concern.

"We'll talk more about this later," Harvey said. "But give us a quick overview what Grant claims about iron and your salmon."

William tipped up his chin. "You know. Iron fertilizes the ocean, more salmon run up the rivers, and we make more money selling fish."

I looked at the ground, pressed my lips together, and counted to five. We would confront the whole iron thing with the Haida environmental council the following day.

Harvey jumped into diplomat mode with an "okay, thanks." A brilliant chemist, she delighted in the glorious complexity of marine biogeochemistry. Pour iron slurry into the ocean and catch more salmon? Too simple and quite likely wrong. A vein in her neck throbbed.

William said, "I understand the UN hired you, Dr. Allison, and Dr. Tusconi to study what happened out here with our iron project. Why is that?"

Noting the "Dr. Tusconi," I used my professional ocean-ographer's voice. "Plus Dr. Ted McKnight. He's arriving in Kinuk today with our research equipment for the cruise. We're all from the Maine Oceanographic Institute. As you know, the UN considers dumping tons of iron sulfate into the ocean an international violation. They want an unbiased team—people not from this region—to visit the site and duplicate some of your sampling to verify results."

William opened his mouth as if to reply, but Harvey cut him off. "We'll talk more about this tomorrow on the ship when Ted's there. Okay?"

William's fists were clenched. "But—"

"Lots of work to do now, William," Harvey said.

He relaxed his hands. "All right." William pointed to a shed above the high tide line. "I'll go over how we count fish."

We followed him up the beach. "We want to get in the water and survey a reach ourselves," I said. "When was your last count?"

"Yesterday."

"Good. We'll compare our data with yours."

"The number of fish changes a lot from day to day."

Harvey and I glanced at each other.

3

IN THE SHED, WILLIAM SHOWED US THE EQUIPMENT HE AND an assistant used on the river. He picked up a device with wheels and revolving metal cups. "We have two current meters."

I nodded. "Stream gauge?"

"It's upstream. Each time we count fish, we record river height."

In the corner, a wooden box overflowed with dive gear—wetsuits, booties, hoods, gloves, masks, and snorkels. Clipboards, waterproof paper, and markers lay on a shelf above.

"And your counting methods?" Harvey asked.

"We enter the river from downstream and slowly move up. Whoever's in the water calls out data to the other person walking alongside. Numbers of salmon and length. We estimate size from a ruler attached to a dive glove."

"One person covers the full width?" I asked

"Yes. The river isn't that wide."

"Time of day?"

"After sunset and on moonless or cloudy nights."

Harvey looked at her dive watch. "It's about four now. Let's go back, eat, and be here at six. Moonrise is around nine."

At camp, wood smoke laced with aromas of grilled salmon and roasted potatoes zinged my taste buds, despite the late lunch.

William gestured toward a log bench. "Sit. There's a story about Salmon Boy I think you'll all enjoy."

Harvey and I and the three other women lined up on the log and tucked in.

William stood with his back to the ocean. Medium-tall and athletic, he wore slim-waisted, worn jeans. Unlike other Haida people I'd met, his face was delicately sculptured with fine features—thin nose, hint of cheekbones, delicate lips. In shadow, his eyes were chocolate-black and when he turned, long lashes stood out against the sky.

William spoke with confidence and dignity beyond his early twenty-odd years. He had the full attention of each woman on the log, including me.

"Long ago, there was a boy who didn't revere salmon. No matter what his parents tried to teach him, the boy walked on the bodies of fish they caught or kicked them out of the way. He said the fish tasted bad and wouldn't eat them. One day, the boy was caught by a big current and drowned. His spirit found the Salmon People, and he followed them far out to sea and turned into a salmon. Two years later, in the spring, he returned to the very river he'd left. But now he was a salmon. His mother fished that river and caught him in her net. She dumped him on the ground and was about to kill him when she saw the necklace he wore. It was the very same one she'd given her son. Very carefully, she carried the salmon back home. There, over seven days, he shed his salmon skin and was human again. To his dying day, Salmon Boy taught his people, especially young boys, everything he'd learned about this fish honored by the Haida people."

The fire crackled and waves sloshed up and down the beach.

Gwen said, "Lovely story, William."

"What a great way to teach Haida children a love of nature," I added.

William nodded quickly. "It is. When I was a kid, an elder would make a fire on the beach—evenings just like this—and tell us these tales. There are so many—the woman who married a bear, how the whole earth flooded, the man who became an octopus."

And glowing creatures that fly?

William pointed down the beach. "Later tonight, we'll set up a sauna beyond Bart there. A teepee made of tarps and line. We pour water onto hot rocks from the campfire, and the teepee fills with steam. At about ten, when Mara and Harvey get back from their snorkel."

Five pairs of eyes watched him stroll away.

Gwen turned toward us. "Snorkel?"

"In a river on the other side of the island. We're counting fish."

"Sounds cold. Better you than me."

"Have you kayaked before?" I asked.

"Never done anything like this. We're only here one night. Tomorrow, the hot pools back on Kinuk'll be heaven. Then we fly home to Vancouver."

Harvey asked, "Is this overnight kayak/hot-pool trip popular?"

"You bet. Folks on Kinuk do well with it, I'd imagine. Looks like they expect us to put up our own tents, though. I need help with that."

Gwen's friend offered, and the trio left for the tent site.

Harvey waited until they were out of earshot, straddled the log, and leaned toward me. "Okay, girlfriend. *What happened?*"

I swung my leg over the log to face her and described my hopeless fight with the outgoing current—how the kayak slapped against the waves, swept past Augustine Island's tip, was awash in fog.

Harvey's eyes widened with each step in the saga. "My god, Mara. Haida Gwaii's one of the windiest places on earth. There's a twenty-five-foot tidal range. With an outgoing tide, all that water sweeping past the island?" She put a hand on my arm. "You're incredibly lucky William caught up with you."

"There's more. The most bizarre thing happened right before William motored up. You won't believe it."

She sat back and crossed her arms. "I can believe almost anything about you, Mara."

"Promise you won't say I'm crazy."

Significant eye roll. "For goodness sake, what is it?"

I leaned closer and lowered my voice. "I'd swept past the tip of Augustine. There was no hope of paddling back. I was beyond panic. Out of nowhere, this piercing shriek came from behind. It scared the hell out of me."

"I'd imagine."

"Wait. Something blood-red zipped by my port side. Its eye—super black—looked at me. The rest was a blur longer than my boat. And the thing glowed."

Harvey's gray eyes were huge. "Damn."

I sat up and brushed sand off my hands. "Of course, it wasn't real. Adrenaline does weird things to your brain. I think it's called Tachypyschia. Time slows or speeds up. People see things rush by in a blur. I'm sure that's what it was."

"Maybe."

Not at all the reaction I expected. "What'd you mean?"

"Think about all the people who see a bright light right before they die. Thousands of identical descriptions from around the world. Even ancient Greeks wrote about it. Seems like there's really something there."

I shook my head. "Nope. There's a biological explanation. I'll send you the link for the paper. It's tunnel vision caused by blood in the eye and oxygen depletion. So-called spiritual experiences all have scientific explanations."

William walked up. He'd heard what I said.

"For Haida, the physical—what you call real—is only one part of our experience. We know animals are powerful, their spirits potent. There's constant talk between us and creatures. Our myths and tales are full of it."

"Do you have a favorite myth?" Harvey asked.

"The story of how Raven brought light into the world. Want to hear it?"

"Sure," we said in unison.

William sat cross-legged on the ground. We swung around to face him. He spoke softly. "In the beginning the world was dark. The Raven was tired of bumping into things. He learned that an old man had a wonderful treasure in his house. It was the light of the universe and hidden in a box inside many other boxes. Through complicated twists and turns of deception, Raven stole the light. It was in the form of a beautiful, incandescent ball, and the bird flew off with it. Raven flew high and far and marveled at mountains and rivers below he'd never seen."

Our storyteller cocked his head from side to side and peered at the ground. He leaned in.

"But Raven was so busy looking at this beauty he didn't see Eagle until that bird was nearly on him. Raven dropped the ball, which shattered on the earth below. Some of the pieces bounced back into the sky, where they remain to this day as the moon and stars. That is how light came into the universe." William leaned back on his arms.

"What a great story," Harvey said. "Maybe your ravens symbolize the space-time continuum."

I looked at Harvey like she was nuts.

William raised an eyebrow. "What do you mean?"

"Einstein. Space occupies three dimensions and time is the fourth. Ravens have the normal three dimensions—height, width, and depth. Maybe their flight represents the fourth. In that way, they'd be part of the physical world but not bound to it."

"Is there a fifth dimension?" William asked.

Harvey shrugged. "Possibly. Some physicists say there are ten."

William stood and brushed off his jeans. "That's wild. Funny. Those physicists would probably scoff at the Haida's beliefs, which seem a whole lot simpler than ten dimensions."

It was time to bring things back to earth. "I wasn't worried about ten dimensions out there on the ocean. I was cursing fates that handed me a kayak with a useless rudder."

"I know," William tossed another log on the fire. "I heard you."

I laughed. "I'll bet you did. They probably heard me all the way back in Vancouver. I was shrieking like a banshee."

"In a dense fog, Raven is a better guide than sound."

Did he mean Raven led him to me? He stared so intensely, it seemed he could read my mind. I shivered as if an ice cube had run down my back.

Down the beach, Bart knelt beside a kayak.

"Excuse me," William said. "I need to do something before we leave." He headed in Bart's direction.

I waited until he was out of earshot. "Harve, do you think William actually believes the Haida legends or tells myth stories just because tourists enjoy them?"

She wrinkled her nose. "What I think is that *he's* sincere and *you're* cynical."

"About animal myths, I agree. Mrs. McCarthy's fault."

"And Mrs. McCarthy is…?"

"My first grade teacher."

"I gotta hear this."

"Before Mom and Dad moved to Spruce Harbor to help set up Maine Oceanographic, we lived in western Maine. Out there, moose were all over the place. One day, a young one walked right by our classroom. We ran to the window to watch. I asked why the moose was alone, and Mrs. McCarthy said its parents had to be close because they lived in big family groups."

Harvey looked skyward. "I'm missing something."

"At dinner that night Dad told me Mrs. McCarthy was wrong. Moose *don't* live in family groups. We'd seen a yearling its pregnant mother chased away. I couldn't believe it."

"That momma moose abandon their yearlings?"

"'Course not. That what my teacher said was incorrect. She must've known it was."

"Come on. You're way too hard on your teacher. You guys were, what, six?"

I raked my fingers through tangled hair and picked off a red snarl. "Doesn't matter if we were two. You *don't* make up nice stories about animals to protect kids. That's just wrong."

"Mara, wasn't it Einstein who said 'if you want your children to be intelligent, read them fairy tales'?"

I pushed up off the log. "Because they use their imagination. But that's very different from what Mrs. McCarthy did."

Down the beach William spoke to Bart, who stood, hands on hips.

"Looks like Bart's getting a talking-to that not's working," I said. William left Bart and strode farther down the beach. It was my turn to vent. "Meet you by the dinghy in a couple of minutes, Harve."

The guide knelt on the far side of the kayaks. Lined up in perfect order, the boats looked like crayon-colored sardines. He appeared to be fiddling with foot pegs in one of them.

I walked over. "Bart."

Bart jerked his head up so fast he nearly toppled over. Thick ebony hair cut straight across his forehead framed large almond eyes and rugged features that hinted at Asian and Siberian ancestry. A black T-shirt with sleeves cut off at the shoulders hugged his chest, and his washed-out jeans were wet and sandy at the ankles.

"Do you know why I was late?"

The guide stood, slowly. He was several inches shorter than my five-seven but made up for his height with bravado. The T-shirt showed off impressive biceps, and tattoos of long, slithery creatures ran down both arms. He crossed them.

"William told me."

I waited for an apology. But he only looked down, out over the ocean, anywhere but at me.

"Bart, have you ever paddled at the other end of the island?"

He shrugged and mumbled, "No."

"Well, let me tell you. The current's a riptide. With a rudder, it's fierce, without one, hopeless. I could've died out there."

He jutted out his chin and glanced at me. "Sorry."

"Has the rudder stuck before on that kayak?"

"*No*. And I checked them all before we left."

"So, what happened?"

He shook his head and shrugged. "Don't know."

I don't avoid confrontation, but we had fish to count and it was obvious I wasn't going to get more out of the guide. Needless to say, the exchange was less than satisfactory.

I snatched a towel from my kayak's forward hatch, left Bart on the beach, and marched off to meet Harvey and William. We were halfway down Kinuk Bay when the dinghy's motor coughed, then shut down.

William swiveled toward the silent motor. "Not *again*."

Harvey and I eyed our watches and each other. William hovered over the motor and muttered in what I assumed was

Haida as he tried to bring the errant machine to life. We drifted back toward the campsite on an incoming tide.

Five minutes. Ten. Twelve.

We only had a couple of hours in Eagle River before the nearly full moon slid over the trees and made the salmon too skittish to count. William's unreliable motor was eating away at that window.

Stone-faced, eyes closed, feet in grungy, sloshing water, Harvey perched on her seat. Harvey hated disorder. I knew she was trying to keep calm in a situation she couldn't control.

Me, I checked my watch every thirty seconds.

At fifteen-and-a-half minutes, the motor finally caught and we spend away.

Near the mouth of Eagle River, we jumped out of William's skiff.

Turing around, I gasped. The Pacific Ocean lay before us, entirely unbroken to the south, north, and western horizon, where the orange sun slid down beneath a gaudy rose sky. An amber ribbon skipped across the sea surface and ended at our feet.

"My god, William. People must come out here just to see sunsets."

"They do."

"Hey, you two," Harvey said. "Let's get going."

We helped William pull the dinghy higher onto the shingle.

I pulled off my windbreaker and ran a hand down my bare forearm. "The wetsuits they gave us on Kinuk don't have sleeves. We'll be in the water for a while and we'll need full wetsuits."

"The wooden box in the shed. Take what you need," he said.

We dug out the smallest wetsuits from the bottom off the box and pulled them over our bathing suits.

I fingered a hole in my sleeve. "Not sure about these. They're at least five millimeters thick but look pretty beat up."

Harvey shrugged and stuffed the rest of the dive gear in a beat-up duffle bag. We walked upstream to the reach where William had counted fish the day before.

Offering to go first, I fumbled with fin and mask straps, pulled on the hood and fins, walked backward into the river, and tried to not kick up stones or make quick movements. In the middle of the river, I slid the mask over my hood and eyes, wiggled fingers into the gloves, positioned the snorkel mouthpiece between my teeth, and slipped under the water. Warmed by the August sun, the river wasn't as cold as I expected. But the borrowed wetsuit was too large and cool water instantly seeped down my neck and over my wrists and ankles. Soon I'd be sopping wet.

There wasn't much current, and gentle movement of the fins kept me traveling upstream at a steady rate. Salmon were easy to spot. Long, sleek gray ghosts, they glided through the water like sluggish torpedoes. From above and in the fading light, I could just make out the crimson underbelly of the males. My bulky form didn't seem to bother them. This was nothing like snorkeling Maine's intertidal where cunner and other fish instantly vanished beneath seaweed cover. Maybe the salmon, a food staple for millennia, sensed the Haida's reverence for them.

Reverence for a fisherman's key prey. Did Maine lobstermen feel reverence for theirs? Respect, maybe, gratitude certainly. But reverence was different. Have to think about that more above water.

I slowly crisscrossed the river, surfaced, and called out numbers and lengths to Harvey who walked along on shore.

Sounds from the world of air—wind, a bird, Harvey's voice—disappeared the moment I slipped under the surface.

Seemingly serene, the muted, dense world of water traveled downhill toward the Pacific in slow motion. But here, as in every river and stream, insect larvae cowered in hidey-holes as fish and other predators hovered above them.

After recording the largest number of fish I'd seen so far, Harvey said, "Mara, can't you speed it up?"

I exhaled hard through my snorkel and squirted her.

Halfway through the reach, I stumbled out and handed Harvey the mask and fins.

"H-here." I wind milled my arms.

"Cold?"

I switched direction. "Wetsuit's way too big. I'm soaked."

"Oh, fun."

I tried jumping jacks with moderate success.

Harvey made her way into the river. We had to finish before the moon was fully up. I studied the eastern sky. Harvey called out numbers, slipped below the surface and came up again, but her progress was slow.

She finned toward me, spit out the mouthpiece, and recited the data.

"Harve, I'm worried about the time."

"Christ, Mara. I'm going as fast as I can. More fish up here."

The jungle blocked my view of the sky. I asked William to run back to the beach to check on the moon.

He returned, panting. "You can just make out a bit of light coming up."

Harvey glided to the side and rolled on her back. She let the mouthpiece fall out. "S-six large, ten medium, t-two small. Jesus, I'm frigging cold."

"Hate to say it, but the moon's rising."

"F-fish."

I chortled.

Harvey slid back onto her belly. She finished just as the moon rose over trees bordering the river.

We jogged back to the shed. Inside, William flipped on the battery-operated lantern. Outside, the window cast a dim rectangle of light onto the shingle. Harvey and I toweled off and pulled on the dry pants and shirts we'd brought along.

Harvey rubbed her arms. "Next time, it's coral reef fish."

In the shed we used a calculator to crunch our numbers. William read out the totals and sizes from the previous day.

"Same half-mile reach, same time of day, one day apart," Harvey said. "We counted a total of two hundred and twelve coho. You got about half that. You saw about twenty percent large, sixty medium, the rest small. We got nearly sixty percent large, thirty percent medium, ten percent small. It's only one reach, but the two data sets are very, very different."

William leaned in to read over both sets of numbers. "Like I said, we see big changes from one day to the next."

We flipped through the pages of his notebook.

"The daily disparity you report here isn't surprising," I said. "But you'd need a whopping big change to tell if there's a fertilization effect."

William bit his lip. "Why don't you explain that."

"You're using this river to gauge the iron's impact on salmon density in your streams and rivers generally, right?"

"Right."

I held up the notebook. "Given this variation, in this reach alone you'd consistently have to see fish counts spike to something like three or four hundred day after day to claim an iron effect."

William shelved the notebook. "Raven takes care of us. He'll see to it."

4

WITH SOAKED HAIR AND LITTLE PROTECTION FROM the wind, Harvey and I shivered all the way back to the campsite. We helped William pull the dinghy above the high-tide line.

"I'm sure Bart's got the sauna going," he said. "Why don't you go in, wash off, and warm up?"

He didn't have to ask twice.

Giggles from inside the sauna-teepee told us things were well underway.

Harvey peeled off her shirt and rubbed her arms. "It's *freezing* out here. Inside, quick."

She pulled the teepee flap aside. We both stepped in. In the middle of the tent, a cluster of glowing rocks the size of small bowling balls illuminated a half-circle of grinning faces opposite us. Except for Bart, they were pale outsiders like Harvey and me.

Gwen from Vancouver said, "You can take my place, Mara. I'm pretty well cooked. It's glorious."

The friend beside her agreed. "Me too. Time to cool off."

Harvey and I made room for the exiting women. Their bathing suits had little skirts, and I assumed a nude sauna with men their son's ages would've been uncomfortable. I didn't know if the Haida were modest, but given my increasingly sagging boobs, bathing suits in the sauna were just fine with me.

Bart followed close behind the women, but he didn't acknowledge us. William took Bart's place.

We settled onto the vacated log. I poured fresh water over

my head and used my fingers—with minimal success—to comb out tangles in my long hair. Eyes closed, I surrendered to the comfort of hot steam.

I was nearly asleep when Harvey said, "William, back at Kinuk, before we left yesterday, I saw you working on what looked like a big bird on the bow of a wooden kayak. Did you carve it?"

I popped open my eyes to catch the sparkle in William's as he turned toward Harvey.

"Do you know," he asked, "the Haida have two clans—Eagles and Ravens?"

She nodded.

"And in the world of birds, ravens are known for their intelligence?"

Harvey nodded again.

"Well, I'm a Raven."

Harvey and I laughed.

With the tiniest twitch in the corner of his mouth, William went on. "Before I was a Watchman out here, I apprenticed with a famous carver on Prince of Wales Island. He taught me the craft of Haida boat carving."

"The wood is?" I asked.

"Red Cedar. We use a mix of modern and traditional tools. Even chainsaws." He grinned.

"Well, your work is outstanding," Harvey said.

"Thanks." His tone sharpened. "Before you both leave, I'd like to talk more about the iron fertilizer."

Given my lethargy, this was the last thing I wanted to discuss. But Harvey agreed, out of tact or the need to know I wasn't sure.

William's face showed red in the glow of hot rocks, his eyes a startling white. "You understand why we did it?"

"Why don't you tell us?" she said.

He spoke quickly. "Two things. One is money from carbon credits. Iron makes algae in the ocean bloom. That pulls carbon dioxide from the atmosphere. We get carbon credits."

Harvey kept her eyes on William. I looked down at my hands.

He kept going. "Ah, like we talked about, Roger Grant says the salmon catch will go up."

I felt utterly exhausted. This wasn't the time to debate Grant's wild assertions about the benefits of iron enrichment—named the "Geritol solution" after the old-fashioned, iron-enriched liquid supplement. "He claims that. William, I'm dog-tired. Let's talk about this in the morning on the ship. Okay?"

William pressed his lips together then said, "You traveled yesterday and did a lot today. Of course."

I scanned my now lobster-red body. "Harvey, I'm done. Meet you outside."

"Be there in two minutes."

I was toweling off in the chilly night air when it happened. William screamed, "Out! Get out!"

Explosions from inside the sauna shattered the evening's peace.

Harvey and William plunged through the tent flap like a single torpedo. He landed on top of her and rolled off with a grunt.

I ran over and knelt beside Harvey. "Tell me! Are you all right?"

Harvey groaned and managed to get up on all fours. I steadied her shoulder while she swung her legs around and sat cross-legged.

She coughed. "The rocks." Deep breath. "They blew up. If William hadn't—"

"Gotten you out, red-hot rock shards would've speared your body."

"Yeah."

On his feet, William extended his right leg back and craned his neck to inspect his calf. In the moonlight, blood streamed down his leg, black as squid ink.

Harvey gasped. "Good lord, William. How bad is it?"

He reached down and came up with a blood-smeared palm. "Surface cuts. Nothing serious. If you're not hurt, Dr. Allison, I'll walk down into the water and soak my leg."

"Harvey. I'm fine—because of you. Thank you, William."

"William, before you go," I said, "Rocks don't usually explode inside your saunas, right?"

He hesitated a moment. "They don't. You've got to know which rocks to use, and I picked the right ones. This shouldn't have happened. I am so very sorry."

"Sounds like it wasn't your fault."

"I've got to soak my leg. See you both in the morning."

He turned away. Harvey called after him. "William, thanks again."

The young man limped down the beach, waded into seawater to his knees, and looked up at the moon.

"Guess he's your knight, too," I said. "Are you okay now?"

"He is and yes, I am. It happened so fast I didn't have time to be scared. But Mara, first the kayak's rudder got stuck and now this? Don't you think that's pretty odd?"

"You bet, and Bart was involved in both. Maybe he's a screw-up, I don't know, but it looks like we'll have to be on our guard."

"As if we didn't have enough to deal with," she said.

I helped Harvey to her feet. In moon shadow, we followed the path up to the tent site.

"Harve, those stories William told us about Salmon Boy and Raven?"

"Yeah?"

"Something important there doesn't jibe with this iron project."

"What do you mean?"

"If the Haida are so tuned into nature, why would they pay Roger Grant to dump tons of iron slurry right off their coast? Besides that, Grant's not even a scientist. From what I can tell, he's a reckless entrepreneur."

"You're right. It's illogical. I wish people weren't so damn complicated. So often, they do things you don't expect. We think Maine lobstermen should care that warm seawater is chasing lobster north to Canada. But most deny climate change is even happening."

Boy, did I know that. My cousin Gordy was a Maine lobsterman. We'd gotten a grant for a pilot project to connect fishermen and climate scientists so they could learn from each other. That Gordy and his buddies called our warnings about a hotter planet "a bunch of crap" made the interaction a challenge, to say the least.

Harvey stopped and put her hand on my arm. "Mara, this UN report's very high-profile. We've *got* to do an excellent job, but how little we know about the Haida really, really worries me. As senior scientist, I feel—."

"You'll be a terrific team leader, and we're the perfect team for this. You know that."

"Hmm."

I knew something besides being an outsider was bothering Harvey but didn't have the energy to talk about it right then. "We've had two near-catastrophes today, Harve. The stuck rudder and exploding rocks in the sauna. At the moment, that's what's worrying me."

She blew out a long breath and walked on. "Like you said, Bart was involved in both."

"Right. Of course, that doesn't mean he's to blame. Could be a coincidence."

"Sometimes I wonder if coincidences are God's way of quietly telling us something."

"Harvey, you don't believe in God. You don't even go to church."

"Maybe it's because I'm past forty, but lately when I'm alone in nature, a spiritual sense—I can't put words to it—comes over me." She held out her arms. "Here, in Haida Gwaii, it feels very strong."

I was amazed. Harvey didn't say things like that. "The archipelago's world-famous for kayakers, sailors, birders—outdoor people like that. But *spiritual*?"

"What about your vision, Mara?"

"Like I said, panic makes people imagine things."

We reached the tent site, an elevated spot well protected from the wind, and set up our tents side by side on a thick carpet of moss beneath a cathedral of red cedar and hemlock. Moonlight, nature's flashlight, showered through openings in the canopy. I'd just finished securing my rainfly with stakes when Harvey crawled out of her tent.

She straightened up. "This is an enchanted wood."

Behind her, a cluster of lantern-lit dome tents glowed in the gloom of majestic giants dripping with water and lichens. I felt tiny in the natural cathedral—trees ten feet in diameter and hundreds high—and sensed the passage of time witnessed here.

"Yeah. It's absolutely extraordinary," I said. "Come on." I lay on my back to take in the cathedral ceiling, moss as my pillow. Stars flickered between the trees. As a bank of clouds blackened the moon, the trees morphed into a looming tangle.

"Bet some of these cedars saw the arrival of the first Europeans."

Harvey stretched out next to me. "When the cedars were seedlings, the Haida were nearly wiped out by measles and chickenpox carried by explorers and trappers. Jeez."

"What?"

"You know. That's what happened to every North American tribe."

We studied the formidable canopy in silent reverence.

Harvey stood and brushed off her butt. "All right, big day tomorrow. Sleep well."

My sleep wasn't sound. Weird dreams woke me. In one, an explosion inside my tent sent dozens of screaming ravens into the sky. In another, an empty kayak bobbed on the sea.

I sat up with a start. It was already fully light. Had I overslept? In the tent beside mine, Harvey quietly hummed. She did that when she was in tidy mode, so I assumed she was organizing her stuff. All was well.

I unzipped my sleeping bag and reached into the duffle for a heavy-duty thermal turtleneck. Today I'd need it for sure. I stepped into the cool, bright morning and stood in front of Harvey's tent.

"'Morning, Harvey. I'm starved. You dressed?"

She pushed aside her tent flap, stepped out, and straightened up. Her champagne hair was neatly combed, clothes like she'd just pulled them from her dresser, and touch of makeup you hardly noticed.

I pushed aside the clump of hair covering my eye and glanced at my crumpled fleece pants and frayed turtleneck cuffs.

After a hot oatmeal breakfast, we pulled down the tents, packed the kayaks, and were on the water before seven. Across the channel on Kinuk Island, a fifty-foot research vessel waited for our ten AM departure. Plenty of time.

Anticipating hot-spring pools on the island, the friends from Vancouver chatted excitedly as they paddled along. I fell back to ruminate.

Ted McKnight would be waiting for us when we reached the Kinuk dock. While Harvey and I counted fish, he'd flown to the archipelago's Skidegate airport with our research gear and taken a boat taxi down to Kinuk so we'd be ready this morning for the one-day cruise.

Late in the spring, Ted and I had started hanging out. As the weather warmed, we spent more and more time together. Now he was always, well, *there*. At work, his office was down the hall from mine, and he didn't hesitate to stop by. In my few hours of leisure, we often did things with Harvey, Ted's half-sister. I loved them both, but the constant togetherness felt stifling, like I was underwater and needed more air.

On the other hand, Ted was an absolutely terrific guy. A new hire at the Maine Oceanographic Institute, he was everything a woman would want—kind, patient, smart—and a blond, blue-eyed stud. We had a lot in common. He'd even taken an interest in Italian opera, a particular passion of mine. Besides all that, the sex was great. We made love, laughed and joked, and made love again. Easy, a joy.

It seemed pretty unlikely I'd ever meet a guy like Ted again. And now he was less than a mile away on the other side of our paddle. The knot in my stomach increased with each stroke.

Harvey slid her kayak alongside mine and matched my paddling rhythm. "Looking forward to seeing Ted?"

I hesitated. Harvey and I talked about pretty much everything, including my palpable fear of losing independence in a serious relationship. But being totally honest about her flesh and blood was awkward.

I went for neutral. "Yeah, sure."

"Mara, I don't know what's going on with you and Ted. That's your business. But working with the Haida on this iron project's a huge challenge. The UN is counting on us. We've got to be a team."

"I know that. But Ted's your brother. I can't—"

"I get it, Mara. Like I said, it's *your* business."

"And you know very well I'm a professional."

"I didn't mean…Of course, you're professional."

We both stopped paddling. Side-by-side, our kayaks drifted with the current.

I used my blade to point at craggy mountains to the north. "It's gorgeous here, Harve. Let's enjoy it."

Harvey glanced at the mountains but didn't say anything. She took off and caught up with the other women. I watched as she started a conversation with Gwen. Harvey was one of the most even-tempered people I'd ever known. The only thing she pestered me about was my insistence on wearing comfortable—in her words, shabby—clothes. Her comment about Ted and professionalism stung me. Naturally, I understood her desire that we work well together. As the most senior scientist, she headed up our team. Harvey was a perfectionist and born leader. An outstanding job would improve the likelihood she'd be the next biology department chair. But I'd never done anything to make her think my personal issues would undermine that goal.

On the other hand, Harvey called it as she saw it. As my best friend, she didn't hesitate to point out my shortcomings, and she was usually right. Much as I hated to admit it, I'd have to make sure my feelings toward Ted didn't compromise our work. There was a lot at risk—the UN assignment, my credibility as a scientist, a cherished friendship, maybe a lifetime partner. No way could I screw up.

But I had to do *something* about Ted. I'd been going back and forth between two options—wait and see what happened or speak with him. Waiting was too passive for me, so I'd decided on option two. At the right moment, I'd explain my need for personal time. Ted knew female oceanographers had to be fiercely independent to get anywhere. We'd talked about that a lot.

I said it aloud—"I need to spend more time alone."

I pooched out air between my lips. The assertion might seem lame, or worse, selfish, to someone like Ted. He *relished* hanging out with his buddies at the Lea Side bar Friday afternoons. And he hosted barbeques—complete with volleyball, brats, and beer—so every single person from MOI, including the seagoing crew, could meet a visiting scientist. Me? Forty-five minutes into Lea Side merrymaking, I'd eye the door and try to remember my last "gotta go" excuse. And my idea of the perfect evening was six, eight at the very most, good friends around my dinner table for lobster risotto and insightful conversation.

Ted didn't seem to mind. In the bar he'd squeeze my hand, say he'd call later, and jump right back in with a verdict on the beer he'd just sipped. Or he'd toast my culinary triumph from the head of my table with a wink and lop-sided grin.

If I owned up to what actually happened when I left the Lea Side, maybe he'd get why alone-time fed my soul. That I tried not to look at the grocery store I'd just claimed as my destination. That the magnet was always the same—outside, quiet solitude. My favorite spot was a tiny preserve on the edge of town hardly anyone visited. The single path took me to a slab of granite that plunged into the sea. On my back, eyes closed, I'd let electricity flow through me with every breath of wet, briny air. I'd step away—leave behind hoarse calls of gulls and endless replay of wave slap on rock—recharged, humming, ready to jump in again.

Could Ted understand how every single day I needed unpeopled time at the end of secret paths? Sometimes it didn't take much—kind of like a plant left out in the sun too long. Just a hit of water did the trick. Other times, I needed longer. A day, even a weekend.

Ted studied plants in college. He'd get it.

At least that's what I told myself.

A half hour later, we beached the kayaks on Kinuk Island. I climbed out, stretched my arms overhead, and looked around. The day before had been so hectic I didn't have time to get a feel for the place. On a rise to my right, steam drifted skyward from several hot pools I couldn't see from down on the beach. A wooden walkway that snaked along the hillside took visitors to the pools from bathhouses half-hidden in the trees. We'd been told another walkway plunged into the woods to the longhouse where we could spend the night after our boat trip.

My gaze slid to the left, where a long pier perched on a row of stout, tall pilings. In Haida Gwaii, the difference between low and high tide reached twenty-five feet. The tide was low, and the pier hung a good thirty feet above sticky mud. Our vessel for the day bobbed gently on a float connected to the pier by a steep, skinny walkway that could move up and down with the tide.

Ted strode up that walkway with the certitude of an athlete. He pushed blond hair off his forehead. In his red and black off-shore jacket, he was ready for the inevitable wind and rough seas we'd face on the Pacific Ocean. When he reached the pier, Ted spotted me, beamed, and waved. I returned his greeting with an equally enthusiastic wave, but it was forced.

We avoided the who-hugged-first issue when Harvey sprinted down the pier to greet her brother. Ambling behind, I grinned and was swallowed into a tight bear hug that should have felt warm and welcoming. Instead, the claustrophobia nearly choked me.

My god, what a cold fish I was. Ted deserved more from me, and I hoped he didn't sense my discomfort.

But I was pretty sure he did.

"You okay?"

Cough. "Ah, fine."

Awkward silence. "Well, not completely. My kayak malfunctioned yesterday. I nearly drifted out to sea."

Ted whistled. "Damn. What's the water temp out there? High forties? Lucky you didn't go over. Did you fix it yourself on the water?"

"No." William and Bart trudged toward us. "See the guy on the right? That's William. He motored up and got the rudder to work."

Ted nodded. "Good man." He motioned toward two canvas bags down on the float. "You'll have to fill me in later. Our equipment's on the boat, and I've been sorting through their gear. We've got a lot to keep us dry and warm out there—heavy fleece jackets and pants, foul-weather gear, hats, and gloves."

Waves rocked the float. My leg muscles tensed. "Bet we'll need all of it."

I scanned the boat. Spots of rust poked through her hull and stained her side, but I was spoiled. Maine Oceanographic Institution's new day vessel was equipped with scientific sonar, two winches, and three types of water samplers. One winch was wired so we could get real-time data from towed instruments. Heavy buoys were deployed with a sturdy A-frame. The ship had radar, iridium phones, depth sounders, and the latest GPS equipment.

I turned to Ted. "How's the ship?"

He shrugged. "She'll do. Fish survey go all right?"

"Okay. Tell you about it later."

A sturdy, white-haired gentleman with a beard to match emerged from the ship's cabin, strode onto the float, and called up to us. "Welcome, folks. I'm Josh Barney, captain of the *Henry George*. Come on down."

We single-filed down the walkway. As we reached the float, Captain Barney shook each of our hands in turn. When he let go of mine, it only hurt a little.

I gestured toward the boat. Close up, the rust was more evident, working deck space appeared small, and bulwark not high enough for an ocean-going ship. "She looks, ah, like a great little research vessel."

"University of British Columbia's outfitted for oceanographic studies close to shore. Have to say, we're not usually this far off the coast. She's a venerable old lady, but the *Henry George* is fast. You'll get your work done and be back well before nightfall. Ah, here comes our crew for the day."

William and Bart marched down the walkway and stopped at the bottom.

Captain Barney pointed at the canvas bags. "No need to wait, lads. Load up this gear."

The "lads" grabbed the bags and disappeared into the cabin with their boss right behind. I stepped aboard as the ship's engines rumbled to life. We pulled away from the float. Holding onto the ship's railing, I watched the hot spring village of Kinuk fade into the rainforest background as the *Henry George* reached an impressive thirty-knot cruising speed.

Harvey came out of the ship's cabin with two jackets over her arm. She handed me one. "Bet you need this."

"Got that right. The temperature was, what, fifty-five on the island? Feels like it's dropped twenty degrees in two minutes." I held up a red foul-weather jacket with "U.B.C Marine" in bold letters down one sleeve. Unlike most friends and colleagues from Maine, I didn't especially relish the cold. Extreme cold seemed to be hazard that followed me around.

"Ya know, Harvey, we could be marine ecologists who study warm places."

"Like coral reefs?"

"Or waters off Mexico or Australia."

"But we've got this spectacular archipelago"—Harvey waved a hand toward shore—"pretty much to ourselves. And we haven't even seen the kelp forests yet."

We'd booked a Haida scuba guide so we could sample kelp. Haida Gwaii brochures boasted an underwater wonderland with giant kelp one hundred fifty feet long. Naturally, we'd be diving in ice-cold water.

I'd just zipped up my jacket, secured its Velcro strips at my wrists, and buckled my life jacket when the ship left the protection of Kinuk Bay, turned west, and plowed into the Pacific's five-foot waves.

Little waves.

Feet apart for balance, I stared back at granite boulders off Augustine Island's tip fifty feet away.

Harvey came closer. "You're quiet."

I pointed at the rocks. "Right there, I slid by the island in my kayak. That's when I really got scared. It was a miracle when William appeared out of nowhere."

"Thank the Haida gods for that. Ah, Ted's talking to William about our track now. You okay to go inside?"

Harvey knew, of course, that I got terribly seasick and avoided enclosed spaces on research vessels.

"You know, Mara, it's really too bad I've got to keep mum about the first time you met Ted. It'd be a great cocktail story."

"You don't go to cocktail parties. But if you do and you tell *anyone* I upchucked on his rain pants day one of a research cruise in front of the whole Maine Oceanographic crew, I'll never cook you another risotto dinner." I waved a hand at the ocean. "Seriously, I'll be fine. It's not that rough. If things get worse, the seasick patch should help."

Harvey yanked open the cabin door. Inside, the aging engine throbbed. I nearly gagged on diesel-thickened air. What looked like sonar, depth sounders, and outdated GPS technology took up most of the forward helm, along with the steering wheel. Captain Barney, at the wheel, stared straight ahead. Bart stood beside him, back to us.

William and Ted leaned over well-worn charts covering half the wooden counter that ran the length of the cabin. They stood as we approached.

Ted raised his voice above the engine noise. "William just showed me where they dumped the iron sulfate. An eddy about thirty kilometers from here."

William stepped aside so Harvey and I could see the chart. We leaned in.

Ted ran his finger due west of Augustine Island. "Just about here."

"So we should be on the eastern edge of the eddy in about an hour?" I asked.

"Right."

I planted my feet apart for balance and leaned back against the counter. "Tell us details, William. Did you add the iron in one spot or spread it out? Why there? Over how many days? Who supervised the dumping?"

If he was irritated by my barrage of questions, William didn't show it. He answered each in turn.

"Roger Grant chartered a trawler for the project. He picked that spot because salmon migrate through it. We added a hundred tons of iron over three weeks and knew it worked because the water looked bright green right away. Everyone in the villages was excited."

"Tell us about Roger Grant. Why did you agree to work with him?"

William's black eyes flashed. "I *didn't* just agree. Some Environment Council members are old. Roger Grant's an outsider. They didn't trust him, couldn't see he's a genius. Some of us—the younger ones—argued with the council. They picked me to be their leader." He pointed at the cabin's window. "All those tiny phytoplankton floating around out there are starved for iron, and we fed it to them. Mr. Grant promises salmon will run heavy and long, like they used to. Besides that, the Haida will be leaders in reducing global warming with marine carbon credits."

Ted jumped in. "How much did the Haida pay Grant?"

William thrust out his chin. "A million dollars."

Harvey gasped. My hand flew to my lips.

Ted kept going. "And if it doesn't work?"

"I just *told* you it's working. We can see how green the water is."

Ted opened his mouth then quickly shut it again. I guessed he was about to argue that you couldn't just look at the water. You needed valid, scientific data.

I tried a different approach, and slipped into teacher mode to reduce the heat level. "William, it's possible your iron enrichment created a phytoplankton bloom. It's happened before. But Canadian oceanographers often see algal blooms out here this time of year. That's the problem. You can't distinguish naturally occurring blooms from iron-induced ones."

The young man shook his head. "You don't understand. Raven is watching over us. The iron worked."

Did William really believe this? Clearly, he was a bright guy. And even Canada's young Prime Minister sported a tattoo on his bicep with planet earth as Raven's belly. Clearly, Raven was an iconic animal in the country.

Harvey brought us back to the task at hand. "William, we've got a plan for today. Take a look and see what you think." She grabbed a pencil and pointed at the chart with the eraser end. "We can deploy an electronic device called a plankton sonde when we reach the eddy where you added iron and run a transect due east back to here. We should detect much higher phytoplankton densities in the locale you fertilized and progressively lower ones as we go east. Okay?"

"What's a sonde?"

"It's an electronic device we drag through the water to get continuous measurements of chlorophyll plus temperature and salinity."

"More chlorophyll means more phytoplankton, right?"

"Correct."

William ran a finger along the proposed transect. "That makes sense. Except it's just one transect. By now, the algae bloom would have spread out many kilometers."

"Excellent point," I said. "We're just getting a feel for the waters now. We'll use satellite imagery to watch the bloom grow over time."

"Satellites?"

"Oceanographers have used this technology for decades to measure phytoplankton in the ocean. Blooms increase light backscatter. So, basically, satellites detect light bouncing back from the ocean surface."

William rubbed his neck and frowned. "But phytoplankton aren't just at the surface. They float around in a three dimensional world. Can a satellite in the sky detect three-D?

I laughed. "It's a problem, and that's a great question. You'd make a terrific marine biologist, William."

Just then, the *Henry George* rose up over a wave, slammed down with a shudder, and threw me at William. I landed against his chest with a "harrumph." He smelled of sea, wool, and, well, maleness.

William held my shoulders before he stepped back. His touch quickened my heart.

"Um, gosh," I said, "So sorry." The ship climbed another wave, and I grabbed the map table to stay upright. "Seems like we're in rougher waters. Maybe I should go outside for a bit." Through the cabin windows, I watched gray-green sea spray spurt high into the air. "But maybe not." I raised my voice. "Captain, are there crackers on the ship? Saltines usually help settle my stomach."

I didn't want to say that the vessel's old engine flavored the cabin's air with sickening diesel.

Captain Barney called over his shoulder, "There's food below deck."

William headed right for the ladder. "I'll get them for you."

"Follow you down," Harvey said. "Need to use the facilities."

William and Harvey clambered down the ladder to recesses below. That left me alone in the cabin with Captain Barney and Bart—both fixed on the messy expanse of ocean now in front of them—and Ted, who was fixed on me.

"What?" I asked.

"I didn't say anything."

"You look cross."

"Do I?" His frown eased. He put both hands out front and flipped his palms up.

He'd seen Angelo—my Italian godfather and only family—use a similar gesture.

"If you mean goodwill, the proper way includes a shrug and maybe one eyebrow raised."

He tried to raise an eyebrow but only managed to look like he had a toothache. We both laughed. That broke the ice, for now.

5

BY NOON, HARVEY, TED, WILLIAM, AND I WERE OUT ON deck getting ready to deploy the plankton sonde. The squall that tossed us around earlier had already passed, and waves returned to gentler twelve-foot rollers my stomach could handle. Even so, we were dressed for heavy seas in life jackets over waterproof jumpsuits and boots. The *Henry George's* deck wasn't nearly as high off the water as those on oceanographic vessels we were used to. Besides that, the ship's bulwark—planking along the side—was short. Both made us vulnerable to icy ocean spray.

William lifted the sonde out of its box and peered at one end. The three-foot-long sausage-shaped device looked like an oversized flashlight. "So, how does this thing work?"

"We'll drag it behind the ship." I said. "The sonde shines a specific wavelength of light at seawater flowing through it. When that happens, chlorophyll—the plant pigment we're measuring—emits a different, longer wavelength. That process is called fluorescence."

William rotated the sonde and considered the other end. "More fluorescence means higher amounts of phytoplankton?"

"Right. The sonde continuously calculates algal biomass so we'll have data along the whole transect."

"Fluorescence is used is all sorts of ways," Ted added. "Lamps, of course, but also brighteners in laundry."

"And in forensics—to see things like blood," Harvey added.

"Enough with the fluorescence lesson, folks," I said. "Let's get this baby in the water."

Harvey hooked the sonde to the electric winch's stainless steel cable. She signaled Captain Barney and rotated the winch arm so it reached out over the water. The *Henry George* slowed to trawling speed. Harvey stepped back. I flipped on the winch's motor, the winch played out cable, and the sonde plunged into the water.

William left to check in with the captain. Silent, Harvey, Ted, and I stared at the winch and sea beyond.

"What is it," I asked, "four months now since we stood on *Intrepid*'s deck and watched the winch drop that half-ton buoy on Peter?"

Ted put his hand on my shoulder. "I can hear his screams like it was yesterday."

I placed my hand on top of Ted's. "Me, too."

Bobbing up and down on swells three thousand miles from the Maine coast, we paid wordless respect to our dear friend and colleague who died because he studied climate change.

We checked the sonde cable a couple of times and returned to the cabin to prepare for the next task—collecting microscopic phytoplankton. Individually as intricate as a snowflake and more stunning than a diamond necklace when linked together, these floating plant-like organisms constituted the bottom of the ocean's food chain. We wanted to see if any species we collected responded to the Haida's iron enrichment experiment—that is, if any particular type took up the iron and outcompeted the others.

There were more modern ways to collect phytoplankton, but the venerable plankton net was appropriate for our quick trip off the archipelago. The thirty-foot-long net at our feet took up the cabin's deck space and then some. It looked like a footless nylon stocking for a giant. The "thigh" end was held open by a yard-wide metal ring.

William squatted and fingered the netting. "What's this for?"

"As the ship pulls the net through the water, microscopic algal cells caught in the mesh will wash down into the collecting bottle," I said. "Phytoplankton are my thing, so back in Maine I'll use a microscope to identify the most common species."

William said, "Cool," and joined Captain Barney.

Ted rummaged through the gearbox for three safety helmets. I knelt down, used a hose clamp to secure a collecting bottle to the small end, and checked to make sure the connection was tight. On my feet I said to Harvey and Ted, "We've got a decision to make. If I tow the net *behind* the ship, we won't need the side winch the sonde's attached to. That way we can leave the sonde in the water and get continuous data. On the other hand, I'll be working from the stern. We're used to ships with decks much higher off the water."

"So if we hit a big mother wave, you could end up in the drink," Harvey said.

I squinted at the water-splashed cabin windows. "Doesn't look so bad, but rogue waves can come out of nowhere."

Harvey glanced outside, bit her lip. "Let's ask the captain."

A minute later, Harvey was back. She zipped up her life jacket and grabbed the metal ring. "He says the seas are supposed to be stable for now, and it should be okay if we work fast. Out we go."

I followed her, collecting bottle in hand. Ted held the cabin door ajar.

As I passed through the opening, I gave him a mischievous grin and jiggled the bottle in my hand. "Why is this end called a codpiece?"

Out on deck, Ted showed a surprising degree of knowledge about the subject. "I've seen ancient Greek figurines sporting codpieces, but most of what we know is from Renaissance portraits and the like. Those guys wore tights and the codpiece was padded. You know, to emphasize men's genitals." He took the present-day oceanographic version, winked, and cradled the thing in his hands.

I rolled my eyes.

Harvey looked at her half-brother and laughed. "Remember that armored pouch we saw in the Met museum?"

"Ouch," I said. "Enough anatomical history. Let's decide who's doing what."

We stretched the net out on the deck and held onto the railing as we made our way to the ship's stern. Harvey scanned the seascape and frowned at gray-green rollers. In the distance, black clouds raced our way. As the *Henry George* rose up on an unusually large wave, spray soaked us.

Harvey ran a hand down her face, shook off the water, and tightened her hood. "Still want to do this, Mara?"

"Yeah. Let's get going. Weather will probably only get worse. All we've got to do is lower the A-frame, attach the net, and play it out from the stern platform. Ten minutes."

We each craned our necks to check out the sturdy A-shaped metal framework over our heads. Attached to each side of the ship's stern and lowered by electronic winches, A-frames tow nets that collect anything from fish to tiny plankton, depending on the net's mesh size and overall dimensions.

Ted looked over at the A-frame's winch. "Harvey, if you operate the winch, I can help Mara with the net."

I nodded at Ted. "Great. Let's go."

"Be right back." Harvey slid her hand along the gunwale, stepped into the cabin to tell Captain Barney what we were up to, and came back with Bart close behind. He must have been bored and wanted to watch the action outside.

She turned toward Bart. "Don't go near the stern. Stay right here. It's safer."

Without a word, Bart leaned back against the cabin door and crossed his arms.

The rolling ship, big clumsy boots, protruding life jackets, and random icy sea spray slowed our progress. Harvey partly lowered the A-frame so we could grab the long cable attached to the frame's pointed end. We clipped the mouth end of the net to that line.

"Harve," I called out, "Play her slowly. I'll walk the net back."

Harvey gave the signal to Captain Barney. The ship's engine droned down as she slowed to a crawl—just enough speed to maintain heading.

At a quarter knot, the *Henry George* felt the waves and rocked hard from side to side.

I held up my gloved hand and called out, "Hold on a sec."

Feet wide apart for balance, I walked back to the stern railing, grabbed it, turned sideways, and yelled so Ted and Harvey could hear me above the strengthening wind. "This damn rail's in the way."

Ted came closer so we didn't have to shout. "Might be. But that damn rail is between you and the deep blue sea."

I ran my hand along the metal bar. "'Course. I'll have to lift the net over it."

Behind me, Ted said, "You'll be on an exposed stern, so for god's sake, be careful."

Harvey shouted, "Good to go?"

I picked my way back, eyed the railing again, and turned toward Harvey. "Yeah, okay. Play out the winch. Really slow."

The winch hummed, then whined. With a shudder, the net's metal ring rose up off the deck and inched sternward. Holding the collecting bottle on the other end, I carefully duck-walked with the net as the A-frame stretched farther out behind the ship. Just short of the stern's edge, I yelled, "Harvey, stop."

The winch's drone faded.

I looked over the railing at row after row of waves with swirling white foam. Vertigo kicked in and I nearly fell over. I grabbed the rail and shook my head.

Ted touched my shoulder. "You okay?"

I blew out a breath. "Yeah, thanks."

Ted stepped back.

"Brace your feet," I whispered. "Supple in the knees. Look at the bottle, not down at the water."

I rotated the neck of the bottle one last time to make sure it wasn't tangled and called out, "Harvey, ready?"

"Ready," she shouted.

"Okay," I yelled. "Lettin' her go!"

Arms extended, I lobbed the bottle. Like a captured bird released from its cage, it sailed into the air and splashed into the sea.

At that very moment, Bart screamed one word that sent terror through anyone anywhere near the ocean.

"Shark!"

I lurched toward his shriek to see the fin. The ship hit a huge wave, rolled to port, and launched me into the air. I careened over the rail.

I seemed to fall in slow motion. Kicking my feet and wind milling my arms, I tried to claw my way through the air up to the ship. On my back, I smacked into water that felt like cement. My neck snapped forward, and I very nearly blacked out.

Frigid water burned my face. Fear shot adrenaline through my body.

I was going to drown. Like my parents. Go under, suck in seawater.

A crashing wave pushed me under. Beneath the surface, I spun in a confusing swirl. I craned my neck backward and winced. Blinking wildly, I squinted, saw dull light above me, kicked my feet, and popped to the surface.

In the trough of what appeared to be a monster wave, all I could see was a wall of green water. Coughing and frantic, I spun around. Did it again. There was no ship—just Haida Gwaii's fury and me.

I was alone in a wild arctic realm alien to my kind. I turned my body right, left, right, left again. I sucked in air in shallow, quick gasps. The terror was like nothing I'd ever known. I rode the next wave up, tried to gulp air, and gagged on seawater that smashed into my mouth. Icy water slithered into my gloves, boots, and down my neck. The gale howled; the indifferent sea roared.

Frantically spinning in search of the ship, I rode the roller coaster wave down once more. At the top of the next crest, a blessed human voice broke through the gale. Ted's, behind me. Hands outstretched, I jerked around.

Toward Ted—life, warmth. Love.

The orange thing directly in front of me made no sense.

"Mara, grab the ring. Grab the bloody ring!"

I reached out, seized the life ring, thrust my arm through its hole, and clasped my neoprene-gloved hands together.

The ship's stern loomed in front of me. A force pulled me to it. Attached to the day-glow ring, feet trailing behind, it felt like my body slid through frigid jelly.

I bumped into the bright blue stern. There, in the shadow of the ship, I was sheltered from the full force of the waves. Finally, I could catch my breath.

Coughing, I tried to see what was above me. Pain shot through my neck. I dropped my head.

"Mara, look at me."

Wincing, I did.

Ted's head was two body lengths above me.

"There's a yellow ladder just to your right," he yelled. "Reach up for it. Hand on each side of the ladder. I'll help you."

My eyes stung like someone had thrown salt in my face. I squeezed them shut and popped them open.

Bobbing up and down with the waves, nothing existed but me and that yellow ladder. My left hand still clung to the life ring. With the right one, I reached up to grab the ladder's right vertical rope.

A stiff blob at the end of arm, my hand barely opened. I slid back into the water.

"Enough of this shit. Get the hell out of this ice bath."

I'd drifted, so I pushed against the bow to be square with the ladder. I flexed my right hand, thrust it up, and grabbed that yellow line.

Suddenly, my arm was held tight to the vertical rope. I looked skyward. Ted's face was even closer now. Both his arms reached down. He'd wrapped one around the ladder's line and secured my arm tight.

"Good, Mara. The other hand. You can do this."

I still held onto the savior life ring. I looked at the thing, hesitated, let it go, swung my body against the stern, and grabbed the other side of the ladder.

"Slide your hand up. I can't reach you."

Ted held my right arm even harder while I inched the left one up. He grabbed it.

"Good. Good. Hold on. You're coming up."

Clinging to that rope ladder, arms extended, I hung like a dead cod on a gaff. The ship's hull slid past me and, for a moment, I was eye to eye with *The Henry George, Victoria, British Columbia*. When my shoulders reached deck height, Harvey grabbed the life jacket and hauled me aboard.

6

ROLLED OFF THE LADDER ONTO MY BACK.

On her knees beside me, Harvey unsnapped my safety helmet, cradled my neck in one hand, and pulled off the helmet with the other. "Speak to me."

The frigid water had numbed my face. I scrunched my eyes shut and moved my mouth around before I tried to talk. "Cold, so cold. Thought I'd drown like Mom and Dad."

Harvey pressed her palms against my cheeks. Her warmth was a salve.

William stood behind her.

Ted yelled over the wind, "William, let's get Mara inside. Make her warm tea. Get blankets. Got it?"

"Got it!"

Ted and William each held one of my arms, helped me to my feet, and slowly walked me into the cabin.

I coughed. "Ted, thank—"

"Later. Let's get you warm."

William went below. Harvey yanked down the cover of the wooden gear-box. I plopped onto it and let her help me out of the jumpsuit. My violent shivering made the job harder.

I expected to be soaking wet, but remarkably little seawater had seeped beneath the jumpsuit. My fleece top and pants were only wet to my ankles and partway up my arms and down my neck.

I held my arms out. "I'm hardly wet at all."

"You were only in the water for something like three minutes," Harvey said.

"You're kidding."

She crossed her arms over her chest. "You've got Ted to thank for that."

Ted leaned against the cabin bulwark. He'd taken off his helmet and pushed hair away from his forehead. "How're you doing?"

"Good. If you hadn't thrown that life ring so fast, I could've drifted away from the ship." I rubbed my arms and looked at him. "No way I can thank you enough."

He shrugged. "Lots of drills on research vessels. It just kicked in."

"Still, what you did was amazing."

Another shrug. As usual, a bit of wayward blond hair nearly reached one eye. Early in our courtship, I sometimes swept aside the lock of hair and kissed him lightly on the lips. With a pang of guilt, I tried to recall the last time I'd done that.

I pushed the memory away, looked into his navy blue eyes, and smiled. "Owe you a year's worth of lemon gelatos."

A private joke. Gelato, Ted's favorite treat, was hard to come by in Spruce Harbor, Maine. He laughed. Harvey didn't.

"Um, you guys have to promise to not tell *anyone* at MOI about this."

"You mean," Harvey said, "things like you should've seen her fly off the stern on her back, arms spinning like a windmill?" Her tone was a bit too sarcastic for my liking.

Ted snorted.

Heat crept into my cheeks. "Yeah. Things like that. Seymour'd relish any tidbit of information."

Our obnoxious Biology Department Chair creatively used whatever he could get his hands on against me.

William carried over a steaming mug. I sipped the hot liquid. It tasted a little like licorice. "Thanks. This is different."

"Herbal tea. An elder on the island, Charlotte, teaches us how to use herbs for tea and medicine. Here's a blanket and some dry clothes from below."

The oversized gray wool sweater slipped over my fleece top. It was scratchy, warm, comfy. I slid on wool socks and used the blanket as a shawl. The dry clothes and warm tea were a godsend. I stopped shivering, and my face and feet went from burning cold-hot to pleasantly toasty.

William took Captain Barney's place at the wheel. The captain limped back, leaned against a window, crossed his arms, and looked down at me. "Mara, *nobody* has ever gone overboard on this ship, even in a heavy sea. It was a rogue wave, but of course I take responsibility for approving the maneuver. I'm so very sorry this happened."

The captain took in my borrowed garb. His bushy eyebrows blended as one, and it pained me to witness his distress. "Captain, I appreciate your saying that. But it was my idea to deploy the net off the stern. I'll be sure to say so in the U.B.C. report."

With a quick nod, Barney returned to his post.

At ten-minute intervals, Ted and Harvey left me to check on the sonde and plankton net. The vessel moved at trawling speed until they finally hauled both onto the deck.

Captain Barney gave his ship her head and steamed back to the islands. I sat on the map table cross-legged and tried to rub salt water out of my hair with a washcloth. Harvey and Ted leaned against the cabin's wall opposite me. They'd already explained how William and Harvey each grabbed one of Ted's legs and pulled him back across the deck while he secured my arms to the ladder.

I dangled my legs to stretch them out. "Harvey, did you see a shark?"

She shook her head. "I was too fixed on what happened to you. You'd disappeared off the stern, for god's sake."

"Me, too," Ted said. "I tried to grab your life jacket, but it slipped right out of my hand. Damn, that was a horrible moment."

"I wish—"

Ted waved a hand. "It wasn't your fault."

"I checked the shark list before we left Maine," Harvey said. "You know, just to see. They're common out here—salmon shark, blue shark, Pacific sleeper, spiny dogfish. More, but that's all I can remember."

William, who'd been standing next to Bart, joined us. "Dogfish Woman's crest belongs to many clans. We see sharks a lot. At the Vancouver airport there's Bill Reid's sculpture. Raven, Eagle, Grizzly Bear and her cubs, Beaver, and Dogfish Woman are all together in a boat."

"That sculpture's huge. What, twenty feet high?" Ted said. "We'll look more closely on the way home."

Bart, who'd screamed "Shark," hadn't said a word. I spoke to his back. "Bart, tell us what you saw."

Bart turned, leaned back, crossed his arms. "A fin maybe thirty meters off the port side right in front of me. Big shark fin. Thought you'd want to know."

I nodded. "Well, yes. Do you see them out here often?"

"Yeah." He didn't wait for another question and turned back.

Captain Barney swiveled in his chair. "Sharks. Yes, we see 'em a lot, though I didn't spot this one. Mara, you look real good. That was a close call. Never happened before, like I said. I'll send you a copy of that report you need to fill out."

Naturally, I understood that the University of British Columbia had regulations and forms about ship safety. "I'll get it back to you right away."

"Good. You all must be hungry."

Suddenly, I was ravenous. "I am."

"Me, too," Harvey said as she looked at Ted.

"You bet."

"William, there are cheese sandwiches below," the captain said. "Help yourselves, folks. We'll be back at Kinuk Island in about an hour."

William climbed down the ladder and returned with a paper bag. Breakfast seemed like a very long time ago. Wanting to eat was a good sign.

In between bites, Ted asked William, "So, what's going to happen when we get back?"

"You'll probably want to use the hot pools, and we'll have plenty of time. Then, we'll walk up to the longhouse to meet with the council."

I ran a hand down my still-damp and sticky hair. "Soaking in hot water would be heaven right now."

Harvey said, "Good Lord, would it."

Ted, who'd just taken a bite of sandwich, mumbled, "Mmm."

"There are men's and women's bathhouses. You can leave your clothes there and use the towels." William might've remembered bathing suits in the sauna because he added with a hint of a smile, "You can wrap a towel for the walk from the bathhouse down to the pools outside."

Harvey brought us back to more important matters. "Who will be in the longhouse? What does the council want to know?"

William finished his sandwich and brushed crumbs off his chin. "The Haida Environment Council—HEC—oversaw the iron fertilizer plan. HEC's head, Gene Edenshaw, will be there, and some other council members. They're, ah, very surprised by the United Nation's reaction to their project. The HEC says they have control over their own waters."

Silent, Harvey, Ted, and I glanced at each other. We were used to fielding questions from fishermen and other Mainers about things like global warming and overfishing. That was hard enough. A group of Haida most likely jaded by hundreds of years of struggle for self-governance would be a *very* different state of affairs. But this wasn't the time to voice our concerns.

Later, the three of us stood on the dock waving at the *Henry George* when a classy fishing boat pulled up. With hefty rods mounted on the back of the enclosed cabin, a pricey navigation unit on top, and three outboards, I guessed this was a commercial charter boat for rich anglers from the mainland. The disparity between the boat and the fisherman who emerged from the cabin was so great I had to cough to cover a laugh. A black, dog-eared baseball cap set off coarse features—large crooked nose, fleshy lips, and oversized ears. The man's black suspenders held up overalls stained with grease, and his faded navy shirt was ripped at the elbows. He yanked open a chest and reached for a large fish tail that stuck out of the ice on top.

We met William at the end of the pier. When he'd left us a few minutes earlier, he seemed anxious to go ashore. But here he was going the other way, back to the dock.

"Who's that in the fancy boat?" I asked.

"Caleb Peterson. He brings fish every week, more often when we've got visitors."

William hurried past us.

I followed Ted and Harvey down a steep set of wooden stairs to the beach and stopped beneath the pier to tie my shoe. So I was alone when angry voices from above startled me.

One I didn't recognize barked, "Not sure? What'd you mean?"

The voices faded. I guessed the pair stepped into the fancy boat's cabin, and trotted to catch up with Ted and Harvey.

In the bathhouse, Harvey and I shared the round wooden hot tub. From a fault line far below, geologic activity heated water that rose to the surface and continuously flowed through the tub. The same was true with the pools outside.

I slipped under luscious one-hundred-degree F water. Suddenly, I was swirling down through grey-green frozen slush. I popped up through the surface with a gasp. When my heart slowed down a bit I said, "It's hard to fathom I was in the frigid ocean a couple of hours ago. Doesn't seem real."

Harvey tossed her head and sent spray across her side of the cozy room. The maneuver looked like something from a sexy ad for athletes.

"Believe me, it was *very, very* real."

"I feel guilty, but it wasn't my fault. Have to say, you seemed pretty pissed off about it, though."

"I don't know, Mara. Danger seems to follow you around. Thank god, Ted was there. He saved your butt." She slid under the water again.

Ted *had* rescued me, and I was now in his debt, which didn't feel great. That selfish thought made me cringe.

Harvey surfaced. "Ready for an outdoor pool?"

I'd eyed one in particular on our way over to the women's bathhouse. "The pool lower down has a spectacular view of Kinuk Bay."

Barefoot and wrapped in beach-size towels, we padded down the wooden walkway. Ted had picked the same pool. Elbows on the pool's outer edge, he floated on his belly facing seaward, his long, lean body a muted olive green beneath the chalky water. The view was indeed spectacular. Beyond the pool, a light onshore breeze roughened Haida Gwaii's waters. Farther off, mother earth had thrust gray jagged mountains thousands of feet up and out of the sea.

Ted rolled over to face us as we approached. "This is a special bit of heaven."

Since we were alone, I dropped my towel on a dry rock and stepped into the pool. Normally, of course, I don't parade about in the nude, and I'm not particularly self-conscious about my body. With my kayaking, running, and yoga, it looked and worked just fine, thank you. But, at that moment, I could feel heat on my cheeks (the ones on my face) because it was obvious Ted was watching me. Of course, we'd seen each other's bodies during lovemaking and joking around in the shower. But out in the open, his gaze felt different, more sensuous.

Had to admit, though, I liked it.

The three of us splashed around the good-sized pool for a while. The memory of my close call on the *Henry George* faded in the heavenly warm water. We leaned back against the side—our extended legs nearly meeting in the middle—to discuss the visit with the HEC.

"Our mandate from the UN is clear," Harvey said. "They want a report from unbiased marine biologists with relevant expertise. One of us should tell the council why we were chosen. If I do say so myself, we're the perfect team."

"Since you're team leader," I said, "you should introduce us."

Ted directed a little wave of water in my direction. "When the UN okayed Maine Oceanographic's recommendation that we would go to a world-famous kayak destination, you hesitated a whole half-second, Mara."

"True. And when you found out about this spectacular place, you were right behind." I rotated my ankles and sent circles of tiny waves across the pool.

"Hey guys," Harvey said. "I'm worried. In my book, you're ready for something like this when you know who thinks what and why. These people are strangers. What do we say to a group of Haida leaders who must desperately need money for their people? They'll see us as white outsiders trying to tell them what to do."

Ted pushed wet hair off his forehead. "No question, it'll be tricky, Harve. But we've got to try to explain what we know. Why most scientists think this geo-engineering is a terrible idea. That's part of our job."

"Sure," Harvey said. "It's how we do it. Must be with the utmost respect. Speaking of respect, let's try to signal one another if we want to add to a discussion someone else is leading. That way, we won't speak over each other."

We dressed in the bathhouse and followed William along a path that cut back into the rainforest. It was late afternoon, with sunset hours away, but moments after the tree canopy closed above us, we walked through muted light. During the quarter-mile trek, we didn't say a word. Silence and gloom set the stage for the serious business ahead.

Bits of bright red appeared through the trees even before we saw the longhouse. The tree canopy opened up again to reveal the short side of a long, narrow building that stood proud in the middle of a large clearing. Blinking, I stepped into the light and stared at the structure before me. On each side of the wooden structure's front door, an enormous black and red eagle greeted visitors. Hanging in a graceful arc, the eagles' beaks met above the middle of the diminutive entryway.

I touched William's arm. "We probably should know something about longhouses before we go in. Is there time?"

He looked toward the sun. "We still have at least fifteen minutes."

In what sounded like the practiced voice of a Watchman, William educated us. "Scientists say my people have been here for at least three thousand years. *We* say these islands were underwater at the time before people. Then the supernaturals stood on the first rock to emerge. My ancestors came later, from the sea."

William gestured toward the forest. "Year 'round, the Haida lived along the coast in this gentle rainforest. Food—salmon, shellfish, elk, and deer—was always abundant. And the towering cedar trees gave them wood for houses, canoes, and many other things. In this abundance, my ancestors lived in permanent settlements. Each longhouse was fifteen to forty-five meters long, about six to twenty meters wide, and each housed many families. Lined up side-by-side, houses in the village faced the water. The fronts were painted, and many also had colorful totem poles carved with families' crests."

I did a quick calculation. A hundred-fifty-foot long, sixty-odd-foot wide structure could house a lot of people.

"I don't see windows," Harvey said. "On the front, anyway."

"In a traditional longhouse, there was only one hole in the roof to let out smoke from the central fire pit. Windows lose heat. We had no glass or anything like that."

I tried to imagine inhabited longhouses. "What was it like inside? I mean, when people lived there?"

William squinted at the structure like he could see into the past. "One big, long room with a sunken square fire pit in the middle. Families slept in bunk beds along the sidewalls. At the far end, stout totem poles colored red, black, turquoise, and white stood guard. Each held up one end of a tree-size cedar roof pole running the length of the building." He returned to the present. "Let's go in."

Single file, we followed William. The front door was only five feet tall, so we all ducked before we passed through the opening. Tallest, Ted had to hold onto the doorframe and bend way down.

We stopped just beyond the door opening to let our eyes adjust. This was a clearly a modern longhouse, with a row of large vertical windows cut into the building's sidewalls. Sunlight that reflected off the cedar interior gave the room a warm glow. In place of the traditional fire pit, a sunken central square about twenty-five feet on a side was lit from above by several large skylights. A series of three steps ran along the full length of all four sides, the top step level with the floor. These appeared to double as benches and stairs down to an empty square I assumed symbolized the fire pit.

In addition to our little party, there were several people in the room. Opposite us—in the middle of the top bench—three people sat, backs straight, in a perfect row. Unlike any Haida I'd met so far, they did not smile in greeting. What looked like two women stood on opposite sides of the long room. Near the sidewalls and in shadow, they were hard to see. Bart was beside one of them.

William called out our introduction. "These are the United Nation visitors. They look forward to speaking with the Environment Council."

The three council members stood—a man and two women. Only then did I fully take in the red and black painting that decorated the whole back wall behind them. It depicted the front of a cartoon longhouse with black sidewalls and peaked roof. Swirls of color showed eyes, claws, and wings. A broad-faced head with a mocking, toothy grin hung below the peaked roof. Lined up, the council members stood directly below that chilling welcome.

1

THE MAN STOOD BETWEEN THE WOMEN, AND SPOKE FIRST. His cadence was unhurried, his voice rich and deep. "I'm Gene Edenshaw. Welcome to Haida Gwaii and Kinuk longhouse."

Gene quickly took our measure. He had a bronzed and open face, keen chocolate eyes, and his brown hair, beard, and mustache were just beginning to go to gray. He wore a wide black headband decorated with a row of red beads in the middle and his eyes smiled easily. I liked him right away.

"After we talk," Gene said, "please join us for salmon dinner. And since the weather promises to be stormy tonight, please accept our invitation to sleep here." He scanned the room and grinned. "As you can see, we have lots of room. Now, please come sit with us."

We made our way to the set of steps on their left and settled ourselves on the top, floor-level one. Since the steps weren't constructed for six-footers, Ted leaned back on his hands so his knees weren't up to his ears.

The younger of the two women had tipped her head as we marched across the room to find a comfortable place to sit. Rich black hair pulled tight into a ponytail framed her broad face. Laugh lines creased dark brown eyes. She wore a kind of scarf across broad shoulders that was fastened mid-waist, black in background, and had hundreds of tiny red and white buttons along the border. It depicted two owl-like creatures that grinned at us from either side of her significant chest.

"I'm Jennie Davidson, and I also welcome you to our village." She spoke with a lilted upswing.

The other woman had yet to say anything, so we waited. Considerably older than Jennie, she looked at us with penetrating black eyes over thin glasses perched on the end of her nose. Her white hair fell down her chest in two long braids secured at the bottom with beaded red bands. She twirled one band between two long, bony fingers with the precision of a watchmaker. Heavily lined, lean, and bronzed by the sun and years, hers was a face that might give outsiders reasons to pause.

She gave us a quick nod and said in a deep, manly voice. "I am Charlotte Webber." Charlotte pressed her lips together and said no more.

I glanced around the room. William had his back against a wall, close enough to hear the conversation. Sunlit, one of the mystery women stood beside him. Her shoulder touched his arm. With ebony hair to her shoulders, smooth skin the color of custard, and a pert nose, she was drop-dead gorgeous. Still in shadow, the girl on the other side crossed her arms and appeared to be fixed on the couple. Next to her, Bart already looked bored.

Harvey stood and began with a few words about the purpose of our visit and introduced each of us. "As you know, the United Nations selected us as a team to review the iron fertilization project. I'm Dr. Harvina Allison, team leader and a marine chemist." She touched my shoulder. "This is Dr. Mara Tusconi, a marine phytoplankton expert. Dr. Ted McKnight has worked on iron fertilization projects elsewhere. Like you, we are only interested in the health of this spectacular marine ecosystem. We want to work with you and learn why you took on this project. We'll try to address your questions as clearly as we can. Perhaps we should start there?"

Jennie jumped to her feet and crossed her arms. "First question is why does the UN think it has jurisdiction over us? The Haida Nation holds title and rights to X̱aayda gwaay."

Harvey answered, "Canada has signed two international treaties designed to prevent marine pollution. In two thousand eight, your country's Parliament voted that ocean iron fertilization should only be allowed for legitimate scientific research. The United Nations considers your fertilization a violation of international law."

Edenshaw took his turn. "But doesn't the ocean belong to everyone and no one?"

I stood. "It's a good question. After the first earth summit, UN governments developed plans for global sustainability in the twenty-first century. This included protection of the earth's oceans. As you well know, humans have taken terrible tolls on the world's seas. Since the ocean and organisms in it know no boundary, UN laws rely on both individual and collective action to protect the marine environment."

Frowning, Jennie vigorously shook her head. "All we've done is add fertilizer to make the tiny algae grow. Farmers have added fertilizer to plants since the beginning of agriculture. What's the harm in that?"

Ted hadn't spoken yet. He leaned forward. "Another really good question, but let's back up at bit. As in agriculture, the elements nitrogen and phosphorous stimulate algae to grow when added to seawater. But, in some places, like Haida Gwaii, nitrogen and phosphorous don't do the trick. Iron appears to sometimes, and we're not sure why."

Charlotte's eyebrows shot up. "Appears to sometimes?"

Ah, I thought. Smart lady.

"Right." Ted went on. "It's extremely hard to know if fertilization experiments work in the open ocean. Adding fertilizer to a field of corn is one thing. You can stand there and measure stalks. Large scale iron, um, enrichment like you've done here, is quite another."

Gene said, "Please explain that."

"Haida Gwaii sits right on the edge of Canada's Pacific continental shelf where cold, rich waters of the northern Pacific mix with Japan's warm offshore currents. You all know this place teems with life. Seabirds in the millions nest on your shores, and there are over twenty species of whales and dolphins. Besides salmon, you have large numbers of herring, halibut, rockfish, and crab. So if you add iron to the water and the salmon run in abundance, that might've happened naturally anyway."

Gene looked directly at Ted. "We do this in the spirit of Lagua who taught the Haida how to use iron long ago. We saw with our eyes what happened when that iron went into the ocean. It greened up."

"As Dr. McKnight explained," Harvey said, "phytoplankton blooms are common here so it's very hard to know if that would've happened anyway."

Gene simply nodded. I didn't think we'd convinced him but was impressed with his professionalism.

William hadn't said a word since he introduced us. He stepped away from the wall. "There's something really important that's gotten lost here. Global warming is a worldwide crisis. Carbon dioxide in the air keeps going up and up. If the iron project works, the Haida Nation will lead the world in a new way to decrease greenhouse gases. With dangers people face with melting glaciers and all the rest, why don't you see our experiment as a good thing?"

The longhouse was quiet as a church as all eyes turned to us. Harvey faced William. "That's truly an excellent question. You're right. If marine carbon sequestration works here, the

Haida will be recognized as international leaders in the fight against global warming. You deserve a lot of credit for facing up to an environmental crisis of this magnitude. We should have said that, and I apologize."

Shoulders back, William acknowledged the comment with a quick nod.

Harvey went on. "But William, you used the word 'experiment' and that's the problem. Scientists conduct experiments in very particular ways because it's so hard to know if an intervention—like adding iron slurry—actually has an impact. As Dr. McKnight said, if you saw more salmon in your rivers after the fertilization, how could you know if that would've happened anyway? That's why the UN declared that any marine iron fertilization projects must be done by trained scientists experienced with this type of work. The man you worked with, Roger Grant, has no training like that at all."

William opened his mouth as if to say something, and closed it again. He returned to the shadow of the wall.

Gene took over again. "From what we've asked, you get a pretty good idea about our concerns. You work as oceanographers. It would be helpful for you to explain how you view this ocean world around us."

I'd dealt with this issue in a high-profile public speech a few months earlier, so I answered. "First off, this is the most spectacular marinescape I've ever seen. The coast of Maine is truly beautiful, but the abundance you have is astounding. Although Maine is home to the American lobster, of course."

Gene grinned. Jennie frowned. Charlotte stared at me.

I held out my hands. "As scientists, we rely on one thing: solid evidence, data. Scientists have done numerous iron enrichment experiments, both large and small scale. Results have been mixed and confusing. So we must conclude that solid evidence is just not there."

Jennie said, "But Roger Grant showed us a scientific study where iron from an Alaskan volcano increased salmon runs in British Columbia. Besides that, there's the carbon credits."

Maybe because he was tired of sitting on his butt, Ted pushed himself to a standing position. "Look, there's no clear link between iron addition and increased salmon runs. That study you mentioned got a lot of press, but most fishery biologists don't think the connection is there. And carbon credits are bought and sold to reduce carbon dioxide emissions by businesses, governments, and the like for *accepted* processes that remove carbon dioxide from the atmosphere."

The front door opened. Cold air swept across my neck.

A raspy male voice bellowed from behind. "And *accepted* means what?"

We turned. Caleb Peterson marched toward us, his long face blood-red, eyes narrowed.

We swung our heads back in Gene's direction as he called out, "Not now, Caleb. You know you've got to wait 'til the full meeting."

Caleb tromped forward and stopped just short of the council. He crossed log-sized arms across his chest and growled, "Why should we listen to some know-it-alls from the states? They know nothin' about us, why we're doing this."

Gene strode over to Caleb and stood before him, toe to toe. "That's not how we treat visitors to Haida Gwaii. These people are just doing their jobs."

Caleb was the first to look away. He dropped his hands to his side, turned around, and stomped out.

Gene returned to the front of the room. "Sorry about the interruption. Caleb is passionate about this business, but that doesn't excuse his behavior."

How many other Haida felt like Caleb?

"We understand," Harvey said.

"I'd like to answer the question about accepted processes for carbon credits," I said.

Gene nodded.

I stood and directed my answer at Jennie. "Tree planting is a recognized type of carbon credit practice. As trees grow, they take carbon dioxide out of the atmosphere. With trees you have a decent idea how much CO2—carbon dioxide—the trees will take up, and you can measure their growth. Hence the acknowledged carbon credits."

Jennie looked confused. "But *algae* take up CO2 too when they grow."

I was about to answer, but Ted interrupted, which annoyed the heck out of me.

"Yes, they do," he said. "But there are two big problems with your scheme. First, you would have to show that iron made the algae grow. As we've said, that's very difficult to do."

Charlotte lifted her chin. "And the other problem?" Apparently, she'd been paying close attention to this discussion.

It looked like Ted was going to respond again. I raised a finger, but he didn't notice. I jumped in.

"Sure," I said. "Charlotte, think about a tree—a sapling. As the tree grows, it takes carbon dioxide out of the air, as we've said. *But* if you cut down the sapling and it decomposes—or you burn it in a fire—that CO2 goes right back into the air. No carbon credits. A major hitch in Roger Grant's scheme is tracking the algae. If they sink and are decomposed—which is highly likely—there is no net removal of CO2. That means no money for carbon credits."

I turned to look at William. He reminded me of a student who'd just failed a major exam. His shoulders sagged, and his glance in my direction was painful to look at.

Gene took over again. "We've been at this a while now. Don't know about anyone else, but there's a little building out there calling to me."

From the pace of Charlotte and Jennie's movements to the door, it looked like Gene wasn't the only one who needed to visit the outhouse. Ted, Harvey, and I walked into the clearing in the front of the longhouse.

"Think I'll use the facilities too," Harvey said.

When she'd disappeared down the path, I turned to Ted, hands on hips. "Do you know you cut me off?"

His eyebrows shot up. "When?"

"William's question about algal uptake of CO2."

"Huh. Sorry." He bit his lip.

Ted looked so guilty, I felt like a jerk. "The back and forth is hard," I said. "There's a lot going on. What do you think so far?"

"Gene's doing a great job. Hard to say about the others. That Caleb's a piece of work, though. Here they come. Back to work."

We all filed into the longhouse.

After we were seated again, Jennie got up. From the serious expression on her face, she could have been addressing the UN assembly. She spoke in the slow cadence of the older Haida. "As visitors, you can't know our history. Over and over, people from away have decimated our islands of trees, fish, and wild creatures. But finally, *we* are the ones who have the power over Haida Gwaii. This iron project, it's ours."

I got to my feet. "Jennie, we do realize we're outsiders who know little about your struggles."

Jennie nodded her head once. "I will tell you about bears. This dance will help you understand in ways my words cannot."

The door opened behind us. Bent over, a bare-chested man stepped through the opening, straightened up, and thrust blackened hands above his head. A massive mask perched on his torso—a red-snouted creature with round white eyes set in bright blue and an open maw that exposed spiked white teeth. The dancer was naked except for a grass skirt that swished with each step. Bear stomped toward us, grunting with each step, and stopped inches from my face. It stunk of carrion and hissed with each breath, but I didn't back away.

The creature swung around. Spinning like a top, it circled the longhouse once, twice, three times. Every eye fixed on the whirling dervish. On the fourth circuit, a wild bear bounded around the circle, its shiny brown fur rippling with each leap. Just short of the door, the man reappeared, stepped through the door, and was gone.

I fell onto the bench.

Jennie began, her diction more pointed. "Hundreds of hunters came here to shoot black bears. Places like Graham Island Lodge bragged that hunters killed so-called 'trophy animals.' This disgusted us. Bear is chief of the forest, a relative we *never* eat. Haida are bears. Bears are Haida."

She paused to drink water from a glass. "Bears here are special—a rare type of black bear found no place else with huge jaws and teeth."

I knew this and more. Ecologists called northwest bears a keystone species. They ate salmon on riverbanks, and scientists had traced the flow of nutrients from thousands of salmon to the upland. In that way, bears brought the richness of the ocean to the rainforest.

Jennie went on. "British Columbia's government ignored the Haida nation's demand for an end to the bear hunt. We flooded them with thousands of letters and e-mails—and won.

In two thousand thirteen, the Ministry of Forests, Lands, and Natural Resources shut down bear hunting here *forever*."

Jennie took another sip. "Then there's logging. When companies ran out of big trees on the mainland, they slashed our forests, and the Crown approved it. It was a land grab. Evil. But in two thousand four, Canada's Supreme Court sided with *us* and against Weyerhaeuser Lumber." Chin up, eyes shining, Jennie looked straight ahead at something we couldn't see. She put her hand on Gene's shoulder and took her seat. Her speech was succinct, heartfelt, and effective. I guessed she'd given something like it before.

"Maybe," said Gene, "you better understand now why we believe that we should control our own waters."

Given the history of white domination Jennie accounted, I itched to ask why the Council agreed to work with a non-native from the States.

It was as if Charlotte read my mind. "What do you think of Roger Grant?"

Harvey took that one. "Mr. Grant isn't a scientist. He's an American businessman. We strongly believe projects of this scale and importance must be carried out by trained scientists who are impartial."

The word "impartial" hung in the air. Gene stroked his chin. Jennie shook her head. Charlotte's face was expressionless, impossible to read.

We described the report we were asked to write. Gene outlined their next step—a meeting with the larger Environmental Council in two days. After that, there would be another Council vote on the iron project.

Gene announced the meeting's end, and we walked up to thank him, Charlotte, and Jennie. When I told Jennie she was a powerful speaker, she looked grateful but tired. Harvey, Ted, and

I headed for the front of the building. Dissection of the meeting was on hold until we were alone. I waited for Harvey and Ted to get through the little doorway, stepped out into the clearing, sniffed the air, and took in the pungent smell of rain. Billowy dark clouds raced by overhead.

Gene joined us.

"Sure looks like rain," I said. "Are there signs you look for that tell you it's going to rain? Bird calls, that kind of thing?"

"Well," he said, "There *is* one thing that works pretty well."

"Yes?"

"Environment Canada's weather radio."

Gene enjoyed my open mouth for a moment. Then he put his hand on my shoulder, threw back his head, and laughed.

FOR DINNER, WE GATHERED AROUND A LONG PICNIC TABLE on the protected porch of a dining building in the bath-house compound. Rain pelted the wooden roof above. Our sleeping bags and pads, plus our clothes, were dry and waiting for us in the longhouse, thank goodness. I was also grateful for the fleece pullover and pants I'd changed into back there.

As if we'd never debated their iron fertilization venture, nine of us—Harvey, Ted, and I, plus Gene, Jennie, Charlotte, William, his girlfriend Anna, and Bart—shared a traditional Haida meal. Three dark blue platters decorated with black animal icons were already on the table when we arrived. They held three items I guessed were appetizers.

William pointed to each one. "Dried seaweed called sguu, pickled sea asparagus, and octopus balls."

I leaned over to examine the closest platter and squinted at what looked like skinny pickles, crunchy black kale, and fried balls. I started with the one that looked familiar, selected a pickle, and took a bite. Everyone but William, Ted, and Harvey was already eating and chatting. The trio waited for my reaction.

Sour and salty, it had a nice crunch. "William, this is great. In Maine we use *Salicornia* as a fresh garnish in salad. It's a salty succulent. Never had it pickled, though."

Harvey and Ted picked up some sea asparagus, nibbled, and tried the seaweed and octopus.

I put a bit of seaweed in my mouth. It melted into a salty flavor with an unusual zing. "Wow. This tastes like the sea." The octopus was last because what I'd had before was leathery. I slowly chewed one of the balls. It was tender and juicy. I licked a finger. "Terrific. How do you collect and prepare this food?"

"We get octopus under large rocks at low tide," William said. "But Charlotte's the expert."

Charlotte reached across the table and touched William's arm. "And you're my top student." She picked up some seaweed. "We collect this in May from the surface of the smoothest rocks and dry it in the sun until crispy. Sea asparagus is best early summer."

Three women in black jeans and red t-shirts removed the empty platters and passed around plates of salmon and roasted root vegetables. I caught one of their names—Lynne—when another server called to her. Lynne, who had intently watched William and Anna in the longhouse, dropped a plate in front of Anna with a loud clunk. William flinched.

With a toss of her waist-length black hair, Lynne turned and marched toward the kitchen. I'd considered the young woman attractive, but the ugly scowl and searing black eyes turned her into a witch. I shivered.

Ted speared a chunk of bright orange fish with his fork and held it up. "What kind of salmon is this?"

William, who appeared to be the local James Beard, said, "Chinook. It's barbequed with bacon jam made with bacon, vinegar, brown sugar, and onions."

We all tucked in. The salmon was melt-in-your-mouth delicious. Seated next to Charlotte, I finished eating and tried to think of something to say to her.

Charlotte held the edge of the table with purple-veined, deeply wrinkled hands and beat me to it. She spoke deliberately and slowly. "Tell me, Mara, why are you an ocean scientist?"

Until that point, this woman showed no personal interest in the three of us. The question caught me by surprise.

"Um, my parents were both oceanographers. We always had people over for dinner. As a kid, I'd sit on the top step of the stairs and listen to them talk about fishing, boats, seals, whales—other creatures—how humans were damaging the ocean. I guess it got in my blood."

"They died."

I covered my chest with my hand. "Well, yes. In a submarine accident."

"When you were—"

"Nineteen."

"Ah," she said, as if that explained everything.

I figured it was my turn to probe. "What is your, um, role here?"

She leaned toward me, and I smelled earth. "As the oldest woman in Kinuk, they call me Revered One. Women are powerful in our society. During the time when fewer than five hundred Haida were left, women held onto the songs, crests, and stories." She straightened up, ran a hand down her braid. "I whisper and people hear me."

The next question out of my mouth surprised even me. "What do you care about most?"

Unblinking, Charlotte stared at the bay below us. She was quiet so long I thought she was in some sort of trance. When she spoke, I had to lean closer to hear her. "The Haida came from the ocean. The sea feeds our bodies and that feeds our souls. Out there is the *only* thing that is important."

Charlotte studied my face. "You and I, Mara, we're the same that way."

I sucked in a quick breath. Charlotte was perceptive, but her earlier statements about my parents made me feel uneasy.

Charlotte turned to Bart, seated on her other side, and William, opposite her. She chit-chatted with them like a completely normal old lady.

Voices got louder as the locals called out, teased, and laughed with each other. I guessed most were probably related in one way or another. As an only child with no parents, living alongside extended family was as foreign to me as a fourth of July picnic to the Haida.

The servers cleared our plates and returned with generous slices of berry pie. After I savored my last forkful, I looked across at Anna and was struck once more by her stunning features and charm. "You know, Anna, you look like some kind of performer. Do you act? Play music?"

"I do rap."

Not what I expected. "Really? Rap?"

"Rap's big with younger Haida."

At one end of the table, Gene called out, "Hey. With some of the old folk, too."

"Can I listen to you online?"

To this, William jumped in. "Anna wrote a song that's gone viral. It's about super tankers, the Northern Gateway pipeline, and our beloved provincial ex-Premier." His intonation for "beloved" indicated the Premier was anything but.

I gave Anna an arm pump. "Wow, an environmental rapper. *Out*standing. Could you do some of the pipeline rap for us?"

Anna glanced at William. After all, she hardly knew us. He winked, and in a clear, confident voice, Anna sang.

Oil, toil. Pipe the oil. Sell the soul. Hole in soil.

Oil, toil. Toil the oil. Pipe the oil.

You've sold your soul.

Look, Look. In the ground. A hole too deep

So deep it boil.

Anna repeated the refrain. We all clapped and whooped. Even Charlotte applauded. William kissed Anna on the cheek, and she blushed.

One person didn't clap or whoop. Just visible around the corner of the porch, Lynne's face was frozen into a piercing glare directed right at William's lover.

9

IT WAS DARK BY THE TIME DESSERT PLATES HEADED FOR the kitchen. I asked Gene how to say "thank you" in the Haida language.

"*Haw'aa.*"

It sounded like "how ah," so I gave that a try.

"Good," he said. "Here's another. *Dáng an HI kil 'láagang.* I thank you."

I tried, "*Dung un kill agon.*"

"Close."

The man was being kind.

"And if you want to say I thank you folks very much, that's *Daláng an HI kíl 'láa áwyaagang.*"

I opened my mouth then shut it with a shake of the head. Once more, Gene threw back his head and laughed.

We thanked everyone—in English—including the cooks cleaning up in the kitchen. People who lived elsewhere on the archipelago called out their goodnights in Haida and English as they disappeared into the night. Ted, Harvey, and I returned to the picnic table to compare notes about the exchange in the longhouse.

Harvey went first. "They were welcoming, of course, and very kind. Professional, you know. But I couldn't tell what they really thought of us and what we told them."

I nodded. "Given their history, you'd expect them to keep their cards close to their chests. Jennie's account was incredible. I couldn't believe it when the man turned into a real bear."

Harvey and Ted glanced at each other. She said, "What bear?"

"You didn't see…? Um, let's talk about it later."

Harvey cleared her throat and said, "Right."

"Gene's a smart guy who'll think carefully about the whole conversation," Ted said. "Jennie asked the question about fertilizer. That and her speech probably means she's the rebel in the group. And Charlotte?" He shook his head. "Don't know. She's an enigma."

"Actually, we had a really nice chat. An unusual woman. Leader of some kind."

That piqued Harvey's interest. "Huh. What'd she say?"

"Couple of things. For one, that my parents were dead."

Harvey raised her manicured eyebrows. "Whoa."

"I asked what she thought was most important."

"And?"

"She said the Haida came from the sea, so only that was important."

Harvey gestured toward the ocean. "Given their history, that's an intelligent answer."

"I still don't get it. Europeans exploited the Haida big time, but they take up with a white guy from the States?"

"William did say that the Haida Nation wanted to be a leader in marine geo-engineering," Ted said.

I massaged my forehead. "That might explain the sentiment, but not why they'd trust an outsider like Grant."

"It's getting late. We've each had a long day," Harvey said. "Here's where I think we are. They know a little about our backgrounds, why we were sent here, and where we're coming from on iron fertilization. I think we worked well together in the meeting. Jennie's description about their history with exploitation was very helpful. Anything else?"

"I'm impressed by Gene's professionalism," I said. "We're fortunate there. Maybe he asked Jennie and Charlotte so we'd see a range of ideas."

"Caleb didn't hesitate to voice his opinion," Ted said. "There's some strong emotions around all of this."

"Lots at stake—a million dollars, the Haida Nation's self-rule, dignity," I said.

We ran through the meeting for a while and then decided it was late.

Ted put his hand on my shoulder. "Quick walk down to the water?"

It was my chance to explain that I needed more time to myself and why. I rotated the ring on my pinky finger. "Ah, sure."

Harvey got up. "Night, kids. Just don't wake me when you get back to the longhouse."

Ted waited while I zipped up my fleece jacket. We'd reached the top of the porch stairs when voices from inside the building startled us. We both stopped dead.

The first was a woman's. It was not familiar. "You *bastard*. We were *engaged* to be married. How could you do this to me?"

A male. William. "I'm sorry, Lynne. Really I am. But things happen. We meet—"

"We?" She repeated the word louder in a higher pitch. "We?"

"Lynne."

"*I* didn't change. You…" The young woman stopped. It sounded like she was crying.

William's voice was pleading. "Please, Lynne. I love you like a sister. But not a wife. I went to S'G̱ang Gwaay Llanagaay and asked my ancestral spirits what to do. They told me that to find peace I should follow my heart. You are not my heart."

Haltingly, she got out the words. "We were born—on the same day. For—as long as I can remember, we were supposed—." She coughed. "To be husband and wife. Everyone, your parents and mine. They all knew. Everyone knew."

William tried again. "Lynne."

"Bastard. Get your hands off me."

A door opened, slammed shut, and a dark figure with long, flying hair ran down the steps. Ted and I didn't move. Another person followed. In the moonlight, head bent, William took each step as if the effort hurt.

Ted and I waited until we were sure he was gone.

We didn't speak until we were nearly to the beach.

Ted said, "Boy, that was painful."

"Young love hurts. But it's so incredible out here. Let's leave what we just heard behind for now."

Unsettled weather had passed, leaving a cloudless sky. Moon shadow defined a steep incline as the path dropped to a ribbon of shingle still exposed at high tide.

We stopped at the water's edge and stood before the Haida sea. Gentle waves slid landward, retreated, slid up again. Pebbles rolling up and back with the water momentarily hypnotized me.

"A little different from the ocean we dealt with today," Ted said.

I blinked and turned to face him. "For sure. I'm always amazed how quickly the ocean can change. From tranquil to furious in minutes. One reason why kayaking's dangerous. Hey, what you did for me today—"

Ted gently put a finger on my lips. "You're okay. That's all that matters. I never want to lose you."

He pulled me in tight and kissed me hard.

Ted stepped back and took both my hands. Moonlight turned his curls silvery, but his face was in shadow. "Mara, what

William said about his heart. I want you to know what's in *my* heart."

"Ted, it's been great. Actually, I'd like to—"

"It's more than that."

My throat tightened. "More?"

"Mara, someday I want you to be my wife."

My mouth flew open. It was a good thing he couldn't see my face. "Um—"

"Not now. We've only known each other for a few months. In a year or two."

I stepped back, dropped his hands, and put one of mine on my chest. My heart pounded so hard it pushed up against my palm. "Um, yeah. Last couple of months we've had a really nice time together." Considering Ted's declaration, that was pretty lame. I added, "But I've not thought—"

"Sorry. I did spring that on you. Between William, this beautiful night, what happened today. It's just, like I said, I never want to lose you. We'll talk about it later."

Ted took my hand. We returned to the path and ended up at the longhouse clearing. Thoughts racing, I didn't remember a thing about the walk.

Careful not to wake Harvey, we crept into the longhouse. Long rectangular slits of moonlight filtered through the windows and illuminated the interior. In a dark corner, our sleeping bags lay on either side of Harvey's. Ted took off his outer layer of clothes and slipped into his bag. I did the same.

"Good night, Mara," Ted whispered. His breathing slowed to a regular cadence.

With a sigh, I nestled into my bag and looked at the ceiling. Despite the taxing day, sleep wouldn't come. My skin itched; my legs twitched. I rolled onto my right side, left, my right again. No good. On my back, I stared into the dark and tried to sort out my jumble of emotions and thoughts.

Ted's statement about marriage had come out of nowhere, and scared the hell out of me. For god's sake, we'd been going out since the spring, and it was only August. Yes, I liked being with him. Ted was great company. We went out to dinner, ran, and kayaked together, and the sex was terrific. But my claustrophobia was very real. I wanted him to understand that I needed time alone and wanted to take our relationship one day at a time.

Marriage had never crossed my mind.

On the other hand, Ted's quick thinking had saved my life. I was in his debt. But surely that didn't mean I owed him something that big.

A story by Dorothy Sayers, my favorite mystery author, came to mind. After Lord Peter Wimsey saved Harriet Vane from the gallows, he asked Harriet to marry him. She declined and said, "I'm sorry. I know I'm being horribly ungrateful…"

Gratitude. That was it. You couldn't marry someone out of gratitude.

Round and round I went with questions and worries. Hours passed. At home, when I was anxious in the middle of the night, a hot shower often helped me sleep. Kinuk didn't have showers, but it did have hot pools. I could go down to the pool we visited earlier and soak in hot water until I felt sleepy.

The moon had set, leaving the longhouse completely dark. I wriggled out of my bag, groped for the flashlight beside me, found it, slid out of my bag, and grabbed my clothes. Ted and Harvey each breathed steadily.

Out in the clearing, I flipped off the light and scanned the sky. With no artificial lights, the stellar display was astounding—the big and little dippers, arc of the Milky Way, and a bright twinkle that might be Saturn. I turned on the flashlight and stepped into the forest. The path was pitch black. I fixed on the tiny circle of light on the footpath to insure no missteps into an unexpected cedar tree or, worse, an eight-legged creature's web.

Despite an extra layer of fleece, I was chilled by the time I reached the bathhouse area. Below, pools overlooking the sea gave off a sulfur smell. I used the privy and stopped in the bathhouse to get a towel. The flow of hot water in and out of the tub Harvey and I had shared kept the single room warm. Back outside in the still, cold night air, the rustle of what sounded like leaves startled me. I directed my light up toward the sound but saw nothing.

"The wind or some critter," I whispered. "An ermine or maybe an owl."

I picked my way down the footpath. The sulfur rotten egg odor grew stronger. It actually was a smell I liked because it reminded me of home—salt marshes, rotting eelgrass, and seaweed washed up on the rocks. The Maine coast. I reached the bottom of the path, threw the towel across a rock, stripped off my clothes, and slid down into the pool. The water was gloriously warm. Just what I needed.

The night was chilly, and I wanted to keep my hair dry. In a high ponytail, it probably wouldn't get wet. But just to be safe, I spread my arms over flat-topped rocks bordering the pool and kept my head out of the water. My outstretched legs floated before they dropped down to the bottom.

My toes touched something absolutely not rock-like.

I jerked back. Water sloshed to the other side of the pool. Just enough starlight reflected off the water's surface to illuminate the horror that slowly emerged directly across from me.

Mine wasn't the only body in the pool. But I knew right away that the other one, William's, was dead.

10

A T THREE-FORTY-FIVE A.M., DAWN WOKE THE RAINFOR-
est on Haida Gwaii. Calls of thrushes echoed through
the village of Kinuk. But this morning, everything was
different.

By six, officers from the archipelago's Queen Charlotte
detachment of the Royal Canadian Mounted Police were busy
gathering information that might be relevant to William's death.
After the police had officially declared William dead, they
contacted a coroner on the mainland. Regulations for sudden,
unexpected, non-traumatic death—especially of someone so
young and healthy—called for an investigation. That meant in-
terviews with key people, which RCMP Sergeant Fred Knapton
conducted in the dining building. I'd found the body and was,
unfortunately, of particular interest.

Knapton interviewed me from one side of a scratched
wooden table. He was a tall, broad-shouldered man too large
for his chair—or the room, for that matter. He'd shed his jacket
and pulled his tie loose. His hair, baby-fine brown and in need
of a cut, fell over his forehead, and a cap—dark blue with a
wide yellow band—sat to his right within arm's reach. It wasn't
the tan broad-brimmed one I associated with the Mounties,
but the bright red and gold crown stood proud on top of the
badge.

Opposite Knapton, I shifted in a metal folding chair while
he fiddled with the tape recorder. I was drained of all emotion,
exhausted from lack of sleep, and shattered by the bizarre turn of

events. Elbows on the table, I rubbed the back of my neck with both hands. "Never done this before."

Knapton slid the recorder to the middle of the table and looked at me. His brown eyes were kind. "You've had a shock. Just answer my questions as best you can. If you recall anything later, you can tell us."

"Before we start, I overheard something that may interest you." I described Lynne's angry outburst. "I'm sure it's just a coincidence that William died soon after that, but—"

Knapton who'd scribbled the information in his notebook, nodded. I got the idea that he already knew about friction between Lynne and William. He turned the recorder on and in a monotone stated his name plus the time, date, location, and circumstances. He asked me to say my name, occupation, and address.

"Thank you. Now, describe what happened in the hot pool."

"Well, like I said, he—ah William—just rose up out of the water on the other side of the pool. Kind of like a seal does, you know."

If Knapton thought that was a strange analogy, he didn't show it.

"Can you describe what William looked like?"

I closed my eyes, tried to picture the dreadful scene, blinked them open. "The stars were bright, but it was pretty dark. I had the impression his face was a funny color, purplish I think. But like I said, it was dark."

"Anything else?"

"His eyes."

"What about them?"

"He stared at me, but was nothing was there."

Knapton nodded.

"You said your feet touched his?"

My legs jerked. "Yes."

"Anything to say about that?"

"His legs felt stiff."

Another nod. "Anything else?"

"I knew something was wrong right away."

"Why is that?"

"Because he didn't say anything. I don't—didn't—really know him, of course, but William didn't seem like the type who'd play Halloween jokes on visitors in the middle of the night."

"And why were *you* in the pool in the middle of the night?"

I explained my insomnia and hope that hot water would make me sleepy.

"Earlier that evening when you left the dining area, you had no plans to go into the pool?"

"No. It was spontaneous."

"So no one else knew you were going to do this?"

"That's right."

"Who else slept in the longhouse?"

"Just my two colleagues. Harvey—Harville—Allison and Ted McKnight. Both were asleep when I left to go down to the pools."

"Did they leave the longhouse during the night?"

"No. I was wide awake the whole time and would've heard them."

"After you left the longhouse, did you hear anything or see anyone?"

"No. Wait. There was something. I went into the bathhouse to get a towel and was startled by a noise when I came out."

"What kind of a noise?"

"Like rustling leaves. I thought it was some animal or maybe the wind." I frowned.

Knapton said, "What?"

"The night was calm. There was no wind."

The room swayed. I leaned forward and cradled my head in my palms.

Knapton said, "Take your time."

I coughed and sat back. "Someone could've been there when I left the bathhouse. That would, um, mean William was... He was murdered."

"All we know now is he was dead when you found him. There's a lot more we don't know—how or why he ended up in that pool, if he died from a natural cause, who last saw him alive, if there was foul play. I'd appreciate you keeping your thoughts and questions to yourself, okay?"

"I'd like to talk about what happened with my two colleagues."

"I understand that. Just the three of you. If you learn or remember anything, contact me right away. Don't worry if it's important. Just contact me."

The chair scraped on the wooden floor as I stood. "One more question, Sergeant Knapton."

He pushed stray strands of hair off his forehead. "Yes?"

"Am I a suspect?"

He looked at me straight on. "We don't know how or when William died, like I said. That's up to the coroner. As scientist, Dr. Tusconi, you pay attention to details and patterns. You puzzle things out. For William's sake—not because you might be a suspect—why don't you apply your talents to this problem?"

"William seemed like a terrific guy. I'll certainly do that."

"If you learn or even surmise anything, pass it along to me. And only me. Don't take any chances, do anything rash."

I slowly nodded. "Yes, and please call me Mara."

Harvey, Ted, and I joined the dozen people who watched as William's body was carried across the pier, down to the float, and onto the waiting RMCP boat. We'd learned that his parents lived on the mainland. It was impossible to imagine their grief as they watched their son borne from the police boat in a body bag. Did William have siblings who'd stand next to the weeping parents? I didn't know.

Gene, red-eyed and tight-mouthed, had his arm around Anna's shoulder. Her sobs were muffled, but when the boat pulled away, she buried her face in Gene's chest and cried without reservation. Her grief was heartbreaking.

As outsiders, we stood apart from the rest. The others slowly left, but we stayed down on the beach, silent until the boat disappeared from view.

"I simply can't take this in," I said. "William, so vibrant and happy just a few hours ago. And now he's dead?"

Ted shook his head. "It is awful, but young people do die. When I was in college, a football player had a heart attack during practice. He caught a toss, clutched his chest, and fell onto the ground."

Harvey toed a loose stone. "It's possible, of course, that William's death was natural. But maybe he was drinking and he drowned in the pool. In the States, alcoholism is an enormous problem with Native Americans."

"Perhaps, but I didn't smell alcohol, and he doesn't seem like the drinking type," I said. "Seems to me it's a pretty big coincidence he died before he was going to defend the iron project to the Environment Council. I mean, right before their vote."

Harvey turned toward me. "Come on. You've been reading too many spy novels. Someone *kills* William because he supported Roger Grant?"

"Think about what Jennie told us. There's a real struggle

going on here. One side wants control over their waters. I'm guessing the other wants nothing to do with rich white outsiders. Powerful stuff."

She tipped her head and scrunched up her lips.

"Christ," I added after a moment.

"What?"

"It'd be dreadful if we had something to do with this."

Harvey stepped back. "What do you mean?"

"Maybe our being here brought something to a head."

"Mara," Ted said. "That sounds crazy."

"At the risk of turning the Haida into gentle Indians, the ones we've met seem like kind people who respect each other," Harvey said. "I can't imagine one of them killing William."

"That Caleb character and the woman who screamed at William didn't seem so kind," Ted said.

Harvey put her hand on Ted's arm. "What woman? What're you talking about?"

We described Lynne's accusations.

"Hard to know what to make of that. Young love's bewildering and can really hurt."

It occurred to me that older love was equally baffling. "I really want to understand what happened to William, but it's just too sad and my brain's in a jumble."

Harvey nodded. "*And* we have work to do."

We headed toward the path to the bathhouse area. "Only two more days left," I said. "We still have to do plankton tows, sample kelp on tomorrow morning's scuba dive, and the big council meeting's tomorrow afternoon. We fly to Vancouver and home the day after that. We've got to plan what we're doing."

"This morning we should work on the UN report. I'll see if Gene'll take us out later so we can sample plankton close to shore," Harvey said.

"The smaller net and bottles are in that canvas duffle in the longhouse," Ted added.

We stepped onto the trail and followed it up. "We've each got our computers, so we can outline the report and start working on our sections," Harvey said. She stopped and gestured toward the forest. "And despite what's happened, we're still in one of the few protected temperate rainforests in the world."

The dining building was the only place where we could work. It wasn't long before my back ached from leaning over to type and my bottom hurt from the hard seat.

I rolled my shoulders. "Ugh. I'm going outside for a walk. Be back soon."

Harvey looked up from her computer. "Just be careful out there."

I stepped from the outhouse and nearly bumped into Charlotte.

"Mara, you study nature. My plant collection would interest you, I think."

Charlotte's braids fell nearly to her waist and her eyeglass chain featured a long-beaked bird spearing a fish. Over her glasses, she fixed almond-shaped eyes on mine. Again, I sensed this was a woman people listened to. It'd be a good idea to spend a little more time with her.

"We're working on our report, and I'd love a break. Thanks for the invite."

I followed Charlotte to her cabin. There was an identical one closer to the dining building. "Whose is that?"

"Gene's."

Charlotte's cabin was small—a tiny porch, one large room, and a smaller room I glimpsed through a partly open door. The big one served as dining room, living room, plus kitchen. It looked and smelled like an old-fashioned laboratory of a doctor or scientist. A wooden bookcase half the length of one wall held hundreds of glass bottles, each bearing white labels and black lettering in the same cursive script. Another wooden case covered the rest of the wall. It had deep shelves stuffed with large sheets of paper, some separated in oversized folders. This was a herbarium—a collection of dried plants pressed and identified to genus and species—and most likely the source of the mothball aroma that perfumed the room.

She motioned to a wooden table that looked too big for the room. "Would you like some herbal tea?"

"That would be nice."

Charlotte opened the bottom spout of a big glass water jug and filled a metal kettle. She carried the kettle to an ancient gas stove, lit a burner with a match, and pulled down a tin from the shelf above.

There were two wooden chairs on either side of the table. I took the one nearest the door. Charlotte shuffled back and slowly lowered herself into the opposite chair.

"When you get old, Mara, I hope you don't get creaky like I am."

"Can I help with the tea?"

"Yes." She motioned toward the stove. "When that kettle boils, there are cups and a teapot on the shelf there."

"You have bottled gas but not running water?"

"There's electricity from a generator."

I nodded. "Charlotte, tell me about your collection. You have so many labeled samples, and your herbarium is impressive."

She leaned back and, with a little smile, looked over my shoulder at her dried plants. "I collected it all myself over the years. We have many rare ones on the islands."

"I've read that the archipelago was a refuge for plants and animals during the last ice age."

"As I tell my students, there are a few ways to think about the great many kinds of creatures. The ice age, like you said, that's one. We also have very different places for things to grow—the rainforest, wet spots, mountains, and the ocean. And, of course, there's the Raven who filled the forests and rivers with life."

The kettle was boiling. I got up, turned off the gas, and took down a black teapot and matching cups. There was a spoon on the counter. "How much tea should I use?"

"About a tablespoon for that pot. But I don't think I'll have any."

I returned with the teapot and mug. "You don't want tea?"

She waved her hand. "Had some Labrador tea this morning. Let that steep for a minute. Not too long."

I was about to ask why two cups of Labrador tea was one too many, but maybe Charlotte had a medical condition.

She put a hand on the table. "Tell me about Maine—what it looks like. I've never been there."

I stared out the window. "It's like this in some ways, very different in others. New England's been repeatedly glaciated, of course, but it's not actively tectonic like here. Maine's a landscape of smoothed mountains, deep troughs, and ground-up rocks dumped on what's now the coast. You've probably seen photos of our coast with waves crashing high into the air around enormous boulders. Inland is so different. When you read Thoreau's essays about the immense Maine forest, you can smell the spruce and pine."

"Wasn't it Thoreau who said 'It's not what you look at that matters, it's what you see'?"

Swirling the teapot, I realized, again, there was more to Charlotte Weber than you'd guess from just looking at the ancient woman seated before me. "That's a great quote. I'll have to remember it." My nose took in the musty, grassy bouquet of old books. "You must know an awful lot about your plants."

"Yes. In this room and here," she touched her forehead, "there's a library of knowledge. I pass on this sacred wisdom to a few of the younger Haida."

"Was William one?"

Charlotte closed her eyes for a moment. "Yes. He was very special, a gifted student." She pointed to an antique dissecting microscope on one of the herbarium shelves. "See that microscope there? He spent hours looking at plant parts."

I poured the tea into the cup. It smelled spicy. "I'm so sorry about William."

She shook her head. "It's done now."

"He was your most promising student?"

"Oh, yes. Bright, thoughtful. He cared."

"But he championed a project that seems so opposed to everything you love."

The muscles around Charlotte's eyes tightened. She stared past me like she was witness to centuries of Haida disappointment and pain. She nodded slowly. "Yes. That man—Roger Grant—seemed to know just what to tell William. Things like the Haida would be famous in the fight against global warming with a new way to get carbon credits. And all the good we could do with the money. Better hospital, schools, all that. He had, as they say, William's number."

I cradled my mug. "Didn't you try to argue with William?"

She sighed "Maybe I should have, but it's not my way to tell my students what to think. I asked questions about Grant and why the iron would work—that kind of thing. William talked about a study on iron and salmon that Grant showed him. It was obvious William was committed."

I realized Charlotte had never stated her opinion about the iron project. "And what did you think about Roger Grant?"

"That is something I would not say aloud to outsiders."

My hands tightened around the mug.

Perhaps noticing my reaction, Charlotte opened the door a crack. "What you've been telling us affected William."

I raised an eyebrow.

"William listened carefully to everything you said. He knew you had years of education to get where you are, and your arguments were based on science and research, lots of it. The contrast between the three of you and Roger Grant became very obvious."

"Wow, I didn't know that."

"He didn't let on in public, but he finally saw Grant for what he was. He talked to me about the hard decision he had to make before the next Council meeting vote in a couple of days. That's between you and me."

I ran my finger around the rim of my cup, let that revelation sink in, and waited for Charlotte to say more.

She fingered the long-beaked bird on her eyeglass chain, glanced over at the microscope, and pressed her lips together.

I changed the subject. "This tea is good. Different from anything I've had."

"I make hot drinks from plants I collect." She smiled. "Except hot cocoa. William especially liked cocoa."

"What do you use the plants for? Besides tea, I mean? Medicine?"

She leaned back in her chair and twirled the band at the bottom of one braid. "All these plants contain chemicals. You know about that. Wax myrtle leaves for fever, boiled cedar leaves for cough, willow for night sweats, blackberry for mouth ulcers."

"Some are poisonous, of course."

"Plants do so much good, but they can be dangerous. You have to know what you're doing. I'm happy you like the tea."

I took another sip, put the mug down, and tried again to get my hostess to open up. "What Jennie said about the Haida taking control with the iron project—that was interesting. But it didn't jibe with your working with Roger Grant. He's an outsider and, in my view, a schemer. Everything the Haida would disdain."

Outside a crow cawed.

"I agree. It's a puzzle."

I studied Charlotte's face for more information, but like a priest who'd just left the confessional, she gave away nothing. I sipped my tea and waited.

Charlotte ran a hand down one of her braids and leaned forward, veined hand on the table. "There are three truths you must know about Haida Gwaii. First, the sea shapes *everything*. The land plants I collect had to learn how to survive salt and storms. Even the earth beneath our feet rose from the depths. For thousands of years the sea has given us salmon, cod, crab, and other creatures, basket reeds, fish bone, gull guano, salt, so much more."

She studied my face. It was hard to not look away. I blinked. "And the second truth?"

"An angry sea is a dangerous sea. You saw that anger off Augustine Island before William saved you."

"So William told you about that."

She shook her head. "He didn't need to."

A chill ran down my arms.

"Maybe an example will help you understand the third truth," she said. "Rivers that flow into the sea are transformed, and they are not. River water remains water, but it is different. So it is with people, animals, and what you call the supernatural. They flow into each other. Different, but the same. You saw that with the bear dance. Man is bear is man."

Given what had happened with Ted and the horror with William, I'd forgotten about the bear. What Charlotte said made no sense. With my vivid imagination, surely I'd gotten caught up in the mesmerizing dance.

I tapped my mug. "You're right, Charlotte. I don't understand. For me, what I touch, see, smell, and hear—that is real and all there is."

"Yes, I thought so, and I am sorry for you."

11

I RETURNED TO THE DINING BUILDING.

"You've been gone a while," Harvey said.

"Charlotte invited me to her cabin for a cup of tea. You should see the place. It's an old-fashioned botanical museum. Reminded me of the days when women collected marine specimens in those long skirts, white puffy shirts, and big hats."

Ted stood and stretched one arm straight up. "These chairs aren't the best. Did Charlotte say anything interesting?"

"Yes, but I didn't understand some of it."

He stretched the other arm. "Like what?"

"People and animals become one another. The same but different."

"Good for fables," he said.

"Gene stopped by, and told us about a place called Ninstints," Harvey said. "It's a good location for the plankton tow, and he's happy to show us around afterward. He says there's more standing ancient Haida totem poles in Ninstints than anywhere else. He wants to communicate with his ancestors about William." She looked at her watch. "We leave in a half hour."

I powered off my computer. "Sounds great all around. After we get back, I'll finish telling you what Charlotte said."

Twenty minutes later, standing in the stern with one hand on the motor's tiller, Gene pulled up to the Kinuk dock in a twenty-five foot inflatable boat. Anna was seated in the bow's one-person seat. I hadn't expected to see her and hoped the trip would lift her spirits.

I stepped aboard and straddled the backseat. Ted handed me the plankton net. We'd already attached the towline and first bottle. The box of collecting bottles was next.

I stashed the gear between the seats. "Nice boat, Gene."

"Too rich for me." Gene looked sideways as we left the dock. "Belongs to Parks Canada so the Watchmen can monitor the islands, things like that."

"Tell us about the Watchmen."

Ted and Harvey got settled and Gene increased our speed. I turned around to face the bow.

"In the early eighties we started a volunteer program to protect the islands from vandalism." Gene cranked the motor and yelled behind me. "People, even some Haida, had damaged totem poles and dug up artifacts. About ten years later, Haida Gwaii became a National Park. Watchmen were hired to protect important sites like Ninstints and educate visitors about the cultural and natural history. I oversee the Watchmen. Some of 'em are women, by the way. William was great at it."

At the mention of William's name, I stared out at nothing, the outboard's steady drone a backdrop.

Gene went on. "Ninstints is a twenty-minute boat ride from here. It's the southernmost island in the archipelago and a World Heritage Site. I'll tell you all about it when we get there." We'd reached the opening of Kinuk Bay. Gene called out, "See the island a few miles dead ahead? That's it."

Gene let loose the motor's throttle. The inflatable bounced through oncoming waves. I held onto the plank seat with both hands. Next to me, Ted grinned when we hit a big one and seawater sprayed us. Our foul-weather gear and life jackets kept us dry, but the cold water and wind stung my face. Ted reached over to wipe off my cheek. I returned the sweet gesture with a squeeze of his hand, tried to ignore my churning stomach, and wished I could fix on his soothing presence instead of my messy sea of uncertainty.

As we approached Ninstints, Gene reduced our speed. "Good place for your samples?"

"Yeah," I said. "Try to maintain just enough forward momentum to keep the net a few feet below the surface. I'll stand back there with you and play the net out."

We slowly traversed Ninstints Bay. When Gene cut the motor, I hauled in the net, stood on the seat, and held the net upright over the side. Ted clambered onto the seat next to me and poured seawater around the mouth to wash debris caught into the mesh down into the collecting bottle. Holding the bottle up to the light, I peered in. It was opaque and light brown. Tens of thousands of microscopic phytoplankton, the marine equivalent of trees, colored the water.

"Great. Gene, let's do fifteen more traverses just like the last one."

"What will you do with these bottles?" he asked.

"I'll use a microscope to count different types of algae in these samples and ones we got off the research vessel. There's a large alga called *Pseudo-nitzschia* that has responded to iron in other places. I'll be looking for that."

He grinned. "And you think Haida is hard to pronounce."

Two hours plus later, I had numb hands, a wet jacket, and bottles full of preserved Haida Gwaii plankton. Their identification would have to wait until I returned to Maine. If the kelp we sampled showed a strong iron signal, Harvey would probably test the plankton as well.

The inflatable rounded a headland and swung into a small cove. I whispered "my god" at our first glimpse of totem poles. With towering spruces as a backdrop, a row of stout, weathered poles stood proud just above the beach. A few lurched sideways, others lay on the ground. Their dignity and symbolism marked this as a timeless place.

Gene pulled up the engine, and the boat slid onto the pebble beach. We climbed out and stared up at the poles. As they'd done for countless years, whales, bears, eagles, and crows stared back down at us with huge, menacing eyes.

Anna slipped away and headed down the beach.

With our help, Gene pulled the inflatable above the day's high-tide line. We gathered around our guide.

"The Haida call this Sga'nguai, which means 'Red-cod island.' At one time, three hundred people lived here year-round in seventeen longhouses."

Harvey frowned. "What happened to them?"

"Nearly all died from smallpox in the eighteen-sixties. Trading with Europeans brought things like metal to the islands. Pole carvers improved their craft and made good money. But it came at a terrible price—diseases for which we had no immunity."

We followed Gene as he stepped up onto rich green turf and paused beneath a well-preserved pole in the center. It stood a good twenty-five feet high, and I craned my neck to follow faces and figures piled on top of each other to the last ragged, decaying icon. Intertwined into patterns with repeating shapes, the designs appeared to be a mystical rendering of something other-worldly, vital.

Gene put his hand on the pole. "Each pole represents a clan—its achievements, stories, and history."

I followed his lead and gently touched the relic. The cedar felt cool and smooth. "So they're a kind of story of the family's ancestors?"

"That's right. When I was a kid, my father left me here for the day. He wanted me to know the place. I wandered around and came to understand that this is partly a graveyard of sorrow. The stories some of the poles tell, it's like the people knew something was coming. More than ten thousand people lived on all the islands out here. Suddenly, people died from disease in every village, some half-in, half-out of their canoes like they were trying to escape something terrible."

Deep in the forest, a crow cawed.

"But let's think about the people when they were alive. You all know Emily Carr, the Canadian painter?"

We each nodded.

Gene spoke to the poles in the proud, clear voice of a preacher. "Carr visited Haida Gwaii in nineteen twelve. She called the people dignified and generous. Some of the women looked so much like people carved on the poles, Carr thought the poles were portraits."

He turned to us. "The totems are mostly decorated with images of animals. These are super-human ancestors the Haida descended from."

Ted came closer. "Did people worship the poles?"

"No, never. They're kind of like a national emblem. One of yours is an eagle. You don't worship the eagle, right? It's a symbol of greatness and power, not a god."

Harvey pointed to a half-rotted adjacent pole. "But these magnificent artifacts are crumbling into the ground. Why don't you preserve them somehow or take them to a museum?"

"In nineteen fifty-seven, about a dozen *were* removed in a big salvage project. You can see them in an anthropology museum at the University of British Columbia. But the ones here remain untouched. Haida believe that even when the poles become part of the earth, our ancestral spirits will still be here."

Like cemeteries. My parents were buried on a hill overlooking Spruce Harbor and the Maine Oceanographic Institute where they'd worked. How many times had I stood there and felt their presence? Body and spirit, a collective human concept.

Gene explained the animal symbology of a well-preserved pole. He pointed to a creature with a long, hanging tongue, short snout, and little peaked ears. "That is bear, an animal with great self-awareness and humility. Above bear is eagle, a very intelligent animal capable of transforming itself. Eagles mate for life and symbolize deep and lasting love between man and woman. Frog is perched atop eagle and signifies rebirth. Butterfly sits at the very top of this pole and is revered for its ability to accept change in the midst of confusion."

Self-awareness, humility, transformation and change, and deep and lasting love. Invaluable traits, certainly.

"Why don't you walk around for a bit? Look out for little jokes—figures carved upside-down and tiny creatures winking or peering out of a creature's ear."

I wandered beneath the poles. Lightly stroking the weathered cedar, I made out salmon people, bears, frogs, and other creatures carvers had released from the wood so long ago. They stared across the ocean at something we mortals couldn't see.

I looked around for Gene. He stood at the edge of the forest and touched the stout end of a toppled tree. Carpeted with moss, the wood crumbled beneath his fingers. In the dripping wet forest, parasitic threads of fungi and other unseen beings were clearly hard at work. Wiping his hand on his pants, Gene called out, "The longhouses, what's left of them, are back here. We've cleared a trail."

Harvey and Ted picked their way over moss-covered mounds toward the trail.

A pole at one end of the row drew me to it. I raised my voice so Gene could hear. "Join you in a couple of minutes?"

Layers of undergrowth muted his "Okay."

Gene had said that the compelling pole displayed features of the trickster Raven more clearly than any of the others. Standing back, I could make out beaks, wings, and eyes. I fixed on a set of eyes near the bottom and couldn't stop staring at them. Suddenly, they twinkled and glowed. I gasped.

I knew that glow. William emerged from the murk off Augustine Island right after the thing with a glowing eye streaked by my kayak. The creature on the totem and William were both ravens. My vision must've been a raven, too.

Blinking, I turned my back on the totem pole and faced Ninstints Bay. Whispers of wind slipped through the spruce. *Mara...Mara...Mara.*

The hush mesmerized me. My feet were glued to the ground. I strained to hear insects, a leaf fall, anything, but life had gone still. Minutes went by. Frozen, I stood and listened.

Finally, I could move, had to move.

I turned and squinted at the spot where I last saw Gene. An elongated black blur with a trailing tail streaked by. I twisted around to see the thing race over the water and evaporate to nothing. It was like the dying moment of a single firework rocket.

"It's this place. My imagination's running amuck."

A single black feather lay at my feet. A feather that hadn't been there earlier. I picked it up, shoved it into my pants pocket, and stumbled over half-buried rocks and tree litter in my hurry to join flesh and blood. I put my hand on Harvey's shoulder. "Didn't mean to be gone so long."

She turned and frowned. "But Mara, it was only a minute."

12

Gene educated us about the longhouses. I only half-heard a "handful of moldering longhouses," "cedar beams lying in moss-covered heaps," "ancient hills of clam shells."

I touched the feather in my pocket, pricked my finger on the quill, and tried to convince myself that Gene's stories about Ninstints had inspired my imagination to create a nonexistent vision. But, damn it, I *saw* a black streak and had a feather in my pocket to prove it.

Gene left us so he could visit his ancestor's homesite. Harvey, Ted and I returned to the poles and view of the bay.

"Want to walk the beach?" Harvey asked.

"Think I'll just stay here for a bit." I closed my eyes and tried to think about anything but the black blur. It didn't work.

Gene touched my shoulder and scared the hell out of me.

"Sorry," he said. "Ah, there's something I wanted to ask. It's about the night William died."

Surprised, I said, "Sure. Go ahead."

"What time did you go into that pool? I mean, when you found him."

I blinked. "Um, a little after midnight. I had my dive watch on. Why?"

"I saw William at eleven that night. From a distance. He was walking up the path to the bathhouses. I told Sergeant Knapton but didn't know when you'd discovered William's body."

Fatigue washed over me. Details of William's demise were

the last thing I wanted to discuss. "So he was alive at eleven and dead an hour later," I mumbled.

"I guess so," he said. Gene clambered down the bank on his way to the boat.

The tide had risen, which made the launch easier. Gene grabbed rubber boots from under my seat, waded in, turned the inflatable around, and steadied it. "Climb aboard, folks."

Harvey slid beside me while Ted settled onto the opposite seat. Anna took the bow again and Gene shoved off.

As we floated away from the beach, Gene referred to Emily Carr again. "Carr writes that the poles never lost their dignity, no matter how crooked or tilted they'd become. Bent over or tipped backwards they might look sad, she said, but they were still forever noble." Gene paused, then asked, "Thoughts about Sga'nguai?"

I looked over my shoulder at poles standing tall and silent. There was profound power here. Dignity, mournfulness, and ancestral spirits. I hadn't been prepared for what I'd experienced. It spooked me.

"Well," Harvey said, "The people who lived here were sophisticated and cultured. Their art alone shows that."

Ted turned around to face us. "They had pride and their own kind of wealth."

"And," I added, "a passion for making the supernatural visible." To that, Anna slowly nodded.

We were nearly back at the Kinuk dock when I realized Harvey was speaking to me. "Mara, you there? You're awfully quiet."

I touched her arm. "Sorry. Guess Ninstints, the whole thing, got to me."

"It's a mind-blowing place."

If only she knew.

Harvey and Ted headed for the longhouse. I wanted to walk the beach, and said I'd meet them at the dining building. Strolling along, I tried to reconcile two incongruent ideas. As a scientist, I trusted what I could measure and see. Visions of birds were figments of my overactive mind. Still, what I saw at Ninstints and off Augustine Island seemed so *very* real. Despite going back and forth a dozen times, I reached no satisfactory conclusion.

Dinner was in the building where we'd eaten the night before. We insisted that we help cook, serve, and clean up. Only Gene and Anna joined us for a meal of lingcod, something I'd never eaten before.

I took a bite. "Gene, this fish tastes fabulous."

"That's one reason why its numbers nose-dived. But it's coming back now."

"So it's a cod?" Harvey asked.

He shook his head. "Lingcod's a type of greenling that lives around kelp. Ugliest fish you'd ever see—dozens of long sharp teeth, greenish with blotches."

Anna hadn't said a word as we prepared dinner, so when she did, we all turned toward her. She looked directly at me. "Lingcod turn from ugly to beautiful food. Like the raven that constantly changes form."

Transformation. The same but different. Charlotte talked about that, too.

The five of us washed and dried the dishes.

"Where in Maine do you live, and what's it like?" Gene asked.

I took the plate he handed me. "It's a village called Spruce Harbor. There's Maine Oceanographic Institute where we work on the water, a good-sized pier for the research vessels, fishing boats in the harbor, shops, a couple of places to eat, and a dozen or so houses. Pretty and quiet."

"Sounds nice. What's the biggest news story in the last couple of months?"

Ted jumped right in. "Mara and Harvey worked together to solve a murder."

Gene raised an eyebrow. "Really?"

Harvey added dried plates to a pile already on a shelf. "I didn't do much. It was Mara. She got the evidence and figured out the bad guys. They were arrested."

She didn't say I nearly died in the process.

I changed the subject. "Gene, the meeting tomorrow with the whole Environmental Council—fill us in."

"There'll be a dozen or so members there besides Charlotte, Jennie, and me. I'll say something about William and ask others to speak if they want. The official meeting will be after that."

"And the purpose of the meeting?" Ted asked.

"We'll give the rest of the committee an update of the project, what we think is happening. Then it's questions for you folks. We have another vote coming up about whether to continue with Roger Grant. So this meeting's real important."

I took another plate. "Since you hired Grant, I assume most Council members agree with the iron project?"

"Most did. But things have changed since we voted to pay him all that money. William was a big supporter, and now he's not here. And since salmon runs are still thin, people are restless."

"So you don't know how people will vote this time?"

"Like I said, William was the iron defender, but now he's gone. Caleb will try to take William's place. Vote could go either way, I suppose."

"Wow," Harvey said. "I didn't realize that."

Based on what I learned from Charlotte, William would probably have voted against continuing the project. Others discouraged by ongoing poor salmon runs, never mind the large financial outlay, might very well have followed his lead. But with William's death, that calculus had totally changed.

I opened my mouth to ask Gene something, but the question faded into the back of my mind before I could articulate it.

Gene wished us a good night and headed for his cabin. I was about to follow Ted and Harvey down the stairs and up to the longhouse when Anna touched my arm.

"Mara, could I talk to you?"

Her deep chocolate eyes searched mine.

"Sure."

"Not here. Somewhere more, um, private."

"Be right back." I caught up with Ted and Harvey and said I'd head up soon.

Anna practically ran down the dark path to the beach. I could hardly keep up. She marched toward the pier, stopped at a large flat rock, and sat down facing the sea.

I joined her. "A favorite spot?"

"For William and me. We watched stars move across the sky, planned our future…"

"Anna, I'm so sorry—"

She cut me off. "What happened. It wasn't natural."

I sucked in a breath. "What do you mean?"

"William. Somebody did it."

Shifting my weight, I tried to see her face. But she was only a dark silhouette against the black night sky. "You think someone killed William?"

"Yes."

I had my own doubts about William's death, but this wasn't the time to voice them. "Anna, sometimes even healthy young men, like William, die from natural causes."

The voice from the darkness was firm and angry. "*No*. My ancestors told me his death was evil, wicked."

Ancestors? I had to be careful. "I don't understand. Explain what you mean."

She stood and walked to the water's edge. I followed. The cold Haida sea slid up and down the shingle.

"At Sga'nguai, I went to my family's ancestral home and heard whispers. My ancestors said William's death was wrong. It wasn't his time."

I didn't know how to respond.

"Mara, you saw the spirit world's messenger. We both did."

I stepped back. "What?"

" On Sga'ngua. The Raven. Like smoke, it disappeared over the water."

My mouth went dry. How could she know? I swallowed and wet my lips. "Anna, what do you want from me?"

"Follow the trail like you did in Maine for your friend. Find out who killed William. His death must be avenged."

I had to tread carefully here. "Yes, I discovered who was behind Peter's death. But don't you see that's entirely different? Spruce Harbor is my home. I know most everyone, their ways, the water, all of it. Here, I'm on foreign ground."

"I can help you."

Mindful of this lovely young woman's burden, I said, "Look, let's wait until William's parents talk to Gene about the coroner's report. What do you think?"

She toed the shingle. "Okay. I guess that makes sense."

In silence, we picked our way up the beach and to the bathhouse complex. After a quiet "Good night," she was gone.

On the longhouse path, I was on autopilot as my feet followed the dense circle of light cast by my flashlight. Anna's insistence that William died an unnatural death unsettled me.

Harvey, Ted, and I had tossed around the idea that William had been killed, but it was very different for Anna to insist that "it wasn't his time." She was from the archipelago, an insider.

Maybe grief had driven Anna to hear voices at Ninstints, but she didn't appear to be hysterical or bewildered. Instead, she came across as a determined young woman seeking help. Also, she readily agreed it was reasonable to wait for the coroner's report. Not the behavior of an obsessive. And, of course, anyone would want to know why a healthy guy in his twenties suddenly died.

On the other hand, a question about cause of death was very different from a claim the person was murdered. Anna had used some pretty strong words. Evil and wicked.

I pictured William—the dancing eyes, easy smile, eager expression. I couldn't imagine why anyone would want to kill him.

By the time I stepped off the path, my head hurt.

Inside the longhouse, Harvey and Ted knelt on their sleeping bags, a flickering lantern between them. They were ghostly glows in a black space said to be visited by capricious spirits.

Harvey pointed to the lantern as I walked up. "The batteries in this thing seem to be giving out. Didn't Gene say something about emergency candles near the front door if we needed them?"

"He did. And I've got matches in my survival kit."

Harvey searched for the candles while I dug in my duffle for the kit. It was, of course, at the very bottom. I pulled it out, found the little tin of matches, and handed them to Ted.

Back with the candles, Harvey looked at the tin. "Waterproof. How does that work?"

Ted took the matches and candles. "Since this building is made of wood, naturally we need to be real careful with this flame." He struck the match and held it to the wick. "You can make waterproof matches by coating strike-anywhere ones in paraffin and putting them in a container that won't leak. Stormproof matches like Mara's are longer than regular ones and stay lit in the wind."

He handed me the match tin. So it wouldn't rattle around, I stuffed it into the nifty waterproof pouch in my pants pocket.

Harvey slowly carried the lit candle over to a metal cup she'd put on the floor. Bending down, she looked like a spirit executing a ritual act. "There. When it melts a bit, the wax at the bottom of the cup will keep it upright. Of course we'll blow it out when we turn in. So, Mara, what's with Anna? I mean, if you can tell us."

Anna hadn't asked me to keep mum, and I needed help. So, with more than a twinge of guilt, I relayed our conversation—without Anna's mention of the bizarre disappearing smoke.

Ted frowned. "Did she say who'd want to kill William and for what reason?"

"No, but she didn't come across as hysterical or anything like that. Maybe, I don't know, we should give her the benefit of the doubt."

"Okay," Harvey said. "Let's just go with this. Who'd want William dead and why?"

"What about William's old girlfriend Lynne?" I asked. "She was certainly out of control when she screamed 'I wish you were dead.'"

Ted stretched out his long legs and rotated his ankles. "People say things like that when they're really angry, but they don't mean it."

"True," Harvey said. "But we read about revenge murder in the news. It happens, and we know nothing about Lynne."

I sat cross-legged on my sleeping bag. "Don't you think it makes more sense to go with the most divisive thing these folks have dealt with? A million dollars for iron fertilization? Lots at stake. There had to be some pretty heated debate."

"Good point," Ted said. "William championed the pro side. Who was with and who was against him?"

Harvey made a fist and stuck out her thumb. "Jennie must be on William's side. She said the Haida had control over their waters. That's one."

"Then there's Gene," I said. "It's hard to know whose side he's on."

Harvey's forefinger joined her thumb. "I agree. Two."

"Speaking of Gene," I added, "while you guys were walking the beach before we left Ninstints, Gene asked what time I found William. Then he said William was alive at eleven. An hour before I found him dead."

Harvey dropped her hand. "So he talked to William at eleven?"

I shook my head. "Saw him in the dark from a distance. William was on the path between the pools and the bath houses."

Ted turned toward me. "Maybe it's because were in 'who-done-it' mode, but that strikes me as kind of odd. Why would Gene tell you what time he saw William and where?"

I shrugged. "Dunno. Maybe he's playing detective like we are."

"Maybe. But still…"

I rubbed my eyes. "Let's keep going with our list."

"What about Charlotte?" Ted asked. "You talked to her for a while at dinner."

"She said the ocean was more important than anything else. So that might make her opposed to the iron project. But she's, what, eighty? And she acted like a kind grandma for both William and Bart. She's a gentle soul."

"What about your visit to her house? Did you learn anything then?" Harvey asked.

"I did, but Charlotte said it was between me and her."

Harvey scrunched up her nose. "So you can't say anything?"

"Um, well, you'd be pleased that William was paying very close attention to our arguments about iron geo-engineering. We were getting to him."

Ted stood, walked around in a little circle, and turned to face us. "Don't you see that probably changes everything?"

"Actually, I don't see."

"Keep going, Ted," Harvey said.

"William championed the iron project. If he changed his mind and voted no, others would probably follow his lead."

Harvey tipped her head. "Yeah, but William isn't here to vote now."

"Right."

"Sorry, brother," she said, "I'm not with you."

"Maybe someone who really wanted the iron project to continue made sure William wasn't around to vote no."

I jerked upright, hand to my heart. "Oh my god. That never…Who would do such a thing?"

He crossed his arms. "I've no idea."

Harvey tipped her head. "Mara, are you okay? You're pale as a ghost."

"It's just that, um, William changing his mind because of us—it's like we're responsible, you know, for his death. All the more reason to figure out what happened to him."

"Hey, girlfriend," she said, "Take it easy. It's a huge leap from William rethinking his vote to blaming us for his death. Right?"

"Uh-huh. Sometimes my imagination takes off on its own."

She gave me a "like-I-don't-know-that" look.

Ted said, "Could we finish our count? Charlotte was three. What about Bart? The stuck rudder, exploding rocks, yelling 'shark' when you're leaning over the stern? And he tries to act tough."

I pictured Bart's sullen expression. "Suppose if I had to pick one person, he'd be it. Still—"

Ted stretched his arms over his head. "Not sure we're making progress here. I'm bushed, and we're diving in the morning. Let's talk about this later."

Just then, a click echoed in the long, empty space. Like the sound of a door closing.

Ted swiveled toward the front door. "What was that?"

I yanked my flashlight from my pocket. "Let's go see."

Outside, we played our lights across the clearing.

"There's nothing out here," Ted said. "Come here, you." He pulled me close. His fleece pullover was soft against my face, chest warm. I closed my eyes and tried to let my body relax. It didn't. Ted let me go and stepped back. "I hope you're not thinking about being a detective again."

Ted's tone was a bit too protective for my liking, but I tried not to let it show. "As I said, let's wait for the coroner's report."

"And if there's a question about how William died?"

"Not sure."

But, even more than before, I knew the answer.

13

AAKA REDISH, HAIDA GWAII DIVING WATCHMAN, MET US after breakfast at the Kinuk floating dock. She maneuvered her twenty-five-foot inflatable so it just kissed the dock's edge. The boat was loaded with scuba-diving equipment.

"Before we take off," she said, "let's go over how you want to take kelp samples. None of my divers have done anything like that before."

"We'll use a tool to take kelp plugs." Harvey pulled a round metal stamp out of a little mesh bag. "It's easy to use underwater. You clamp it around a kelp blade and squeeze. Back in Maine, I'll analyze the plugs to see if kelp took up any of the added iron. That way, we get an idea how far the iron traveled and if there are near-shore impacts."

"Isn't there some iron in seawater anyway?" Aaka asked.

"Yes. But the iron slurry has a distinct isotopic signature compared to background iron."

Either Aaka understood what Harvey meant—the number of neutrons was different in the slurry's iron—or she didn't want to ask.

"Got it."

Aaka swung the inflatable away from the dock and we took off. With a huge grin and laughing chocolate eyes, she radiated positive energy. As Kinuk village disappeared from view, some of the tension that'd gripped my body drained away. The legendary kelp forests with their underwater zoos waited for us. Just what three troubled marine ecologists needed.

Hair flying in the wind, the spirited guide shouted above the roar of the outboard. "You're marine scientists, and I'm so excited for you. Divers come to Haida Gwaii from everywhere in the world. Our waters are full of the most gorgeous, fantastic creatures you'll ever see."

Aaka was clearly an experienced businesswoman who knew how to psych up her clients.

Harvey straddled the seat. "Like what?"

"We've got more than twenty types of whales and dolphins, giant octopus, barracuda, dozens of fish, countless starfish species—purple, red, orange, you name it—plus anemone that are pink, yellow, green, chartreuse. It's a neon circus down there."

I yelled, "The few starfish we have in Maine are pretty boring color-wise. Here it's a biology bonanza. Can't *wait* to get under the water."

"There's a shallow strait littered with starfish not far from here. You all okay to take a little side trip before we go to the dive site?"

Our grins said we were.

We reached the strait. Aaka cut the motor so the boat would drift silently across the kaleidoscope of starfish. When the guide said the echinoderms were littered, she wasn't kidding. They came in every shade of purple I could think of—magenta, violet, lilac, raisin. Orange ones were rust, pumpkin, coral, and tangerine, and reds showed as scarlet, burgundy, and ruby. There were sun stars with ten or more legs and others with five. Smaller bat stars looked like holiday cookies. Leaning over the soft sides of the inflatable, Ted, Harvey and I called out, "Look at that one out there" and "This is mind boggling!" while Aaka named species after species.

Finally, my gut hurt, and I sat up. "You can understand why evolution is a hard sell for some people. Look at the diversity of life right here. Even when you know about the mechanisms and time scale, it's still hard to comprehend how all these life forms could've come about."

Aaka nodded. "Haida creation stories are filled with fantastic, bizarre events. It's boring how they teach evolution in school. I like to spice it up with our wild myths."

The concept intrigued me. "But you know the myths aren't real, right?"

She looked out across the expanse of ocean. "It's hard to explain. Part of me knows they're stories, but another part accepts their truth."

Like Charlotte said, the same but different. Could I simultaneously believe and not believe in the supernatural? The concept was foreign. Thinking about it felt like I was trying on someone else's clothes.

Funny. Harvey regularly urged me to forgo my comfy fleece and cotton for something more exotic and fashionable.

I looked at Harvey and smiled.

"What?"

"Just thinking you're right sometimes."

She tipped her head and pursed her lips—a "what-the-hell?" gesture.

Aaka beached the boat in a protected harbor. Before we slipped under the water, we had to organize all the cold water diving paraphernalia—thick wetsuits, neoprene gloves, hoods, boots, and fins, plus weight belts, tanks, regulators, masks, buoyancy control devices (BCs), and gauges that measure water depth and tank air pressure. We'd communicated with Aaka from Maine and knew she had excellent, if a little old, equipment plus years of experience diving in Haida Gwaii's waters. That was critical. We weren't going deep—maybe seventy-five feet at the most—but frigid conditions and fast currents made Haida

Gwaii scuba risky. Aaka had made sure we were experienced cold-water divers with Open Water Certification.

Finally, we were suited up and on our way out to kelp forests off Rose Harbor.

As we motored over water so clear you could count snails on the bottom, Aaka described the dive site. "I picked a spot where there's enough current for a good kelp bed but not so much you'll have to fight it. We'll stay down for forty minutes. That way, you should have plenty of air and time to take your samples but won't be too terribly cold."

Despite Aaka's perkiness, in fifty-degree water we'd get plenty cold. Encased in the thickest wetsuit I'd ever worn, I shivered.

At the dive site Aaka anchored the boat bow and stern, and set out the dive flag, I looked around. Off the port side, foot-wide ribbons of kelp fronds, the seaweed version of leaves, floated across the surface. Up to two hundred feet long, the kelp were attached to the bottom by holdfasts strong enough to resist the pull of a wild sea.

Harvey and I were dive buddies. Aaka partnered with Ted. Standing beside me, Harvey lifted the heavy steel scuba tank up onto the inflatable's squishy tube and steadied the tank while squatted on the deck and wrestled my arms into the harness. I secured the chest and hip clasps. She handed me one end of the twenty-five pound weight belts. "Damn, this thing's heavy."

I leaned over a bit to raise the tank off my back and swing the belt around my waist, straightened up, and snapped the belt tight. "We'll be pretty buoyant in these wetsuits. Hope this is enough weight."

We switched places. Harvey grunted under the weight of her tank. "Whoa, this *is* heavy. We should sink okay. But if not, we can always get more weight." She secured her weight belt.

A regulator was already attached to each tank. We checked and rechecked our gauges. Accurate tank pressure readings were critical. It was hard to predict how much air we'd use in cold water where we'd be bucking currents. If we ran out at seventy-five feet, we could always slowly release air in our lungs and rise up to the surface. Even so, sucking on a nearly empty tank would be undeniably scary. Since knowing our depth was also critical, each of us had a dive watch that gave accurate depth readings.

Harvey checked to make sure Ted's kelp punch was safely in a pocket of his BC, along with the sampling bags she'd already numbered. She and Ted would sample kelp from two different depths in the kelp forest. "Let's review our sampling method, bro."

"I'll do the transect higher up," he said. "There's twenty bags. For each transect, I'll take five plugs from separate blades of kelp two to three meters apart. One plug per bag and four separate transects," he said.

"You got it."

Aaka handed each of us a dive knife in its sheath. "This goes in your BC pocket. If you strap it to your leg, it could snag on the kelp."

I slid the knife out of its protective cover. One edge was serrated, the other looked razor sharp. "I assume this is for something in particular?"

"Believe me, you get wrapped in kelp, you'll need it."

I pocketed the knife. "Remind us how to avoid that."

"When you're in the kelp bed, slowly push it aside with your hands in front, palms outward. Whatever you do, *don't* turn or swirl. You'll end up bound like a Christmas tree on its way to market."

Trussed in kelp slime would be an absurd terror. I practiced the kelp crawl in my head.

Finally, we were ready to get in the water. With rigid hulls and fat, flexible tubes as gunwales, inflatable boats were perfect for scuba diving. Finned feet inside the boat, Harvey and I sat comfortably on the soft gunwale and faced Ted and Aaka, who did the same. We each spit onto the mask's faceplate so it wouldn't fog, pushed the mask against our face, and pulled the strap over our head. Harvey, Ted, and I opened our mouths wide and settled the bulky regulator mouthpieces between our teeth.

Aaka looked at Harvey and me, brown eyes huge inside her mask. "All set?"

We both nodded.

"Great. Let's go through the kelp safety rules again. She held out her thumb. "One, don't swim deep into the kelp bed. Go only to where you can see the edge, then *slowly* turn around, and swim back. It's easy to get lost in kelp." Her forefinger came up. "Two, use your compass to see which way is in and which way is out." Middle finger. "Three, your buddy might be your savior. Swim five to seven feet apart and make sure you can always see each other." Next finger. "Four, never swim in kelp to or at the surface. We'll swim out of the bed and then go up." Little finger. "Five. Kelp loves to tangle you. Secure anything that can snag and be *especially* careful the kelp doesn't yank out your regulator."

More than a little daunted, I nodded.

"Good. Mara and Harvey, you go first. When you're all set, Ted and I will join you."

I pressed my mask against my face with one hand, leaned back, and crashed into the Haida sea.

Even though I knew it was coming, I squealed when frigid water hit my face like sharp icicles. I shucked on the regulator, rolled upright, and popped to the surface with a gasp.

Beside me, Harvey said something into her regulator that sounded like "goddamn" and "cold." I nodded as glacial streams of water oozed down my neck, up my sleeves, and around my ankles.

Aaka leaned over the side of the boat. "You okay?"

In unison, we gave her a thumbs-up.

"Have to clear my mask," I said into my regulator.

"Okay. See you in a sec." Aaka disappeared from view

Underwater, I had to tip my head back three times and exhale hard to get water out of my mask. I surfaced as Ted and Aaka swam over. Aaka made a circle over her head with her arms. "Okay?"

The three of us repeated her gesture.

Aaka took the regulator out of her mouth and hung onto the boat. "Great. Let's go down the bow anchor line slowly. That'll make it easier to regulate the pressure. Mara, Harvey, why don't you go first?"

With a quick flick of my fins, I floated to the anchor line and grabbed it. Harvey did the same, and signaled me to go first. Assuming she wanted to take her time equilibrating her ears, I nodded and slipped under the water.

The everyday sounds of Haida Gwaii—voices, birds, and slapping water—were gone in an instant. I'd left the airy world and entered the muted, dense undersea domain of fish, kelp, and seals.

At first, my own in-and-out "Darth Vader" breathing swamped all other senses. I took a moment to make sure seawater didn't seep into my mask, blinked, and looked around. Just a few feet below the surface, I was in a realm utterly foreign and immediately treacherous. Light—bright, warm, friendly—had morphed to muted blue-grey. Icy fingers of water invaded tiny channels at my neck, ankles, and wrists. What I did every moment without a thought—inhale, exhale—hinged on a phone-booth volume of air squeezed into the tank on my back.

I checked my depth gauge. Then hand over hand, I gingerly followed the anchor line down. Seawater pressed in on me with greater force each time I grabbed the line.

Water is astonishingly dense and weighs a whopping sixty-four pounds per square foot. For each twelve inches I descended, pressure on each square foot of water increased by sixty-four pounds. Hence the need for the regulator clamped between my teeth. The first part (stage) reduced high tank air pressure to a breathable one. Stage two allowed me to exhale air with the same force—pressure—as the surrounding water.

Since evolution didn't design human ears to withstand underwater pressure, ears are a particular problem for divers. Every five feet or so, mine began to hurt. If I didn't stop to equilibrate inside/outside pressure by swallowing, yawning, or holding my nose and snorting gently, I'd likely end up with punctured eardrums and an aborted dive.

About twenty feet down, I checked the depth gauge and craned my head back. Harvey held onto the line and hovered right above me. My bubbles joined hers and glided up to the surface. Aaka and Ted, who hadn't submerged yet, were black silhouettes with big fins against a dull yellow sky. The hull of the boat loomed over me, a wavy, dark blob.

Foot by foot, I made my way down the line, clearing my ears all the way. A couple of times, I glanced up to make sure Harvey's dark profile was directly above. Apparently, she had no difficulty adjusting to rising water pressure because her progress down the anchor line matched mine. I stopped to read my depth gauge once more. Thirty-five feet. I looked up. Aaka and Ted were just above Harvey on the anchor line. So far, so good.

Aaka had asked us to stop at forty feet before we descended further. When my gauge registered that depth, I held onto the line, waited, and looked around. What looked like snowflakes streamed by. These were plankton, tiny animals and plants at the mercy of the currents. Herring-size fish zipped past in crowded schools. Like swarms of bees, they arched up and down in uniform precision. Beyond the fish, a wall of yellow-gold kelp swayed back and forth and stretched to the sky. We'd swim over to the kelp forest at the end of the dive.

Aaka dove down, righted herself, and hovered beside me. "Wookay?"

With my thumb and forefinger in a circle, I signaled "okay." Aaka drifted up to Harvey who repeated the gesture.

Aaka backed up and held her fist in front of her facemask—the "hold" signal. She ascended, checked with Ted, and came back down. Thumb down, she signaled "descend."

Hand-over-hand and pausing to adjust to the pressure, I moved down the line. My fins touched bottom at seventy feet, and I pushed outstretched arms forward to back away from the line. Hovering just above the bottom, with my mask and ears clear and breathing like Darth Vader, I looked around.

Aaka had anchored the boat on a small flat area between a rock wall and the kelp forest. Smart lady. We could examine the different habitats without going very far. The bottom was carpeted with an array of pink and purple life. Bubblegum-tinted anemones waved hundreds of fleshy tentacles into the current. They looked lovely, but each tentacle was designed to eject a threadlike harpoon that paralyzed shrimp or little fish that got too close. Little armies of round fuchsia sea urchins glided among the anemones and left trails of scraped-off rock behind them. Even the fish were red and pink. A well-camouflaged coral-and-green fish rose off the bottom, startled me, and slid past my facemask.

We circled Aaka and waited for her to show the way. When she seemed satisfied each of us had cleared our masks and ears, and had plenty of air and no concerns, she pointed in the direction of the rock wall and held up ten fingers. Ten minutes. Then she rotated a hand around her wrist. About ten minutes for us to explore the wall.

Aaka and Ted took the lead. Harvey and I waited so we could follow without bumping into them. Side-by-side, we reached the wall and slowly swam alongside it.

An astounding abundance of creatures lay below and beside us. Carpeting the wall were bright yellow sunflower stars, huge blue-top snails, orange-peel nudibranchs—big snails without shells—that looked like dragons, and beds of plum-rose anemone. But it was the larger animals that most drew our attention. We trailed a giant octopus until it slithered into a crevice impossibly small for its bulky body. A grunt sculpin looking like a dwarf-striped pig tiptoed across the rock, a cartoon ballet dancer. We floated above an old man's face that stuck out of a hole—the wolf eel, a long eel-like fish with an enormous head. The creature demonstrated the terrible crushing power of its jaws when it grabbed and clamped down on a good-sized sea urchin. Urchin spines really hurt, something I knew too well, so I cringed as the fish munched on its prey. But it simply swam away, spines spilling out of its teeth.

Before we knew it, Aaka and Ted swam back to us. She pointed to the kelp forest, our next place to visit. I checked my watch. Only twenty-five minutes to go. On our way, we stopped to gape at an ocean sunfish, *Mola mola*. Longer than I was tall, the fish appeared to be an enormous flattened round head with a tail. A sea lion swooped down to take a look at the sunfish, saw us, flipped its fin-like tail, and sped away.

Close up on the seafloor, the kelp looked like a bunch of swaying, skinny brown trees. Instead of roots, each one grasped the bottom with its holdfast, which looked like oversized chicken feet with toes dug into the rock. I craned my head back. Each stipe reached for the sun, its ribbony fronds swinging back and forth with the current.

Aaka stuck her thumb toward the surface—the "ascend" signal. Together, we used our fins to glide upward. To stay vertical, I had to kick harder against a current we hadn't experienced earlier. Aaka stopped about halfway up the kelp canopy and indicated we could swim through it slowly with our respective buddies. She held up her hand and held out five fingers. Did we remember the five safety rules?

I ran though the list in my head and turned toward at Harvey. She nodded, as did I.

Aaka made quick circles with her forefinger, moved her hand up and down, and tipped her head. I understood she had warned us about a down current and nodded.

Ted and Aaka floated up about twenty feet before they glided in. I gave Harvey the "wait" hand signal so we could take a moment to just look at the forest first. She nodded.

Above us, kelp fronds glowed red-yellow in filtered sunlight. Akin to a forest of real trees, *Macrocystis* rose straight up from the bottom to the surface, and their fronds looked like branches with leaves. About halfway up the kelp canopy where we were, there was enough room for us to safely swim among the fronds. Divers were at risk at the surface, where the kelp was thicker and denser.

Harvey pointed toward the kelp, and we slowly slid in. Speckled light from above dappled across the rich brown fronds. A little farther in, the water turned blue-green as the canopy grew denser. Harvey pulled out her punch, stopped every couple of meters, and slipped samples into the plastic bags. She touched my arm and signaled we should return to the canopy edge. Reluctantly, I slowly turned around and swam beside her out into open water. There, we checked our air pressure. Both tanks were over half full. Good.

We entered the kelp again. Harvey pointed to the surface, where a school of blue-gray fish swam between swaths of brown kelp and patches of bright blue water. She glided in front of me and stopped to take a kelp sample.

Above, the school scattered when a seal swooped down and headed right for us. As the seal swirled like a top, sunlight scattered off white blotches that covered its body. It went right for me and stared into my facemask. Enormous dark eyes and a downturned mouth gave the animal a solemn expression at odds with its playful behavior. After inspecting my mask, the seal backed up and circled me.

Turning, I followed its movement and marveled at the perfect design. The sleek, torpedo-shaped body, stubby fore flippers, and dual hind flippers allowed the animal to zip through water with minimal effort. With its blubber insulation and adaptations—tolerance of lactic acid and ability to re-inflate lungs underwater—this was a mammal that could stay submerged for hours.

I held out arms wrapped in neoprene. Creatures from above, we had dropped into the seal's domain with lots of noise and tons of bubbles. Without high-tech protection from the cold, plus imported air, weights and buoyancy regulators, we were about as vulnerable here as we'd be on the moon.

In an instant, the seal was gone.

I turned to look for Harvey. Out of nowhere, a downcurrent grabbed me and threw me deep into the kelp bed. Ragdoll in a wetsuit, helpless against the tremendous pull, I spiraled down, down, spinning with the swirling water.

14

ARMS FLAILING, I TRIED TO FIGHT THE SINGLE-MINDED surge—grab onto something, anything. It was pointless. There was no way to stop the sickening downward spiral through a torrent of river filled with seaweed.

My body spun more slowly and finally came to a stop. I closed my eyes. The world spun around again. Bile bubbled up into my throat. I popped my eyes open and took deep breaths to calm my nauseous stomach.

Throwing up into a regulator was a very bad thing.

I did a quick inventory of my body. Nothing hurt and, thank god, every piece of gear looked to be in place. My mask still covered my face, the BC wrapped tight around my chest, and fins were attached to both feet. And most critically, thanks to my death clamp, the blessed regulator was still in my mouth. Hyperventilating and scared shitless, I sucked air and scanned my body again. It was astounding, but all appeared to be well.

Except for one thing.

Like a mummy, I was shrouded in kelp.

I twisted left and right as far as possible within the seaweed constraints. Tried kicking my feet and pushing my arms out. It was no good. Kelp stipes and fronds wound around and around me. Perfect slimy ropes.

There was no way to know my depth or how far down I'd gone into the kelp forest—and, of course, where Harvey was. Somehow, the pressure gauge on my tank had slipped out of the BC where I'd secured it and was just visible beneath a kelp frond. I squinted to read the numbers. Three-hundred psi. Well past the turnaround point and, because I was sucking air, slipping down fast. I closed my eyes and listened to my yoga teacher's voice in my head. Slow and steady. In…out…in…out. That's it. In…out.

When I'd calmed down some, I assessed my situation once more. It was bloody dangerous and laugh-out-loud ridiculous.

Trussed in kelp, I could run out of air in minutes.

I tried to ignore the physics underway in my tank. When divers use up most of their air, each inhalation is more labored and painful. It's like trying to suck water through a straw from the bottom of a nearly empty glass. At some point, there's no water to suck.

Preoccupied by the danger facing me, I didn't notice the seal at first. The creature peered into my mask. Gotta be a hallucination brought on by fear and low oxygen, I thought. The vision's nose bumped my faceplate. My head jerked.

It blinked. I blinked. Eye to eye, we communicated via thought.

"So you've never seen a human wrapped in kelp?"

She—I felt the creature had a female temperament—blinked twice. I took that as a negative.

"Help?"

No response. Of course not. This wasn't Lassie, for god's sake. She left my field of view. Panic returned. I was alone again.

Moments later, she was back. I tried again. "Help?"

This time, she tipped her head. Then, as gently as a doting mother, she bit into kelp blades that constrained my right arm. Pieces of brown kelp floated upward. With the free arm, I reached for the BC pocket.

The pocket was just big enough for two gloved fingers. I grasped the end of the knife and by inches, pulled it out.

My friend eyed the knife, backed away, and tipped her head again.

I nodded. Our eyes met once more and, with a swirl of her sleek body and a tail swish, she was gone.

The blade easily sliced through my kelp restraints. Moments later, I was free. Light streamed into the kelp from my left, so I turned in that direction. Gingerly, I used the "kelp crawl" to glide through swaying seaweed. The final blades wiped my faceplate, and I popped out of the canopy into glorious open water.

I looked up. The sun, higher now, was a wavy circle of bright light at the surface. The boat's hull, dark in bright blue water, swung slowly on the anchor lines. Best of all, Harvey floated ten feet directly above, fish-eyes behind the mask fixed on me. I looked at my dive watch to confirm that we were at a safe depth.

I pointed to the anchor line. She stretched her arm down in my direction and made a big circle with her thumb and forefinger. "Okay." I repeated the gesture.

With a couple of flicks of my fins, I reached the line and held on. Harvey did the same and looked down. I stuck up my thumb. She nodded and we both crept up the anchor line. My tank neared empty, and each inhalation took more and more effort. The boat looming above had to be closer, but it didn't look it.

Desperate to reach the surface and suck in fresh air, I only wanted to let go of that goddamn line and use my fins to zip up to the surface. But my training kicked in, and I stopped at regular intervals to clear my ears and let blood gases equilibrate.

Finally, my goal was within reach. I broke through—into the realm of air-breathing creatures.

I spit out my mouthpiece, sucked in cold, clean air, and pushed the mask up off my face. Salt water stung my eyes, but it didn't matter a bit. Harvey hung onto the boat's hull. I grabbed the hull line.

"Jesus, Mara. What the hell happened? One second you were right there, gone the next."

I took in a breath and blew it out. "Current. Sucked me down."

"Current? What current?"

"The—" Another inhale. "You didn't feel it?"

"No. You were there in the kelp, then gone in a flash. I swam out to see if you were in open water, looked down, and there you were. Right below."

Quick calculation. Harvey's maneuver would've taken about thirty seconds. "Um, how long was I out of view?"

"Well under a minute."

I coughed. "Um, seemed longer. Hey, let's get out of this ice bath so we can head back. A soak in that hot water'll be a dream."

Aaka was already in the boat. Standing, she looked down to regard her three charges. "Weight belts first. Super slow. For goodness sake, don't drop them or they'll end up on the bottom."

I unsnapped my belt and raised one end just high enough so Aaka could reach down, grab it, and haul the heavy thing into the boat. She repeated the gesture with Harvey and Ted.

"Great," she said. "Tanks next."

One by one, we unfastened and slipped out of our scuba tanks. Aaka reached over the side and pulled each tank up the gunwale and into the boat.

Our gear aboard, we hoisted ourselves over the inflatable's soft gunwales—another reason why the boats are so popular with divers—and fell into the boat.

Aaka pulled up the anchors and started the outboard. She didn't gun the motor until we were well away from Rose

Harbor. To keep out of the wind, I sat on the floorboards and leaned back against the gunwale. No go. I shivered violently in my soaked wetsuit.

My tank was within reach. I checked the pressure gauge. It was dangerously low.

While we were underway, Ted handed Harvey his kelp samples so she could stash them in a plastic box. She couldn't control her freezing hands, and Ted had to help her pop the lid.

"What'll keep the plugs from going bad?" Aaka asked.

Harvey rotated her jaw so she could talk. "There's preservative in each bag. Back in my lab, I determine if kelp assimilated the Haida's iron."

We helped Aaka tie up on the dock.

She said, "You guys are frozen. Scoot up to the bathhouses. I can deal with this stuff."

The boat's hull was littered with tanks, weight belts, fins, and everything else we'd used.

"You sure? There's a lot of gear here."

"Yeah. Part of my job."

Harvey and Ted picked their way through the dive debris, stepped onto the dock, and headed up to the pier.

I'd just started down the dock when I turned back. "Aaka, did you see a harbor seal near the boat?"

"Funny you ask. At the end of the dive, a seal swam around the boat like it was looking for something. When you surfaced, it watched you for a moment and disappeared."

"Right. I saw it, too. Hey, won't you join Harvey and me in the bathhouse? That way I can properly applaud your terrific dive-guide skills."

She grinned. "I just might take you up on that."

The tide was much lower, which made the ramp between the floating dock and pier steep. Lost in thought, I slowly made the climb and tried to make sense out of two bizarre events. First, a gust from nowhere carried a single feather on Ninstints and now a seal freed me from kelp? I could easily dismiss the savior seal. Nitrogen narcosis, also called raptures of the deep, could result in hallucinations when divers breathed gases under elevated pressure. Dismissal of the kelp mummy wrap was more of a stretch, but that could've been part of the delusion. After all, Harvey said I'd disappeared for less than a minute.

I reached the top of the ramp and took in the sweeping view. Damn. Why couldn't I just cool it, forget about what happened—for now anyway—and enjoy myself? I was in an ecologist's paradise with stunning scenery and magnificent animals, like seals and whales, and kelp critters in a riot of colors.

But like my mother had always said, I wasn't the cool-it type.

My mind replayed the advice my mother, a marine conservationist, had given me when I started college.

If you want to be an exceptional scientist, you must be open to completely new ideas—ones that aren't in the textbooks.

In my back-and-forth about the visions, there *was* a quality of an exceptional scientist I'd ignored—open-mindedness. After all, if Alexander Fleming had dismissed the odd idea that mold could kill bacteria, there'd be no penicillin. With creative thinking, Rosalind Franklin used her fuzzy X-ray diffraction images to draw the double helix structure of DNA. Maybe I was missing something with my stubborn ideas about reality.

Huh. The idea was intriguing. I was getting nowhere obsessing about feathers and seals. I could let the fixation go for now, and be open to what might happen. Instantly, this seemed right. Something important was just beyond my reach. It wasn't a scientific finding, like Fleming's or Franklin's. It was about me, personal.

With a lighter step, I walked along the pier. Below, a row of wooden dinghies bleached gray, olive, and brown crowded each other above the high-tide line, suggesting that the Council meeting would be well attended. Harvey and Ted had stopped halfway down the pier. Fixed on something, they leaned on the railing and looked down. I followed their gaze to see a crowd of people around the hot pool where William had died. They all gaped at the pool.

Well, what used to be a pool.

The water had drained out. Now, there was only a big dry hole.

15

I CAUGHT UP WITH TED AND HARVEY. "JESUS. WHAT THE hell happened?"

"Not sure *when* it happened," Ted said, "But a seismic shift below must've caused *what* happened."

"Just one pool drained?"

"As far as we can see," Harvey said.

I hugged myself. "D-damn coincidence it's the one where William died."

Despite the confusion outside, Harvey and I took our time in the bathhouse. After all, we'd been immersed in fifty-degree water for nearly an hour and chilled to the core on the ride home. I slipped down into warmth, pushed hair off my face as I surfaced, and knotted it into a tight ponytail. The knot held for a change.

My core temperature had returned to normal by the time Aaka arrived. She stripped off her clothes, dropped into the tub without a word, leaned her head back, and shut her eyes. Her faced was scrunched up like she was in pain.

I touched her shoulder. "Aaka, what's the matter?"

She slid under the water, came up, and raked her hands down her face. "Um, what's happened out there."

"That water drained out of the pool?" Harvey asked.

"It's the one William died in."

Aaka looked like she was about to burst into tears. Was she related to William? I didn't want to pry and wasn't sure what to say. Harvey looked at me and shrugged.

Aaka broke the tension. "William and I were lovers. We were going to get married."

Now I was utterly confused. Anna had said *she* and William talked about marriage.

"Oh," was all I could manage.

Harvey was more gracious. "Aaka, how terrible this must be for you. I'm so sorry."

Aaka's eyes filled with tears. She slipped under the water again.

When she came up, I went for a neutral question. "Have any of the pools emptied like this before?"

She shook her head. "Not that I remember. This is going to freak people out. Especially the older ones."

"Yes?"

Aaka clicked into guide mode. "For Haida, hot pools are sacred. They've been here for centuries. Longer."

"And they attract tourists," Harvey said.

"That, too. If more drain, it'll be a disaster."

"Speaking of tourists," I said, "where's your dive operation and where do you live?"

"Up on Moresby Island. I usually dive there but came down a lot to—" She looked to the side and squeezed her eyes shut.

"You're a terrific guide. I'd recommend you to anyone. You know the currents, the natural and cultural history. You're very safety-conscious. I'm sure Harvey agrees."

"Absolutely."

Aaka pushed herself up onto the edge of the tub. "This is a dangerous place to dive. We've had a couple of deaths. Last one got tangled in the kelp."

My stomach flipped.

Our dry clothes hung on the bathhouse pegs. We toweled off and said good-bye to Aaka. We'd paid her earlier and told her to look for another check—our tip, a generous one. She said she needed time alone and asked us to thank Ted for her.

Harvey and I stepped outside.

"I feel so bad for her," I said.

"Yeah. It was hard to know what to say."

Ted was waiting for us outside the men's bathhouse. We walked down the path to join the crowd.

Twenty-odd people circled the empty bowl. Hunched, pale, and tight-lipped, Gene stared down at the dry hole.

I walked over to him. "Gene, what happened?"

He straightened up and blinked. "Oh, um…Mara. Let's see. I was out here this morning and noticed the water level was down. When I came back later the pool was dry."

"Has it drained before?"

"Not that I know of."

Ted asked, "Gene, would you like us to find out if there's been tectonic activity out here? Would that help?"

"Probably not." He glanced over his shoulder. People around the pool clustered together in little groups. "They believe it drained because something bad happened here."

"What do *you* think?" I asked.

"If it was only the drained water, I'd pay attention to the geologists."

"There's more?"

Gene stepped away from the pool, out of earshot from the crowd. We followed. He spoke so quietly we had to lean in to hear. "William's parents called me this morning. They were upset and confused."

I frowned. "Confused? Why?"

"Let me back up. The coroner ordered an autopsy because William's death was so unexpected. I guess that's routine."

I pictured William's body on the table for an autopsy. The image was gruesome.

Gene continued. "I don't know the details. From what his parents said, it's difficult to determine if heart failure or drowning is natural or not."

"So they think maybe someone—" I didn't have to finish the sentence.

"Anna talked to them. She's convinced William was, ah, murdered."

The foul word hung in the air.

"I don't get it," Ted said. "No offense to Anna, but she's probably not thinking straight. Why would William's parents listen to her?"

"That's the part they didn't want to talk about. Apparently, Anna gave them a name."

Anna's words rang in my head. *Someone did it.*

"Damn serious thing to do," Ted said.

I put my hand on Gene's arm. "What happens now?"

"Don't know. Coroner has to decide. I just hope it's quick so we can put this behind us."

"Gene," Harvey asked, "are you going ahead with this meeting?"

"There's nothing we can do now, so yes. And talking about something besides William and what happened here might help."

Great. We'd be speaking with a roomful of locals faced with the death of one of their own and sudden drainage of the pool he died in. Someone sniffled, and I cringed at my insensitivity. The people gathered around the hole in the ground were struggling with grief and an inexplicable event. My concerns were trivial in comparison.

Gene looked seaward. I followed his gaze. Rows of waves rolled across the bay.

"Where's my head?" Gene asked. "Almost forgot to tell you about the storm. A typhoon remnant, I think that's what the weatherman called it, in the Pacific unexpectedly turned east. It's heading our way now. They'll keep planes in Vancouver. No morning flights from here to the mainland, and who knows when they'll go again. You better change your plans. The meeting won't start for a half an hour, and you can use my phone. Door's unlocked."

As Gene walked away, we frowned at the clouds.

"Damn," Harvey said. "Now what?"

I put my hand on her shoulder. "We call the UN's travel agency. They'll take care of the flights. Bummer for sure, but there's nothing we can do about it."

Gene quickly circled the pool and headed up the path. People trailed behind him. We were the last to leave. I paused in front of the spot where William died and caught up with Harvey and Ted.

"It's too weird," Harvey said, "A young man dies in a pool that's dead?"

"You know, William could've died someplace else if he was killed," Ted said.

The idea that someone had carted William's body down to the pool before I arrived was too shocking to consider. "Let's not make stuff up. We don't know what's going on."

"Sure. It was just an idea."

In his cabin, Gene had a reliable phone connection to the mainland. We crowded into the tiny back room to make our calls. The travel agent told us told us not to worry—she'd take care of everything.

"Nice to have a professional handle this," Ted said. "Usually, I'm on the phone waiting for"—he air quoted—"'the next available agent.'"

We called a colleague at MOI. Arthur studied sea-floor spreading and would surely know about fault activity off British Columbia.

Luckily, Arthur was at his desk. He knew all about the tectonic event. "The Pacific and Atlantic plates meet along the Queen Charlotte fault, so you'd expect seismic activity there. Magnitude six earthquake early this morning about ten kilometers south of the islands."

We were on a speakerphone.

Ted leaned in so Arthur could hear him. "Wouldn't we have felt that?"

"Not necessarily, if it was shallow."

I spoke up. "Arthur, it's Mara. Would you expect more earthquakes in the next few days?"

"Gimme a minute." Over the speaker, we heard his fingers on the keyboard. "Right. Magnitude five aftershocks were measured following the earthquake. Wouldn't be surprised if there are more."

"So more pools might be impacted?"

"Could very well be."

We thanked Arthur, said we'd see him in a couple of days, and hung up.

Harvey looked at the phone. "Arthur's a good egg."

I nodded. "He is. Now if we're asked, we can sound intelligent about tectonic activity out here."

"Let's go over the issues before the meeting," Harvey said.

Ted leaned against the wall and crossed his arms. "Top on my list is whether what we say matters. You heard Gene. Like with the tectonic event, some will barely listen."

Ted sounded frustrated, which I understood. As scientists, we relied on data, evidence, and theories based on key principles. Sudden releases of energy in the earth's crust caused plates to shift. Earthquakes were the result. But people who treasured the heated waters for their spiritual and healing powers might not care a whit about tectonic plates and earthquakes. Our reasoned arguments about the iron fertilization project might not have much impact either.

"Maybe some won't care to listen, but others probably will," Harvey said. "All we can do is respect what they say and try to be as clear as we can."

"The issues with the iron are the same," I said. "They violated international law. In such rich waters, it's extremely difficult to tell if iron fertilization works, and they've been duped by Roger Grant."

Grim faced she added, "What's different is who'll be there. I think this will be a free-for-all."

16

WE DUCKED THROUGH THE LONGHOUSE DOOR. THE long room echoed with murmurs, like the inside of a church. People ranged in age from about twenty to eighty. A few wore black vests decorated with red symbols, but most were just dressed in regular street clothes. I could have been in Maine at a town meeting.

Council members had spread out across three sides of the pit benches. What I guessed were observers stood next to the walls. The only one I recognized was Bart. The row of steps nearest the door was empty. Gene waved and pointed to the unoccupied seats. We walked over and sat down, like three ducks in a row.

Gene welcomed council members and visitors and outlined the agenda. He'd begin with brief remembrances of William—a memorial service would take place soon. After he reviewed the iron project's plan and progress, he would introduce the UN visitors. The rest of the meeting was open for comments and questions, including ones directed at us.

In his tribute, Gene described William as a bright, curious young man. He was an outstanding Watchman who tackled every challenge with passion and commitment, including the iron controversy.

Several others, mostly women, added their memories. With tears running down her furrowed face, Charlotte said she'd known William since he was a baby, and loved him as one of her own. The nods and sniffles said her remembrance hit home.

Gene ran through the project's chronology. He reminded members what the council had paid Roger Grant, plus the dates and amounts of iron added. The UN visitors, he explained, were oceanographers familiar with iron fertilization projects and charged with evaluating the iron's impacts on Haida Gwaii's waters.

At first, council members directed questions at Gene. How much iron slurry was it again? Where was it added? Didn't the water green up? Salmon fishing was still poor. Why was that?

When council members appeared satisfied with Gene's answers, he formally introduced us. After a polite moment, the questions began. I was used to fielding belligerent, sometimes nasty, questions from lobstermen who didn't like my answers—mostly about climate change. Compared to them, these folks were genteel.

A bookish woman with owl glasses went first. "You're only here a couple of days. How can you tell anything from that?"

I stood. "Excellent point. But first, each of us would like to thank the Council and others here today for your generosity. You live in an astoundingly beautiful, precious part of the world. We will never forget Haida Gwaii."

A few looked surprised at my comment but most just smiled and nodded.

To address the first question, I described our trip out to the fertilization site, how we'd sampled the water, and our use of satellite imagery for situations like this.

Owl-glasses woman said, "You've certainly been busy. That's very helpful."

The questions went on, and we took turns fielding them.

"Haida have watched over these waters since the beginning of time. Aren't we our own protectors?"

"Roger Grant tells us we'll get lots of money from carbon,

um, credits, I think he called it. Are you saying we won't?"

"It's been weeks since that iron was dumped. I'm still not catching salmon. When's that going to change?"

"Before that iron was thrown into the sea, the ocean was in balance. Now it's upset. What will happen?"

Caleb, the guy who'd barged into the first meeting, stood away from the wall across the room when he spoke. "The ocean greened up right after iron was added. Anyone could see that. How can you tell us it didn't happen?"

We emphasized again that the satellite photos would help us determine the iron's impact. So, no, we had not come to any conclusion.

Caleb stepped toward us and crossed his arms. "Roger Grant's worked with us. Spent time here, like he's done other places. You come in for what, three days? Then you go. I put my money on Grant."

Gene stood and faced Caleb. "Enough. These are our guests."

At least half a foot taller than Gene, Caleb pressed his lips together, narrowed his eyes, and glared at his accuser. The muscular man looked like a bull about to charge, but Gene didn't flinch.

Gene cleared his throat and turned back to the group. He said, "The new Council vote is the day after tomorrow. That will give you time to think about what you learned today and talk to other members if you want." Gene then called an end to the meeting and gave a surprise announcement. "The *Haida Queen* should be anchored off the dock by now. The captain's invited us for a buffet dinner. You'll remember the food was great last year. And there's a storm on the way. The captain is hauling anchor after the buffet so they get back to the mainland before it gets too windy."

While Gene spoke, I watched Caleb. Red-faced, he still held clenched fists to his chest and continued to focus an angry scowl at Gene. But people didn't appear to notice. With the meeting over, people closest to Caleb just walked away like he was a statue. Maybe his aggressive behavior was a familiar nuisance best avoided.

There was one exception. Bart, who'd witnessed the meeting from the wall near the front of the room, stepped from a shadow, stared at Caleb, and cracked his knuckles. What was that about?

Voices interrupted my musing. Several people had approached us on their way out. Ted and Harvey were answering more questions, so I joined in to help. When we finally stood alone on the pit steps, I reached back to massage my lower back. The meeting had lasted almost two hours. No wonder I was tired.

Only a couple of people remained in the longhouse. Anna was one. She looked out a window at the far end of the room.

Harvey said, "Hey, let's walk on the beach to clear our brains. I guess dinner's on some boat."

I glanced back at Anna. "Be with you in a couple of minutes."

Harvey looked over my shoulder. "Right."

Anna appeared to be lost in thought and didn't seem to hear me walk across the wooden floor. "Anna?"

She twirled around. "Huh? Oh, hi."

"Could I speak with you?"

She looked around. "Here?"

Nobody was near. "Sure. I've been standing for a while. Let's sit on the floor."

The wall was a good backrest. We leaned against it, legs stretched out. I twirled my ankles. "That's better."

Anna stared at her feet.

"I understand you talked with William's parents—"

"So?"

Her tone surprised me. She'd been so polite before.

"Nothing wrong with that, of course. But you upset them with your claim that someone hurt William. I assume you meant Lynne. It's a very serious thing to say. For one thing, you have no proof."

Anna studied her feet again. I had no idea what she was thinking.

Finally, she said, "There's proof. Or close to it."

I didn't want to argue that "close to proof" made no sense. "What are you talking about?"

"It's Lynne. She studied herbal medicine with Charlotte."

Clearly, I was missing something. "And?"

She got up. "You should know. Some of those plants are deadly."

I pushed myself away from the wall and stood to face her. "Are you saying William died because Lynne poisoned him?"

She met my gaze. "It's a good possibility."

I shook my head. "Anna, surely you understand you can't accuse people of murder just because you don't like them."

"She's got a record."

"Lynne?"

"Assault. She beat someone up. They had to go to the hospital."

I cleared my throat, unsure where this conversation as going. "That's terrible, but it doesn't mean she murdered William."

Anna got to her feet. "What if I showed you something— dried herbs—I found hidden in Lynne's room?"

Frowning, I shook my head again. "They could be anything."

"I'm pretty sure they're *not* just anything. They're poison."

That was it. Hands on hips, I demanded, "Look, Anna, what do you want from me?"

Her eyes flashed—black, piercing. "People aren't listening to me. But you're different. They respect you. What if we compare the herbs I took from Lynne's room with poisonous ones?"

"But wouldn't Lynne notice they're missing?"

"She left most of the package behind. She won't notice if I take some."

"Anna, I don't know…"

She stood tall and crossed her arms. "William told me he saved your life. You owe him something. A lot. I'm just asking you to look at a dried plant, after all."

I placed my hand on my chest. She was right. William had saved me, and I did owe him. Against my better judgment, I relented.

"Okay. Get the plant. I'll meet you in the dining building in about an hour."

With a quick "thanks," she turned and marched toward the door. I watched until she'd slipped through the front doorway. I didn't feel great about what I'd agreed to, but it seemed the only way to put an end to her accusation. What could I tell about a dried herb? Even if I could ID whatever was in Anna's bag, that wouldn't mean much. The only way to know for sure about plant toxins was to perform chemical extraction and analysis. Certainly, that wasn't going to happen here.

So I'd look at the plant and very likely say I didn't know what it was. Then that would be that.

Harvey and Ted were on their way back from the pier end of the beach when I caught up with them. The *Haida Queen* had motored in during the meeting and was attached to the dock by a gangway. Waves on the bay were noticeably higher, but the boat barely moved.

I wasn't sure what I'd thought the *Haida Queen* would look like, but the huge two-story barge-type affair wasn't it. We stood on the beach and stared at the ship.

"I was expecting a large sailing vessel," Harvey said.

"What does it remind you of?" Ted asked.

I thought for a moment. "One of those river boats where you gamble. Huh, maybe that's what this is."

"There was an article in the flight magazine," Harvey said. "British Columbia is taking in a lot of money from gambling. It's very controversial, like in the states. Gambling addiction and all that."

"Maybe the Haida nation gets a cut," Ted said.

Harvey began walking toward the ship. "Whatever it is, I hope the food is good. I'm starving."

Ted and I strolled behind. He took my hand. "How'd it go with Anna?"

I recounted the conversation.

"Accusing Lynne like that, it's serious, but Anna's in a bad way. After all, she was William's fiancée."

I said, "Well—"

He stopped walking, and so did I. "What?"

I held up both palms. "Aaka says *she* was supposed to marry William."

Ted grimaced. "Ouch. That complicates things."

"And Lynne thought William was going to marry *her*. Apparently, William left three women with the impression they'd get married. It's a mess. William seemed like such a good guy. But now I wonder if he two-timed Aaka, Anna, and Lynne."

"If he did and one or the other found out, they'd be plenty angry," Ted said.

I groaned. "That just increases the 'who had motive' issue. We already had Bart and Lynne, maybe Caleb. Now there's Anna and Aaka."

"Let's go with Occam's razor. When there are competing hypotheses, we choose the simplest one. Nobody killed William. He died of a heart attack. A natural one."

"I'd like to believe that, but I really sense something's amiss here."

We were well behind Harvey. I turned to look at the western horizon. Sunset wasn't for a while, but the undersides of long, thin clouds already glowed pink.

Ted took my hand again. "Let's forget about this bad business for now and watch the sky. Looks like we can do that if we eat on the upper deck."

"That'd be nice."

Low tide had made the ramp connecting the pier to the dock especially steep. Ted stepped down first and turned to make sure I didn't trip.

What a great guy, I thought. Any woman would be lucky to have him. My next thought wasn't so pleasant.

If I didn't watch out, some other woman would.

Later, sated, I sat cross-legged on a high platform, facing west. The remains of the buffet—chicken bones, olive pits, and pie crumbs—lay between Ted and me.

Ted leaned back on his long arms to watch the nightly show. "You think the sunset looks different here? I mean, from Maine?"

I considered the scene. Waves on the expanse of the ocean before us glittered reddish-bronze beneath the setting sun. A bank of clouds from the west raced toward us. They were an eerie gray-green color, but the ones directly above the sliver of red sun were a swirl of purple, red, and orange. Dark purple peaks poked into the gaudy clouds. "Have to admit, much as I love Maine sunsets, the mountains here make these truly spectacular."

As if on cue, a dolphin flew out of the water and disappeared with a splash.

Ted laughed, slid over, took my hand, and kissed it. "Sure can't beat that."

My arm stiffened. Ted let go of my hand. "Mara, something's clearly the matter. Can you tell me what it is?"

Lots was the matter, all of it impossible to explain. A vision off Augustine Island, an underwater hallucination, a seal that saved me, a gust from the Ninstints forest that dropped a feather at my feet, how I might be losing my mind. No, I couldn't tell Ted any of that. But I could try to be honest about my feelings toward him. He deserved that.

"Ted, I love you. Truly, I do. You're terrific in every way. But it feels, I don't know, too much. I need more time alone."

Against the darkening sky, his eyes were deep navy. The pain I'd caused was hard to see.

"Is there anything I can do? I mean, to help?"

"If there were, I'd tell you. But it's not you, Ted. It's me."

Sadder than I'd ever seen him, Ted stared at the sunset. When we took the companionway down to the main deck in silence, the western sky was pewter gray.

Harvey met us near the gangway. Even from a distance, I could see she was distraught.

"What's wrong?"

She gestured toward the stern. "After eating, I checked out the roulette wheel. Not to gamble. To see who was."

Harvey knew the odds of winning were about the same as a June snowstorm in Maine. Not impossible, but extremely unlikely, especially given the changing climate.

"You'll never guess who was at the wheel."

Ted and I looked at each other and shrugged.

"Gene."

We didn't know Gene well, of course, but the image of him kissing a lucky rabbit's foot and placing a bet didn't match my impression, to say the least.

"Maybe not what you'd expect," Ted said, "but, you know, so what?"

"He and that guy Caleb were competing. It got pretty nasty. That's them barking at each other."

To see what she meant, I walked toward the raised voices. Ted was right behind me. We stopped in the threshold of the large open room. At the far end, waiters were hurriedly clearing the buffet tables where we'd gotten our food. At our end, there was a long wooden bar, a cocktail area, and three large tables with green surfaces. At each gambling table, a man in a white shirt and black vest was in charge of the roulette wheel or a card game.

At the moment, nobody played roulette because a man stood between Gene and Caleb. It looked like a scene from a rowdy game like ice hockey or rugby. The flustered referee held Gene and Caleb back with outstretched arms and desperately looked around for help. He was about to get it because a hefty guy, maybe the manager or a security cop, was running toward him.

I turned away. "I've seen enough. Let's get out of here."

We joined Harvey on the dock, which rocked to and fro with the building waves.

"Damn," I said, "if you hadn't told me that was Gene, I wouldn't have recognized him."

"Got that right. Pretty awful."

"Maybe Gene was drinking," Ted said. "That turns some people mean. Or maybe Caleb did something inexcusable that really pissed Gene off."

"Or the other way around," Harvey said.

"Gene did something to incense Caleb?" I asked.

"Caleb yelled something about Gene cooking the numbers. Or going to cook the numbers. Whatever that means."

"Caleb strikes me as someone who mouths off."

Harvey ran a hand through her hair. "Thought I had a decent idea who thought what and who to trust. Now, I'm not at all sure."

As team leader, Harvey in particular needed to understand the motivations and stances of the Haida's main players. I wanted to help, but there was nothing to say or do.

On the pier, we stopped to get a sense of the weather. A bank of clouds raced overhead and wind whipped my hair around. I left Harvey and Ted where the path turned up to the dining building. They planned to use Gene's phone to check in with the travel agent before they headed back to the longhouse. On our way, I explained that I was going to meet Anna and why.

"Plant ID sounds safe, but with what's going on here, be careful," Harvey said.

"And watch this storm," Ted added. "It's coming in fast."

Anna was waiting for me when I stepped into the kitchen. "Thought you might not show up."

"Sorry. We ate and watched the sunset." No need to tell her about Gene.

She slid a clear sandwich bag across the wooden island we used to chop vegetables. "Here."

It was nearly dark in the room, but I didn't want to waste generator fuel. "Are there backup batteries so you could you switch on the overhead light for a while without turning on the generator?"

She nodded. "We've got some powerful batteries for the kitchen."

In the light, I lifted the bag to eye level. In addition to ground-up leaves, I was surprised to see what looked like intact dried flowers. "Do you know anything about these flowers?"

Anna opened her mouth like she was going to say something. Then she closed it and shook her head. "No."

"I can't tell anything from the leaves. But the flowers look pretty distinctive. Do you have any plant identification books?"

She shook her head again. I squinted at the bag. The flowers *did* look very unusual, which might help with their identity. My scientific curiosity kicked in.

"I'm going to call someone in Maine who might help me. My grad student. Gene's letting us use his phone."

"Can I come?" Anna sounded excited.

"This is a long shot. Okay? But, sure, you can come."

It was many hours later in Maine compared to British Columbia, but Alise, my student, was a night owl. Bright and enthusiastic, Alise was also a little crazy. It seemed like she colored a swath of her hair purple, red, or orange just to give the more conservative scientists something to talk about besides their research. I didn't care a bit. She was an excellent scientist, up for anything, and great company.

Luckily, her cell phone number was easy to remember. She picked up on the first ring.

"Alise here."

"Alise, it's Mara."

"Hey. How's it going out there?"

"Good. I've got a puzzle and could use your help with an Internet search."

"Sure. Got my computer right here. Gimme a sec. Okay, fire. What should I search?"

"How about plant poisons?"

"You know there are tons."

"For plants that could grow on the coast in the Pacific Northwest."

"Hold it." There was clicking in the background. "Okay, got a good page."

"Look for ones with distinctive inflorescences." I described in detail what I'd seen in the plastic bag.

I could hear the computer keys.

"Here's one that looks good."

"Go ahead."

"*Veratrum viride*, variety, um, *esch*, um, *scholzianum*. Boy, that's a mouthful."

"Tell me its distribution."

"This variety grows in Alaska, British Columbia, the Northwest Territory, and other places. Um, from sea level up pretty high."

"Good. Now please describe the plant, mostly the flowers."

"Let's see. Herbaceous perennial. Tall. Leaves arranged spirally. Numerous flowers on a large inflorescence with branches—"

"Hold up. I've got to take notes." Anna had turned on an overhead light, so I could see a pad and pencil on Gene's desk. I grabbed both and scribbled.

"Got it. Keep going."

"Um. Inflorescences with branches up to seventy centimeters. Flowers are five to ten millimeters long and there are six green or yellow-green tepals. What's a tepal?"

"It's used when you can't tell the difference between a sepal and a petal."

"Learn something new every day. Okay, fruits are capsules about one to three centimeters long."

"Seeds?"

"Right. Ah, they're flat, around ten millimeters, and are released from the capsule that splits when mature."

I scanned my scribbles. "That should do it."

"One more thing, Mara."

"What's that?"

"*Veratrum viride*'s common name and toxicity."

"Of course. Go ahead."

"False hellebore, also called Indian poke or Indian hellebore, is highly toxic. It slows respiration and leads to cardiac arrest."

Anna and I looked at each other.

"Mara, you still there?"

"Yes. Sorry. Is there something else?"

"The plant's commonly used by Native Americans."

"Alise, you're a gem. See you in a couple of days."

I dropped the phone into its cradle. Anna leaned against the tiny office's wall.

"Well, that was interesting."

"Sounded like it," she said. "What next?"

"I'd like to look at the inflorescences close up. Do you have anything that magnifies?"

"Kids come out here for a nature outing. Identifying plants and animals, you know? I'm pretty sure there's something like that in the dining house. The children work on projects there."

We walked back in the dark. Leaves skittered across the circle cast by my flashlight, trees on either side of the path swayed back and forth, and cold rain spit against my cheeks. While Anna searched for the magnifier, I waited in the kitchen. She returned with a good-sized magnifying glass and slid it across the wooden island.

I used it to look at my hand. "This will work. Let's get that overhead light on again. I'll take a look at these flowers. Also, a tall stool would help a lot."

I carefully poured the contents of the plastic bag onto a white paper towel. For the next twenty minutes, I peered through the magnifying lens at the inflorescences, consulted my notes, picked up the lens again, and rotated bits of flowers to get a better look. Anna was a silent observer.

Finally, I put the lens down and rubbed my eyes with the back of my hands.

"What do you think?"

I blinked and sat up straight on the stool. "Anna, I'm not a botanist. These would have to be officially identified by an expert. But what I see matches the description Alise gave us. Right after William died, I met the coroner's investigator, a Sergeant Knapton. I suppose I could tell him about these plants and let him decide. That's all I can do."

With a tight smile, Anna nodded. "That would be great."

"It's too late now. I can call him in the morning. On one condition, though."

"Yes?"

"You must promise to accept his decision, even if you don't like it. If Knapton says he wants nothing to do with these plants, that's the end of it. Okay?"

Anna's "Okay" was a little too quick. I got the idea she was confident Knapton would be very interested in her plants.

Personally, I didn't think so.

When I got back to the longhouse and told Harvey what I'd found, she sat cross-legged on her sleeping bag and tapped a finger on the end of her nose. She did that sometimes when she was thinking. "False hellebore? Sounds vaguely familiar, but it's been a very long time since I studied plants."

Ted leaned back on his arms, legs sprawled out in front. "But lots of plants have nasty chemicals. Foxglove has digoxin, poppy morphine. For apple seeds it's cyanide. The hellebore's toxicity probably means nothing."

Stretched out on my bag and pad, I closed my eyes for a moment. My day had included a scuba dive with a bizarre ending, a two-plus-hour Environmental Council meeting, Gene losing it on the gambling boat, and staring at dried plants through a magnifying lens for too long. I was bushed.

I sat up. "You're right. But Anna was so determined, it seemed like she'd go off on her own. This way, the RCMP get the information and decides what to do. Not me and not Anna."

The storm had begun to make its mark on Haida Gwaii. Rain battered against the skylights, and wind lashed trees around the clearing. A bout of rain sounded like marbles smashing into the skylight.

"Thank goodness the rain wasn't too bad on my way over. So, what did the travel agent say?"

"There were only two seats on the ten AM flight from Sandspit to Vancouver day after tomorrow," Harvey said. "Ted and I have tickets for that. She put you on the noon flight. If that's not okay, one of us can take the later flight."

"Actually, that's good. There's a little museum in Sandspit I'd like to visit."

I didn't want to say I'd have a little more time in Haida Gwaii to look into William's death.

"What about the trip home?"

"No problem. We're all on the same red-eye, just the next day."

Rain pelted the windows on the side of the building.

Cross-legged near the lantern, I cast a long shadow in the empty room. "This sounds like a hurricane."

Harvey slid into her sleeping bag, rolled onto her back, and put her hands behind her head. "Aren't typhoons the same as hurricanes?"

Ted rifled through his duffle. "They are. Low-pressure center, strong spiral winds."

"So this one might do some damage," I said.

"Hadn't thought about that," Harvey said. "I wish this was our last night here. It's been a fascinating few days, but I'm ready to jump on that plane and head back to Maine. Tons of work to catch up on."

"Then there's Connor, of course."

At the mention of her lover's name, Harvey grinned at the ceiling. Lit by the lantern, in profile, she looked like a human version of a contented Persian cat—perfect, sleek, and smiling.

She turned her head in my direction. "Sure you're okay to leave a little later?"

"Absolutely. I'll look around."

She smirked. "Oh, lots to do in Sandspit, population one hundred."

"No, seriously. I looked online before we left. There's a museum next to the visitor's center."

Harvey sat up. "I'm wide awake. Any ideas what we can talk about?"

"We could go through our list of suspects again," Ted said.

Tired as I was, I rallied. "Let's do it."

"Who first?" Harvey asked.

"Wish I had my whiteboard," I said. "Let's see. Anna accuses Lynne. But there's no direct evidence."

Ted walked back and forth as he talked. "For Lynne, what evidence is there?"

"Just plants Anna found in Lynne's room. That's pretty thin. And who knows how they got there."

"If Anna knows about Aaka, she'd be awfully angry," Harvey said.

"I can't imagine Anna hurting William."

The possibility hung in the air.

"That's Anna and Lynne," Ted said. "Who else?"

"Caleb's an angry guy," Harvey said.

"Motive?"

"Don't know."

"What about Aaka?" I asked.

"Like Anna," Harvey said. "Can't imagine her killing anybody."

Harvey rubbed her eyes. "*This* is making me tired."

"Let's go with Occam's razor and then to bed," Ted said.

Harvey and Ted talked about what awaited them at home. I rummaged around in my duffle for my toilet kit and ran through what I missed in Spruce Harbor. The picture-perfect little harbor with lobster boats swinging on their moorings. The Neap-Tide, my favorite hang-out eatery, on Water Street. Foggy mornings when I got wet walking down the street, screeching gulls overhead.

Then there was my little cottage at the end of a dirt road that overlooked the sea. Angelo de Luca, my godfather, had helped me fix up that treasure.

Angelo. God, how I missed him. A widower with over-flowing Italian generosity and love, Angelo had opened his arms and heart to me when my parents died. Angelo would meet us at the bus station. I smiled at the thought of his bear hug.

By the time I finished brushing my teeth and hair, Ted and Harvey were both nestled into their sleeping bags. I switched off my flashlight, padded over to my bag, and slid in. Ted was beside me. I reached over to touch his arm. He didn't stir.

In the dark, I lay on my back and listened to Ted's steady breathing. Deep down, I knew he could be the love of my life if I let him. But something I couldn't name or express held me back. Something more than needing time alone. Overwhelming loneliness came over me, and I blinked back tears. I desperately needed to talk to someone.

In the fifteen years since my parents had died, I'd perfected personal traits that served me well in grad school and at the Maine Oceanographic Institute—independence, self-confidence, hard work. I'd studied like crazy at MIT, and proved to my male colleagues a woman could be a damn good oceanographer. I'd followed my parent's professional path, like I was born to study the sea. Nothing got in my way.

The personal costs of my stubborn independence had only dawned on me a couple of months earlier. That took a vicious attack in a parking lot *and* being kidnapped and nearly dumped a mile offshore. Those near-death horrors helped me understand what Angelo, Harvey, and probably Ted already knew. Trust people who love you with secret worries, and they can help.

Out here on the Haida Gwaii archipelago, there was no-body I could talk to about Ted. I loved Harvey like a sister, but she was Ted's half-sibling and couldn't be an objective listener. Angelo. I needed to talk to Angelo.

In Sandspit I'd be alone for a couple of hours. Wi-Fi con-nections were reliable there, and it'd be afternoon in Maine. I'd reach Angelo and tell him everything.

With that resolution, I slipped into a deep sleep.

17

THE STORM SWEPT PAST THE ARCHIPELAGO DURING THE night. By mid-morning, the sky was cloudless and air smelled cool and fresh. Other than branches and leaves that littered the clearing and puddles of water in low spots, nothing was damaged at the longhouse.

We took the walkway to the dining building and peered into the kitchen. Empty. The path down to the water gave us an inkling of Kinuk's severely battered shoreline.

The day before, the gentle incline took us right down to the shingle beach. Now the path abruptly ended at a cliff half as tall as a house. As far as we could see up and down the beach, the unbridled sea had gouged out deep chunks of earth.

Gene was on his hands and knees under the pier. It looked like he was inspecting the pilings. We slid down the dirt incline on our butts to join him.

He got up and put his hands on his hips. "I've seen some pretty bad storms, but this one's a doozy. Looks like the wind must've been worst at high tide."

Ted walked closer to one of the pilings. "These look okay?"

"Yes, thank goodness. Let's go get some breakfast, coffee. I'm starving."

On our way back, we scrounged around for logs and planks that had washed ashore. Gene directed the construction of a makeshift inclined walkway up from the beach to the eroded path. Energetic as always, he didn't act one bit like a man with a hangover. It was hard to believe he was the same person we'd seen at *Haida Queen's* roulette table the night before. Gene cooked up a breakfast of scrambled eggs, toast with homemade blackberry jam, and coffee.

I filled my mug with more coffee from the pot. "How often do you get a food delivery?"

"Caleb brings over fresh fish at least twice a week. Salmon, ling cod, whatever's out there. Once a week, he brings staples—fresh vegetables, milk, that type of thing, from Skidegate or Old Masset. Most people live in those towns." He winked. "You worried there's not enough food?"

"You've taken excellent care of us."

"You bet. Speaking of Caleb, he's doing damage survey and needs help. Usually, William goes with him. You folks up for it?"

"Damage survey?" Ted asked.

"In the park, we have to keep track of erosion, debris buildup on the beach, oil leaks from ships, that kind of thing."

"Gene, Caleb's a pretty rough character," I said. "We don't want to spend the day with someone who'll be nasty to us."

"No question, Caleb gets carried away. He's obsessed about this iron project, so you've seen him at his absolute worst. Today, you'll see a completely different side of the man."

Ted, Harvey, and I looked at each other.

"You're sure, he'll be, um, pleasant?" I asked.

"I do," Gene said. "And you'll find his ecology disaster excursion very interesting."

Caleb's boat, the *Spirit of Tanu*, was already at the dock when we got down there. Instead of his grubby fishing gear, Caleb wore an official-looking khaki shirt and matching pants, along with the usual black rubber boots. Without the scowl, his coarse features gave him the look of a friendly lobsterman you'd see on the cover of a Maine travel magazine.

Charlene D'Avanzo

Gene was right. A very different Caleb welcomed us like an obliging neighbor. "Hey, glad for the help. Step aboard."

We pulled away. Caleb motored slowly in shallow water so we could assess the damage to Kinuk Island. The erosion was impressive. Despite the protection of Augustine Island, Kinuk's westward-facing shoreline hadn't escaped the scouring action of the angry sea. Caleb snapped photos. At the end of the island, he set the motor at trolling speed to keep the boat from rocking.

We crowded around the chart table in the fishing vessel's cabin. Caleb pointed to our position. "We're right here between the tip of Augustine and Kinuk. I'll head for Sga'nguai—Ninstints. Any erosion there'd be a disaster."

The image of Haida Gwaii's spectacular totem poles dangling on their sides over a crumbling cliff face was sickening.

"Are you worried about the poles?" Harvey asked.

Caleb put a stubby finger on Ninstints Bay. "They didn't put the village in a place exposed to storms. It should be okay. But we have to check."

Caleb opened a notebook and recorded what he'd seen on Kinuk.

I asked, "Are you already seeing impacts of climate change out here?"

"It's hard ta sort out, but we're pretty sure."

"Why?"

"Last spring, some scientists from UBC came out here for the week. We showed 'em around, and they did a workshop for us. They said warming on the BC coast is the fastest in Canada. In Queen Charlotte Sound, they're seeing temperatures at the ocean's surface going up five times faster than what's happening in the *whole earth*."

Huh, I thought. Gulf-of-Maine temperature where we lived had also increased at an unprecedented rate, partly because the melting Greenland ice sheet shifted Gulf-Stream water north. Warmer waters pretty much ended Maine's shrimp industry and led to explosions of green crabs that decimated clams. I knew little about warm-water impacts off BC but suspected salmon were at risk.

"Warmer waters means rising sea level and bigger storms. Think you're seeing that now?" Ted asked.

"Yup. Both."

Rising sea level and massive storm surges. In the not-so-distant future, a significant portion of the Haida Gwaii archipelago was going to wash into the sea. The Haida nation would have to adapt, or disappear with the land.

Harvey, Ted, and I were out on the *Spirit of Tanu*'s bow when we rounded the headland and motored into the calm waters of Ninstints Bay. The totem pools looked exactly as we'd left them. I let go of the railing I'd been gripping.

Caleb put the motor into neutral and joined us. "Like I said, people who lived here knew exactly what they were doing."

"So, what's the drill?" Ted asked.

"Looks like there's no erosion, but we need to see. That means taking measurements from the poles to the edge of the berm." He gestured over his shoulder. "I got boots you folks can use in that big plastic box in the cabin."

As Caleb motored closer to shore, we looked through the storage tote stored under the chart table. He had an assortment of gear for his fishing clients—waterproof jackets, bibs, hats, and gloves. Boots were in the bottom of the box. There were even a couple of pairs for smaller feet. I kicked off my hiking shoes and pulled on boots.

Caleb called over his shoulder, "When we anchor is when you can get off. Transom's down low."

He was right. I stepped off the stern, and water didn't even wash over the top of my boots.

Caleb had a couple of those big yellow measuring-tape reels foresters use. We worked in pairs to stretch the tape from the base of each pole to the edge of the berm. Caleb recorded the data in his notebook.

I paired up with Harvey and avoided what I'd secretly named "the weird feather spot" by picking poles farthest away.

Back on the beach, Caleb took the reels. "Now we go to the west side of the park. There'll be damage out there for sure."

We followed the same routine for the next four hours. Caleb motored close to shore, we jumped out with the equipment, and Caleb anchored in deeper water and waded in. At intervals along Moresby Island's western coast, we measured the height of the scoured bank plus distance from the eroded berm straight back to the nearest large trees. At each site, Caleb got the GPS coordinates with a handheld device, recorded the data, and took photos.

Washed-up debris littered the beach all along the coastline, but the volume and variety of debris at one site was astounding. In addition to the usual plastic bottles and pieces of netting, we saw shoes, ripped pieces of clothes, lots of soda cans, plus kitchen paraphernalia such as plastic plates and jars.

There was a pile of plastic dolls in perfectly good condition. I picked one up. "How does something like this get here?"

Caleb took the doll and looked at her face. "Container ships. You folks must know about that oceanographer who tracked toys kids use in tubs for, what, twenty years? From a wreck in Alaska all the way ta Scotland and Maine."

"Sure. He and the yellow rubber ducks were famous. Helped people realize how much junk gets dumped into the ocean and where it goes."

Caleb waded back to the boat and returned with a cooler of food and drinks. The chicken salad sandwiches made with bakery bread were delicious, and ice-cold soda hit the spot. Clearly, Caleb knew how to take care of his rich clients.

Sated, I lay back and closed my eyes to enjoy the warm sun on my face. There was a light offshore breeze and waves gently sloshed up and down the beach. I tried to imagine we were on an unspoiled Caribbean island, but when I opened my eyes, the piles of trash said otherwise.

I sat up and brushed sand off my arms. There was more in my hair, but that tangled mess required a hairbrush. "Caleb, is environmental patrol a regular job for Watchmen?"

"I do most of it, lots more then I need to."

"All this debris on your beautiful beaches. Do you get discouraged?"

"It's hard to look at, but there's nothing I can do. Big successes like the cannery keep me going."

Harvey sat on a log the storm had dumped on the high-tide line. "Cannery?"

"Lots of Haida used to work in canneries owned by rich people on the mainland. But that was a long while back, and fish stocks are way down now. That's why this iron thing's so important. Anyways, we—there's a group of us—blocked this new cannery. That was a big, big deal."

I waited for him to say more about the iron project, but he didn't. "Tell us about the proposed cannery."

He shook his head. "First of all, it made no sense with fish numbers way down. And they wanted to build right near an old village site."

Caleb was an unexpected teacher, and we needed to understand the iron fertilization scheme in a larger context.

I kept him talking. "Did the Haida environmental movement come about because of overfishing?"

"That happened way back in the seventies. Guy named

Gujaaw took on a logging company that was supposed to clear-cut a big tract right here on Moresby Island. As a kid, Gujaaw hunted and such on Moresby, so it was special."

"Did Gujaaw win?"

"Took ten years for changes. It was the late eighties, I think, when three elders dressed up in red and black blankets. They stood in the middle of a logging road on Lyell Island. Got arrested."

Harvey leaned forward on her log. "Did they go to jail?"

"Nah. Too hot for the government. Polls showed BC folks on *our* side for once. Charges got dropped when no new cutting permits were allowed."

"Then what happened?"

"Haida Gwaii Watchmen started. We're here to protect the natural, historical, cultural heritage. All together."

"Wow, Caleb. That's a great story. Good environmental news for a change."

Caleb sat tall and his dark eyes shone. "Sure is." He waved a hand at the ocean. "Right here, lucky thing happened a couple years ago. There could've been a big spill when a Russian ship lost power in rough water not far offshore. If she broke up, diesel fuel would've covered these beaches." He spread out his arms.

"Like the Exxon Valdez," Ted said. "Oil still seeps out of sediment into Alaskan waters."

"Yeah, like that. We got lucky. The Russian ship got towed to safer waters."

My butt was going numb. I shifted position. "Did that make people more aware of what might happen with the tar sands?"

"You bet. Just last week we had a rally in Masset. We're calling for oil-free coastlines on the mainland, out here, too. Tar sands mean tankers by the hundreds hauling the stuff down the north coast."

The rap Anna had sung was about the massive tar sands project—huge deposits of tar-like bitumen. The shallow tar sand mines looked like giant black bomb craters.

I pictured William urging Anna to sing her song for us. They seemed like such good friends, and now she was alone. I wondered if William had a brother or sister who might comfort Anna but knew nothing about his family.

Caleb," I asked, "Did William have any siblings? You know, someone who might take Anna under their wing?"

He pulled one of his impressively large earlobes. "Um, let me think. Okay, I remember. William talked about an older brother name of Robert, Richard, something like that. They were really different and didn't get along. Robert, whatever, made lots of money in banking I think it was. Said William was a loser for being a Watchman. You get the idea."

I nodded. It was amazing how unlike siblings could be. William's brother sure didn't seem like the type to befriend Anna.

I had a final question for Caleb, an important one. "Caleb, I'd like to ask you about the iron project."

He eyed me, then nodded.

"I heard the Haida were excited to be leaders in reducing carbon from the atmosphere. Did Roger Grant explain that? I mean, how it would work?"

He looked at the ocean and squinted. "Let me think. Um, Mr. Grant said carbon'd be traded for like, you know, wheat, corn, all that."

Carbon trading on the stock exchange. The inkling that this was important slipped through my mind and was gone in an instant. I'd have to read more about it when I got back.

Caleb glanced at the sun. "Time to go."

The tide was on its way up. Caleb waded out to bring the *Spirit of Tanu* closer in. He climbed aboard, pulled up the anchor line, and let the boat drift shoreward. Ted held out a hand to help Harvey and me step onto the transom shelf.

Caleb opened the throttle on the way back. Even in the cabin, we had to yell to be heard.

"This is a great boat," Ted said. "You do a good business with fishing charters?"

"Some of the best saltwater fishing in the world out here. My people get salmon fifty pounds and more. Big halibut, too."

"So it's good money?"

We slammed into bigger waves, and I nearly ended up on my ass. Caleb slowed down. I stationed myself more firmly against the cabin's bulkhead next to the wheel.

"Money? It's good during season, but that's short. I got a wife, kids, a house, all that. Living out here's not cheap."

"Can you do the charters and be a Watchman at the same time?" I asked.

"Gene's good there. I'm Watchman full-time half a year."

I was curious about Caleb's relationship with Gene, and Caleb had just provided a good lead-in for a question. I kept it vague. "Um, you guys good friends?"

"Not sure Gene's good friends with anyone. He's kind of secretive if you know what I mean."

Gene didn't strike me as secretive, but I kept that to myself. I moved closer so I didn't have to yell quite so loudly. "Caleb, just wondering. What's your take on William dying and the pool drying up?"

He gripped the wheel and his face muscles tightened like he'd clenched his jaw. He was quiet so long I thought he wasn't going to answer.

"Don't have an opinion on that."

Caleb dropped us off at the Kinuk dock and thanked us for our help. I watched him speed away in the *Spirit of Tanu*. Out in his boat doing important environmental work, Caleb was in his element and completely different from the angry man we'd seen earlier. People were complicated, and I had to be careful about rash judgments. That seemed to be a hard lesson for me.

18

PARTWAY DOWN THE PIER, I STOPPED TO LOOK OUT OVER the bay. From up high, Kinuk's new scars weren't visible—just the expanse of blue-green sea and mountains in the background. Haida Gwaii was a world-renowned tourist destination, and visitors saw only the beauty. Given the stunning land and seascape, that was understandable. But our work here, including what Gene called "the ecology disaster excursion," showed us the inevitable impacts of human exploitation on an ecological jewel fifty miles off the coast of British Columbia.

Harvey and Ted were halfway up the trail to the bathhouse complex when I caught up to them.

"You going to the longhouse?"

"Thought we'd find out the deal for dinner first," Harvey said.

At the junction of the main path and the one leading down to the pools, we saw Gene walking toward us. He moved slowly, head down and shoulders slouched, like an old man. I guessed he'd visited the pool where William died.

He saw us, straightened up, and quickened his steps. "How'd it go?"

I said, "Like you said, it was really interesting. Depressing, too, of course. And Caleb was a completely different person out there."

"He's passionate about the environment. If you're on the other side of him, though, watch out. Guess passion goes both ways." Gene looked west. "It's six or so. You folks hungry?"

"Caleb took good care of our stomachs," Ted said. "We can wait. Whatever's best for you."

"How 'bout in an hour. We'll have something simple."

In the longhouse, we took advantage of daylight to organize our stuff and pack. We dumped out our duffle bags and made piles of dirty clothes, clean ones we'd wear the next day, toiletries, and gear we wouldn't need. That done, we sat on the steps in the middle of the big empty space. The bold back mural appeared bluish gray and muddy in the waning light.

"What struck you most about today?" I asked.

Harvey curled a lock of blond hair behind her ear. For the trip home she'd changed into black fleece pants, a red turtleneck, and a spanking clean red fleece pullover. "What we learned from Caleb. The environmental history. Especially the protest against the lumber company."

"Can't you just picture three stately Haida in those gorgeous black and red robes standing there, refusing to move?"

Ted leaned back on his long arms. "You know, the Penobscot Nation in Maine organized and just won a big battle."

"Really?" I said.

"The EPA sided with the Penobscot and ordered the governor to improve water quality to protect fishing on the reservation. Given the Nation's sentiment about the governor, they must've loved that."

Beyond what I'd learned in grade school and read in the news, I knew little about Maine's Native Americans, including their environmental struggles and victories. "I've lived in Maine my whole life and you've been there, what, four months? It sounds like you know a lot about this."

Harvey rolled her eyes. "Mara, Ted and I invited you to go with us to an open meeting, but you said you had too much work. Don't you remember?"

Work always came first for me. "Oh, yeah." To change the subject I added, "Don't know if you heard me, but I asked Caleb what he thought about William's death. He wouldn't say a thing. Do you think that's kind of odd?"

Harvey got to her feet. "Not sure what to make of that. We better head down. Maybe we can help Gene."

We pulled the kitchen door open. The room smelled of hot oil. I was startled to see Lynne at the stove. As far as I knew, she hadn't been on the island since the night William died.

Gene sliced fish on a wooden cutting board. He used a foot-long knife with a thin blade that curved up. It looked like a small version of an ancient Chinese fighting sword.

I stood next to him. " What's that?"

"Halibut." He turned toward Lynne. "I'm just about done here. Let's eat out on the picnic table. Why don't you carry out the plates and silverware?"

Lynne walked by without acknowledging Harvey or me.

I leaned in. "Gene, that's a nasty-looking knife. I've never seen one like it."

"Coho fillet knife. Cuts through flesh like butter."

I shivered.

We sat down to eat.

I'd only taken a few bites when I had to ask. "Lynne. Haven't seen you lately. Where've you been?"

"On the mainland."

"Lynne helps out when Anna's away or there's a large group." Gene asked about our day with Caleb.

"He told us about Gujaaw, the logging company protest, and some recent successes," Ted said. "Really interesting."

I glanced at Lynne. She paid no attention to us or what we had to say.

"What's the difference between a person and a tree?" Gene asked.

Harvey shrugged. Ted shook his head.

Smirking, I said, "What?"

"One's illegal to hit with an ax."

We groaned.

"One more. What do you get when you cross an environmentalist with direct action?"

We waited.

"Arrested!"

Lynne got up and left.

Gene became serious. "What about native tribes in Maine? I'd bet they're a force to be reckoned with. Was there a turning point for them like lumbering was for us?"

"I'm not sure," Harvey said. "But I think it was about the right to unlimited fishing and hunting on the reservations."

"And now," Ted said, "native people in Maine are fighting against some fishing limits on species that really do need to be managed. It's like their push for power has gone too far."

Gene leaned forward. "What fish?"

"Eels. The money for baby eels—elvers—is astounding. What do you think they're getting per pound?"

"A hundred dollars?" I guessed.

Ted motioned upward with his thumb and turned toward Harvey.

"Three hundred?"

Thumb up again.

It was Gene's turn. "Five hundred?"

Ted shook his head. "*A thousand dollars* per pound and going up. I saw a photo of a sign that said fifteen hundred."

Gene whistled. "Japanese market?"

"Yeah," Ted said.

I was astonished. "I knew it was high, but that's unbeliev-able. Huh. In the US people think of Native Americans as, you know, big time environmentalists. But many tribes desperately need money. That pits poverty against their environmental ethic."

I opened my mouth again to say "Like with the Haida and the iron." But with Gene right there, I changed my mind.

It was twilight by the time we'd finished the dishes. Lynne had disappeared. Gene said he'd see us at eight in the morning and left.

I turned to Harvey and Ted. "Up for a final walk by the water?"

Harvey shook her head. "Sorry. I'm bushed."

Ted looked down at his feet. "Ah, me, too. Bushed."

Down on the beach, I sat on the flat rock where Anna had said she and William were going be married. The evening show was well underway. A rose-lavender sky had turned the glassy bay a showy pink. But I felt unsettled, and even the bright colors didn't lift my spirits.

Ted was a big reason for my disquiet. I was miffed he didn't want to join me. Miffed and guilty. Maybe his patience was running out. If so, I couldn't blame him. We'd been in the archipelago less than a week, but given my raw emotions, it felt a whole lot longer. Between disappointing Ted, the angst around the Haida's iron controversy, the inexplicable visions, and, of course, William's death, I was spent.

A voice startled me. "Mara."

I jumped up and faced Lynne. Her face was taut.

"My goodness. You scared me."

"I want to talk to you." Hands on hips, her words spilled out. "Anna accused me of—of—poisoning William with plants she found in my room. She even said something to his *parents*. You know about this. Why are you involved? You're not even Haida."

I kept my voice calm. "Anna asked me to identify some plants. I tried to ID them and will pass the information along to Sergeant Knapton. He's investigating William's death."

"Did it ever occur to you that Anna put the plants in my room?"

"Yes, it did. I intend to say so to Knapton. Of course, he'll realize that as well."

Lynne's shoulders dropped. "Oh."

"Were they your plants?"

The warrior was back. "No!"

"Hold on. Any idea how they got in your room?"

She shook her head.

"Who here knows about medicinal plants?"

"Charlotte's had a couple of students. William, me, Anna. Others who aren't around now."

"Who knew the most?"

"William, besides Charlotte, of course. Nobody knows more than Charlotte."

"One more question, Lynne. Why would anyone want William dead?"

She choked on the answer. "Nobody. William was special." She spun around and left without saying good-bye.

I picked my way along the shingle before it got fully dark and wondered how Lynne found out I'd identified the plants. The Haida were probably a close community in the Vancouver area where William's parents lived. Anna was in communication with them, so maybe Lynne learned about the plants from William's mom and dad or a cousin. Something about that pricked at the far recesses of my brain.

"I'll remember when I least expect it," I said to myself.

At the bottom of our makeshift ramp up to the path, I took a last look at Kinuk Bay. On the horizon, lavender had turned to gray, and black strands interrupted the smooth surface of the water. Kelp. Beneath the still waters, sleek seals with human eyes flew through the sea forest.

I wanted to say one more farewell. Cross-legged at the edge of the empty pool, I stared at the spot where I'd last seen William. I closed my eyes and pictured him alive—laughing at his joke about smart ravens, telling us the salmon-boy story, and, of course, motoring up in his beat-up dinghy to save me. I didn't believe William had died of natural causes, but had no proof. Just a possible identification of a possible plant that might have been used by a killer. Too many possibles and maybes.

I was in William's debt. Doubly so, given his rescue of my closest friend in the sauna. I needed to figure out what had happened to him.

No. I *would* figure that out.

19

THE HAIDA GWAII AIRPORT WAS IN SANDSPIT, A HALF-hour boat ride north of us on a good day. We were down on the Kinuk dock at eight a.m. In the distance, an inflatable motored toward us. Gene, right on time. How he looked at the roulette table flashed through my mind—the red face, snarl, and clenched fists. A very different Gene pulled up to the dock. We handed him our duffels and stepped into the inflatable.

Gene pointed to three sou'westers. "The trip up to Sandspit's not that long, but it's bumpy out there. Don't want you to get soaked on your last boat ride through the islands."

As he puttered away from the dock, I turned back for one last look. At the edge of the rainforest, the very tops of the spruce vanguard glowed gold in the morning sun. Steam from the bathhouses vanished into a cloudless gray-blue sky. Kinuk village looked at peace.

But, of course, it wasn't.

We quickly reached the end of the bay. Gene turned north, away from Augustine Island, Ninstints, and the cold, harsh Pacific beyond. We passed Rose Harbor, where seals carved watery paths through kelp forests that swayed with the incoming tide. I pictured the seal that had peered into my facemask, freed me from the kelp, and saved me. God damn it, the creature had been real. I couldn't be honest and try to convince myself otherwise.

I told myself to relax and enjoy my last boat ride in Haida Gwaii. I'd talk to Angelo about the visions in Sandspit.

The inflatable bounced against the waves as Gene pointed out Burnaby, Lyell Island, and Skedans—exotic-sounding places I'd probably never see.

"Every centimeter of Burnaby Narrows is covered with the gaudiest sea critters you can imagine," Gene said. "When there's a full moon and the tide's real low, you can walk across and pick them up. I found a day-glow orange snail with neon green fringe and bright pink antler-type things."

Compared to that, my savior seal wasn't so odd after all.

Gene went on. "In eighteen seventy-eight, George Dawson visited a village called Tanu when he worked for the Canadian Geographical Survey. He took a famous photograph showing village life—a totem pole carver, clothes drying in the wind, food boxes covered with cedar bark and neatly tied with cords for a sea voyage."

"Wasn't that right before the measles epidemic?" Harvey asked.

Gene's face clouded. "It was. An anthropologist found a mass grave there. Now it's a historic village—and home to black bear. I see more bear in Skedans than anywhere in Haida Gwaii. One even charged me when I was there."

"What did you do?" I asked.

"Grabbed a piece of cedar and hit him on the muzzle as hard as I could. Bear took off, thank goodness. Their claws can rip a man apart in minutes."

"I know a geologist who was banging on a big rock," I said. "She didn't know a black bear was on the other side. The bear ripped off both her arms."

Harvey asked, "Hey, could we change the subject?"

To reach Sandspit, Gene had to leave the protected waters of the archipelago. The boat slapped hard against the waves. We had to hang onto the seats so we wouldn't fly off.

Out on the open water, an orca breached not fifty feet from the boat. Glistening in the morning sun, its rich black skin set off bright white markings on the animal's belly and sides, under its mouth, and above its eyes. The killer whale slipped beneath the surface. Ted, Harvey, and I leaned over the side of the inflatable and peered down to see where it had gone. The orca stuck its head out of the water, and Harvey launched herself backward and bounced off the opposite side.

"Jesus. Scared the daylights out of me."

"Funny," I said. "That toothy grin makes orcas look friendly. But they eat seals, sea lions, and whatever they can catch."

"And whales, even baby ones," Gene added with a wink.

Compared to Kinuk, Sandspit looked like a megalopolis. A massive stone breakwater protected the marina and fifty-odd boat slips. We passed a hundred-foot sailboat with Mount Moresby as its backdrop. Postcard perfect.

Gene cut the motor and coasted alongside the floating walkway closest to shore. "This is it, folks." He pointed to the right toward a peninsula jutting into the water. "Airport's out there, as you know."

He jumped out and wrapped the inflatable's bowline around a cleat while we unloaded our bags.

"Like we promised, you'll get our report within ten days," Harvey said. "After that, it's up to the UN to decide what to do about the iron venture, if anything."

"Well, I can't imagine a better UN crew. You folks take care."

Ted shook Gene's hand. "And I can't imagine a better guide and teacher. You're dealing with a difficult situation."

Harvey was next. "Mind if I hug you?"

Gene laughed and held out his arms. "Haida are big on hugs."

When it was my turn, Gene bear-hugged me as well. I stepped back and took both of his calloused hands. "Ted's right. You've done an amazing job with a powder-keg situation."

Gene blinked as if confused by a troubling though. He quickly recovered, and a grin spread wide on his broad face. "Please come back."

We watched until the inflatable disappeared behind the marina's breakwater.

Harvey looked at her phone. "Whoa, full bars here. Plane leaves in an hour. We better head out to the airport now."

I walked between Ted and Harvey into town.

"Sure you don't want to try to change your ticket?" Harvey asked.

"Nah. Like I said, there's a little museum here I really want to see." I didn't mention my need for private time to call Angelo.

Big on hugs, too, Harvey gave me one before she and Ted took off for the airport. "Don't you *dare* miss that plane."

Missing planes, buses, and other means of transportation was our little joke. Harvey hated to hang around terminals and the like and didn't allow much leeway time. Traffic jams had made her late more than once. I always got to the airport or bus station hours ahead of time. That made her crazy when we traveled together.

"You know me. I won't."

Ted strolled away and said over his shoulder, "See you in a couple of hours. Have fun."

I turned down School Street in search of a good cup of coffee and wondered why Ted hadn't hugged me. Ouch. I wanted it both ways.

I'd think about Ted later.

Halfway down the street, I found the perfect place. A blackboard outside The Sandspit Café boasted "best coffee in town" and "homemade muffins!" I ordered coffee and a blueberry muffin. "Okay if I sit outside?"

The woman behind the counter had blue-black hair pulled back into a tight ponytail and bangs cut perfectly straight across her broad forehead. She reminded me of Bart that way. Come to think of it, I hadn't seen him for a while.

She slid an oversized mug of coffee toward me and said, "Of course, dear. How about I warm up your muffin?" Like a typical Canadian, her "about" sounded like "aboot."

A white metal table and matching chair outside took advantage of the morning sun. I sipped good coffee, closed my eyes, and lifted my face toward the warmth. With slow yoga breaths, I tried to let tension from the last few days drain away.

It didn't work. I was still as tense as a spiny lobster in a crevice with a circling wolfish above.

William's unsolved death was a big part of it. I'd failed him, and was about to abandon the quest and fly away to New England. I relaxed my grip on the mug and flexed my hand.

Besides that, my treatment of Ted felt lousy. The rest was Haida Gwaii itself.

Beautiful as it was, the archipelago had taken an emotional toll on me. The richly interwoven natural, cultural, and spiritual domains made the islands unforgettable. But something in that interwoven fabric challenged me to the core.

As a scientist, I put my money on what I could see, smell, hear, and record with instruments—observed phenomena, data. Spiritual claims couldn't be tested, and fell outside what existed. Other people experienced "unexplained events."

I did not.

But my experiences over the last few days had been overshadowed by doubt and an irrational fear I didn't know what to do with or understand. Like most people, I'd had my share of personal trauma and raging emotions—mainly when my parents died. But that was a knowable phenomenon.

Feathers that magically appeared, oversized ravens that streaked by run-away kayaks, and sentient seals—these experiences challenged me to rethink my worldview. I felt like I was on a cliff edge about to fall off.

The café waitress placed a grapefruit-sized muffin in front of me.

"My goodness, that's big."

She flipped her ponytail with one hand. "We got big eaters in Sandspit. You here for a while?"

"No, on my way home. I've been in Kinuk with some friends."

"Oh. Hey, I heard what happened to William Edenshaw down there. Just terrible. Knew him when he was a kid. Came here to fish with his dad and brother. My husband ran a charter boat, bless his soul."

I stared up at her. "William has a brother?"

"Sure does. Richard. They look alike but couldn't be more diff'rent."

"What do you mean?"

"William, he was a gentle soul who liked being on the boat, you know, out in nature. Not for the sport of catching fish, my Bill said. But that Richard, he was real competitive like his dad. Practically kill himself to get the most fish."

"Richard doesn't sound like the nicest guy."

"Truly, I think he ran to nasty."

"William became a Watchman. What happened to Richard?"

"Lives in Vancouver, I think. Heard he's doing, what's it called, like on Wall Street?"

"A trader?"

"That's it. A trader." She flipped her ponytail again. "Well, I need to be getting back."

I watched the waitress until she disappeared around a corner. Something she'd said seemed important, but it was just out of reach. I sighed. It was intriguing how everyone knew everyone on Haida Gwaii. Family and friends, all connected. Maybe that was it.

I bit into the muffin and washed it down with coffee. Comfort food. I ached to be in Angelo's kitchen again, drinking his espresso and nibbling on biscotti. My only family. I checked my watch. Time to call Angelo and Knapton.

Knapton answered on the second ring.

"Sergeant Knapton, it's Mara Tusconi. I have some information you may find, ah, peculiar."

"Go ahead. I'm interested in anything you've got."

"Anna, the woman who spoke with William's parents?"

"Yes?"

"She said she found some suspicious plants in the room a woman named Lynne uses when she's on Kinuk. Lynne used to be William's fiancée."

"Yes. I'm taking notes. Okay, go ahead."

"I'm not a botanist, but I did try to identify the plant. It might be false hellebore, native to this area and poisonous."

"Where are you? How can we get this plant?"

"Sandspit, on my way home. Why don't you contact Gene Edenshaw. He'll know where Anna is."

"Good. I will."

"Of course, someone may have put the plants in Lynne's room."

"I'm aware of that."

"Are you considering William's death suspicious?"

"Mara, you're not family so I can't say much. We always look hard at an unexplained death of someone so young and healthy. And we did find something this time. With the new, ah, evidence, William's parents have asked for more tests. I've agreed. Maybe your information will help us narrow our search, who knows. As you can imagine, it's often a needle in a haystack."

I could imagine. Given thousands of possible pollutants, environmental chemists needed details about compounds to test for. The same would be true for human fluids and flesh.

I gave Knapton my contact information in Maine.

"Thanks, Mara. We've got forensic experts who deal with plants and poisons. Who knows, this could be the lead that opens up the case."

I prayed Knapton was right.

One more call—Angelo. I needed and wanted his help, but that didn't make asking for it much easier. I'd always assumed strong people were independent and didn't burden others with their troubles. But in the last few months, it was amazing how much I'd learned about myself and others when I opened up.

I wanted to see my godfather's face when we spoke. There's a video app on my phone that doesn't get much use, and I had to fiddle around to get the thing to work.

Angelo picked right up.

"Angelo, it's Mara."

"Sweetheart! Where are you?"

"I'm still on the islands off British Columbia. Ted and Harvey took the first island hopper to Vancouver. I'm on the next one. You got the message we're delayed a day?"

"I did."

"We catch the red-eye from Vancouver this evening. I've got video on my end. Set the phone up so I can see you."

Angelo's features—gray eyes, mop of curly white hair, and ready smile—filled my little screen. I wanted to reach into the phone and touch him.

"Can't wait to hear all about the place and what you three have been up to."

"Um, do you have a few minutes to talk?"

"Of course. Is something the matter? Are you okay?"

"Fine, mostly. A young man we knew died. And a few odd things happened."

"Someone died? That's awful."

"It was, but let me back up. On my first day, I was, ah, in my kayak and a bit of danger. Right before a Haida Watchman motored up in his skiff to give me a hand, a huge bird swooped down and zipped by the kayak. I can still see its eyes—pitch black like in some Haida's painting of the Raven—then glowing. They call the bird the trickster."

"Dio mio. Go on, dear."

I hesitated for a moment and decided Angelo didn't need to know—not now anyway—that I'd discovered William's body. "William, he's the Watchman who helped me, died the next day in a hot pool. And soon after that, the hot pool drained. It's still empty."

"Oh no, he died? Why?"

"Police are still investigating."

As a mechanical engineer, Angelo was curious about why the pool suddenly drained. "And the pool. Was there tectonic activity out there?"

"Yes. We called Arthur. You remember him? The geologist. He said there had been."

"Have to look that up."

"The next thing happened on an island where there are old totem poles lined up right above the beach. It's a World Heritage site. Haida carvers decorated the poles with animals piled on top of each other. Gene—he was our guide that day—explained that the carvings depict a family's spiritual ancestors."

"Sounds fascinating, Mara."

"It was. Harvey and Ted followed Gene into the forest. I stayed behind, looked out over the water, and tried to imagine life there hundreds of years ago. Suddenly, the forest got still and a black blur zipped by and evaporated over the water. I found a big, black feather by my feet."

Across the thousands of miles, Angelo nodded like he'd heard such things before.

"The last, um, event was the oddest. We dove in the kelp forest. Harvey and I were buddies. In the middle of the kelp, a current out of nowhere carried me down. I got tangled. But a seal appeared, bit into the kelp, and released me. Later, Harvey said I'd disappeared for a half-minute, but it seemed much longer."

I squinted at the screen and tried to gauge Angelo's reaction. He looked thoughtful.

"So the feather, seal, and the rest frighten you?"

"Each one alone might not. But together, I don't know, it feels powerful. I can't explain it."

"Actually, Mara, it doesn't surprise me you're susceptible to strange events like these, considering what you say about the place."

Not the response I'd expected. "What do you mean 'susceptible'?"

He smiled. "You *are* half Italian and half Irish. Both believe in the spiritual."

"The Irish have their wee people, fairy folk, and all that. But Italians?"

"For us, it's mostly religious, I think. Remember when you used to go to Mass? All those statues and paintings of Gwen, the apostles, and angels? For some Catholics, that's very real. The incense helps, of course."

His mention of incense triggered the pungent scent and a long-forgotten memory. "Haven't thought about this in years, but when I was ten or eleven, I had a vision in church. It was a special holy day because the priest walked up and down the central aisle swinging that metal incense holder on a chain. The smell of frankincense, myrrh, whatever, was powerful. The church had a painting of an angel I liked. She had auburn hair like mine that fell down her back in curls, red-gold wings, and a flowing white dress. I was at the end of my pew when the priest swung the incense right in front of me. When he passed, I looked at the painting on the far wall. The angel winged out of the painting and whispered into my ear. I don't remember what she said."

Angelo nodded. "There, you see? What did you think at the time?"

"I didn't have breakfast before we went to church, so I figured that was it."

Angelo's chuckle was contagious. I laughed, too, and it felt great.

"A while back, before you were born, Mara, I had a revelation in church, too."

"You've never mentioned it."

"Saw no need to. It was soon after my bride died in that car accident. I was so young and loved her so very much. Figured life was over for me."

Angelo in despair? It was hard to imagine.

"I didn't see a vision like you did. It was—this is hard to explain—a presence."

Angelo narrowed his eyes like he was trying to see into the past.

"The, um, presence didn't say words out loud. I heard them in my head. She—the voice was female—said my darling was with me, always would be, and that this time of trouble would pass. I was destined for important work that would save lives."

"And your engineering teams *did* save lives. The marine acoustics and all the rest."

"We did."

I glanced at the time in the top corner of the phone. "Angelo, I've got to go to the airport."

"You'll be fine, Mara. These things aren't rational. They're something else entirely. Give that intense brain of yours a rest."

"Okay."

"We'll talk more about this when you get back."

"I love you, Angelo."

"And I love you, Mara. More than you can ever know."

I ended the call, carried my mug and plate into the café, and asked for directions to the museum. It was right down School Street. On my way out, I picked my duffle up off the ground and shouldered it. Walking slowly toward the museum, I mulled through my conversation with Angelo.

My godfather had been my rock, beloved friend, and stand-in parent ever since my real parents died in a submarine accident when I was nineteen. In winter, we chatted in front of the fire in his living room with bay windows that looked out over the Maine coast. When the weather was warm, we sat outside on his patio, sipped wine, talked, and watched the sun set over Spruce Harbor. Angelo was a renaissance man who knew about history, art, fishing, people. I trusted him completely.

Angelo didn't think my visions were odd given my heritage. I relished my parents' legacy. If my genetics made me "susceptible" to the spiritual, maybe I wasn't losing my mind. "Give your brain a rest," that's what he said, and it felt just right. For the moment, anyway, I'd let my subconscious sort through the meaning of my visions.

I enjoyed my relief for a moment before guilt returned. I was about to leave Haida Gwaii and had done precious little about William. Near the end of the street, a "Welcome Centre" sign greeted me. I paused in front of the entrance. Angelo's message might help me understand something about William's death if I let my subconscious mind work on that problem, too.

I climbed the steps in quick anticipation.

20

THE DOOR OPENED INTO A SMALL, EMPTY ROOM. MAPS were strewn across a Formica counter. On the opposite wall, a display held brochures advertising adventure trips and bed-and-breakfasts.

"Hello?"

"Back here. Please come in."

Next to the display, a sign labeled "Museum" hung above a door. I stepped through.

Facing me, a woman sat behind a table littered with what looked like long, thin sticks. Scissors, a knife, and twine lay in front of her. It looked like she was about to make a basket.

She stood. "There's only me here today. Do you need a map or anything?"

She was tall with long, curly blond hair and pale skin. Since it was a Haida museum, I assumed she was of Haida heritage but didn't want to ask.

"Actually, I'm here to see the museum."

She smiled and held out her arms. "This is it. The Haida Heritage Centre is in Skidegate. We're a kind of a satellite."

"I'm on my way to the airport and don't have much time. Could you quickly show me what's here?"

"Of course. I'm Marion. I volunteer here."

"Mara Tusconi. I've been kayaking around Kinuk with friends and I'm on my way home to the States."

She pushed aside a chair and walked to a wall decorated with traditional clothes. One item was a poncho-like cape. Next to it hung a skirt. Both were made of animal skin. A pair of moccasins lay on a little table along with beads and other small artifacts.

"This year we're focusing on Haida women. This little display gives us a chance to talk about the Haida matriarchy."

"I'd be very interested in that. What are the clothes made of?"

"Deerskin. These are replicas, of course."

The cape was particularly striking. The cream-colored garment was decorated with hundreds of white shells, attached with bits of red ribbon. White fringe ran along the cape's border.

Sharon fingered a piece of fringe. "We're doing this display because most historical depictions of First Peoples—what you call Native Americans—only show men in celebration garb. But women wore such clothes as well. Haida are a matrilineal people. The chiefs were men, but even that title was passed through the female line. The Eagle and Raven groups, they were matrimoieties."

A bright red V-shaped inset gave color to the cape's front. I pointed to a large blue bead at the bottom of the V. "Wow. That's a gorgeous blue."

"In the 1800s, bright beads from Venice, places like that, were highly prized along the Northwest coast. Especially blue ones."

"How did the beads get all the way out here?"

"Traders. Back then, traders valued beads, furs, metal." She laughed. "Now, traders deal with intangibles like stocks."

The room tipped sideways for a moment.

Marion cocked her head to the side. "Are you okay?"

I blinked. "You've been very generous with your time. I really appreciate it."

I passed through the visitor's center, stepped outside, and checked my phone. In fifteen minutes, I absolutely had to head up to the airport. But before that, I needed to think. On one side of the building a bench beneath a tree was empty. A quiet spot. Perfect.

I dropped my duffle onto the bench and sat next to it. The word "trader" echoed in my mind. Marion said fur traders had brought beads to the archipelago. Interesting. But someone else had used the term in a different way, one that was vitally important.

I whispered it aloud. "Trader. Trader. Trader." Glancing down road, I knew who it was. The waitress. She'd said William's brother Richard was a trader. Okay. So what? I closed my eyes and tried to calm racing thoughts. Trade. Trade what? People traded things like the Haida did with their beads. No, not right. What else? Trade. Trade deals. I shook my head. Not even close.

It came to me in a flash. Carbon Trading. Right after he had described William's brother as rich banker, or something similar, Caleb had explained that carbon credits were traded on the international market like pork bellies, wheat, corn and all the rest. I didn't make the connection then but did now.

Richard was a trader and very competitive. He had to win. He and William were very different, and Richard probably saw William as a tree-hugger. But the iron project, that was something right up Richard's alley. Lots of money to be made and an aggressive American entrepreneur to work with. Canada would be out front on carbon credits, a leader in international trading. Richard would make a ton of money

I could see it all in my mind's eye. Richard had heard about businessman Roger Grant's geo-engineering scheme and saw the waters off BC as Canada's chance to get the jump on marine carbon trading. Richard contacted Grant and told him about the Haida's anger toward outsiders who'd taken everything from them. He explained that Grant could sell the iron project as the Haida's alone, a way to make money for their people selling carbon credits with the added bonus of bountiful salmon runs. Richard had convinced William with praise about Roger Grant's forward-looking ideas. The Haida would be seen as leaders in international carbon credits with a new way to fight climate change.

I imagined that things went well at first. Tutored by Richard, Grant knew how to approach the Haida leaders, what to say, what not to say and do. William stepped forward as champion of the project. The first slurry experiment was a success. The ocean greened up. People on the archipelago were excited. But time went by and salmon runs were still thin. Then the UN sent in a team of scientists who questioned the whole idea of iron geo-engineering, carbon credits, and all the rest. William was swayed by the experts' arguments, and it looked like he would vote against continuing the iron project.

If he did, the iron fertilization project off Haida Gwaii would be dead.

Dead. Could it possibly be that Richard had killed his brother to keep this scenario from playing out?

Detectives apply three criteria in murder investigations. Motive. Means. Opportunity. I considered each one.

Wildly lucrative carbon-credit trading could be Richard's motive. Knowledge that his scheme was in jeopardy required inside information, but with all the family connections on the archipelago that wouldn't be difficult. Means? Richard had fished off Haida Gwaii and could easily get out to the islands. He'd have visited Kinuk and knew the layout. Opportunity? That was more difficult. To do the deed Richard needed help. Someone he knew. Someone with access to William.

I glanced at my watch. My suspicion of Richard was probably a crazy idea. Even if it wasn't, I was about to leave the islands and couldn't act on it. Sergeant Knapton seemed interested in false hellebore. Maybe he'd also be intrigued by the idea that Richard might be behind William's death. I had nothing to lose by suggesting it.

I picked up my phone, found his number, and went right to his voice mail. "Sergeant Knapton, it's Mara Tusconi. I've got something important to tell you. I'm on my way to the Sandspit airport and will call again from there."

I was walking past the marina when my phone buzzed. Text message. I reached into my pants pocket and pulled it out.

A message from Queen Charlotte Air.

The plane scheduled to leave from the Sandspit airport at twelve noon had maintenance trouble. We arranged for a floatplane to fly you from Skidegate to Vancouver. Go to the Sandspit marina. A water taxi will pick you up and transport you to Skidegate.

Skidegate was minutes away on the other side of the strait. But a floatplane all the way to Vancouver? I hoped the trip wouldn't be too bumpy.

Just as I arrived at the marina, a powerboat with a small cabin pulled up to one of the floating walkways. I was surprised to see Bart jump out and tie it off. He looked around and waved at me. I walked toward him.

"Bart. Are you the water taxi? Pretty fancy boat."

Still in his T-shirt with cut-off sleeves, Bart wore jeans that weren't ripped or dirty. It looked like he'd made an effort.

The words came out rapid-fire. "Ah, it's my cousin's. He's got the taxi business in Skidegate. I was there and knew what you looked like. He asked me to get you."

Cousin. Of course. Everyone had relatives in the archipelago.

"Climb aboard. You can toss me the duffle." He looked behind me.

I glanced back. We were alone on the dock. "I've got it. Thanks."

Bart stood at a console in the middle of the boat, started the motor with a key, and pulled away. In the cabin, what appeared to be a man in a red jacket looked forward. Probably another passenger. We motored out of the marina and were well past any other boats before Bart kicked into high gear. The water was pretty calm, and I leaned back against a side railing.

Bart swung the boat in the direction we'd come from early in the morning.

I yelled, "Bart, isn't Skidegate to the north?" I pointed over my shoulder. "Behind us?"

The passenger turned around, slowly removed his sunglasses and pocketed them, and strode toward me. "It is, but that's not where we're going."

21

THE GUY STUDIED ME WITH COLD, PIERCING EYES, LIKE A raptor's. Stunned, I knew the terror of a trapped animal.

With a toss of my head, I stepped toward him. "You're Richard."

"Ah. The brilliant Mara Tusconi figured that out. Thought you would."

What appeared as a graceful outline on William's face was sharp and stone-hard on Richard's. William's chocolate eyes invited you in. Richard's were unreadable, dirt-brown. With long, manicured fingers he stroked a beard so patchy I could see blotches of red where his skin showed through.

"Richard, what are you doing?"

"Taking care of business."

"I don't—"

"Actually, I think you do. That's the problem, the business I have to take care of."

"Where are we going?"

"Where no one will find you."

He was deadly serious. My throat tightened. I had to keep him talking. That'd worked for me in the past when I'd faced a dangerous man.

"Why?"

He looked skyward. "*Please.* I'm not stupid, Dr. Know-it-all."

"I don't think you are stupid," I said. "But why you don't you assume I am and tell me what's going on here."

We'd reached open water, and the boat slammed through waves. Spray soaked my ponytail, and icy water ran down my neck.

Out in the open, it was hard to converse. I raised my voice. "Could we talk up there in the cabin?"

"Worried about getting wet? You'll be plenty wet soon. Suppose so. Try anything, you'll end up with a broken neck. I'm a black belt."

I held onto the gunwale and picked my way forward. The ocean was a confusion of green, white-capped waves. I considered jumping overboard. With no boat in sight and fifty-degree water, I'd die from hypothermia in minutes. Bad option.

I reached the cabin.

Richard said, "Stop there."

I lifted my chin. "Like I said, could you tell me what's going on?"

"Let's not play games."

"You think I know something."

"I'm afraid you know pretty much everything."

"But how would—?" It hit me in a flash. Bart. Of course. How could I have been so incredibly dense! "Bart told you."

"Dr. Tusconi gets an A."

"Bart's been spying on us?"

"The longhouse has great acoustics. You can hear what people say from pretty much anywhere."

The night before last—when Ted, Harvey and I had tried to figure out who might want William dead—Bart would've heard an earful. Words and phrases ran around my brain.

"Bart told you we'd figured out William was going to change his vote. We wondered if someone might care enough to stop him. So what?"

He rubbed his stubby beard and cracked his jaw. "Besides that, you said your visit might've triggered William's death. You *had* to figure out what happened to him. Said you owed William that."

"But—"

"I read all about you, *Dr.* Tusconi, on the internet. How you solved the murder of that scientist in Maine. You're clever, smart. Bart tells me you're fierce, like a raven, he said. How you went after him with a vengeance over that kayak rudder. Even when you left the islands, you wouldn't let this go. You'd easily find out who I was, what I did for a living. It's not a big leap to the rest."

"But William had his whole life in front of him. He was your *brother*."

Richard looked past me. Coal black hair, skin pulled tight against the spectral face, empty eyes—this was malevolence.

"William was weak, no vision, no spunk. Mamma's boy. Dad despised him. The Haida fantasies—ancestral spirits, children's myth stories—William bought all that crap."

Bart's hands clenched the steering wheel. Nostrils flaring, he fixed steely eyes on Richard.

"Think about it. The ocean's huge," Richard said. "Billions to be made in carbon credits. I had to be out front on it."

His indifference toward his flesh and blood sickened me.

Richard swiveled around to look through the cabin window. "Bart. Turn here."

Bart hesitated.

"*Now*," Richard snapped.

Bart clenched his teeth and turned the wheel hard. The boat raced toward a narrow inlet. Unlike the rest of the archipelago, we approached what looked like a low-lying swampland. It reminded me of the Everglades where I'd canoed. There, boaters who failed to exactly follow signposts got helplessly lost in a maze of intersecting mangrove-bordered rivers. If the Haida swampland was anything like that, a lost soul would never be found.

Richard acted the guide. "Different from the rest of Haida Gwaii, isn't it? Unless you know where you're going, you get completely turned around."

We entered the swamp maze, and the boat skimmed over flat water. Richard went out on deck and barked directions. Bart turned to port at one intersection, port again at the next, starboard, port. The route was as twisted as Richard's mind.

Bart called out, "Gas is gettin' low."

Richard snarled, "You should've put more in."

"Didn't know it was so far in here."

The forest was like nothing I'd ever seen. Tall, straight, skinny trees along the water's edge sprouted only a few stumps of branches, each shrouded in bright green moss like gangrene limbs. Behind them, yellow-green hummocks cloaked with more moss appeared to be smoldering remains of dead trees. The forest beyond looked dense and impenetrable.

A soggy landscape as foreign as any I'd experienced.

In his fancy red offshore jacket, jeans, and boat shoes, Richard took in the scenery like this was a nature trip. But I knew this was an enemy with a mission, certain he could carry it off without a hitch. There would be no flaws in his plan to get rid of me. Only luck and my cunning would save me. I sent a prayer to my parents.

Richard looked me up and down. The hair on my neck stood at attention "You're clever, Dr. Scientist, and persistent as hell. You'd make a good trader."

I gave him the best pique I could muster. "I don't care about money."

"Then you're a loser, just like William. Save nature, save the world." Richard pointed to a beach on a point ahead. "Bart. There."

Bart steered in that direction. Richard squinted down at the water for a minute, then ordered Bart to cut the motor and throw out an anchor. I stepped onto the deck and scanned the scene. We were at least a thousand feet from shore, a straight shot ahead. Roughly the same distance to starboard, a volcanic rock dome stuck out of the water and blocked the view of the shoreline beyond.

The anchor caught, and the boat stopped swinging. Richard looked skyward. "It's getting darker. Wind's picking up. Bad weather's coming faster than I thought. First bitter storm of the year. Big storm. Without protection, the cold will kill you."

Cold. Why did it always have to be cold?

"Bart, check her pockets for a phone or anything useful like that."

Bart patted my pockets, reached into the left one, and pulled out my phone.

"Toss it overboard."

Bart threw the phone far off the port side. I nearly let out a squeal as it disappeared beneath the water.

"Pat her down again so you don't miss anything."

Bart winced but did what he was told. "Nothing."

Richard smiled like the Cheshire cat. "Mara, overboard. Do it, or Bart will throw you in."

Straight ahead to the beach was a fairly easy swim—in warm water and a bathing suit. Of course, Richard would watch to make sure I didn't make it.

22

I JUMPED INTO THE HAIDA SEA AND ROCKETED DOWN.

The vicious cold hit me like a bare-fisted punch. I was encased in water so intensely frigid it felt red-hot. Bitter spikes pierced my naked face.

Despite the pain, or maybe because of it, I didn't black out. Feet on the bottom, I forced myself to focus and look up.

Forget the cold. Beat the bastard.

The boat loomed overhead, motor in the back, starboard to my right. Richard would assume I'd take the shortest route to shore—straight ahead in front of the bow. Instead, I would turn away from the boat in the direction of the rock outcrop—and swim underwater most of the way.

Soaking wet, my fleece pullover and pants were weights that pulled me down. I swiveled and breast-stroked underwater.

Adrenaline kicked in.

The water was gin-clear. Scattered clusters of thick kelp lay across the surface. After a half-dozen strokes, I kicked to the surface directly below a kelp clump, stuck my face in seaweed, sucked in some air, submerged, and breast-stroked again. Clothed, I pulled through molasses.

Surfacing through the kelp the fourth time, I took in air with gasping gulps. Petrified Richard could hear, I twisted to check out the boat. The motor was going. Good. No way they'd hear anything over that.

I went under again but came up after only two strokes, panting like a panicked dog. My heart thumped so hard and fast

I was sure it'd burst through my shirt.

Hypothermia. Get the hell out of the water.

The rock loomed directly in front of me. I kicked to it, grabbed attached kelp, and hand over hand, pulled myself to the other side. Out of Richard's sight.

I sucked air in quick gasps. My pullover made treading water harder. I pulled it off and threw it to the side. Land was a direct shot.

I pictured Angelo on the beach. Had to get to him.

I lay on my belly and tried to swim. My tennis shoes kept my feet afloat, so that helped. But with all four appendages frozen stumps, I could only manage to shove my arms forward, one at a time. Sloggy dog-paddle.

Shove right. Left. Right. Left.

A little closer to shore.

My limbs were heavy weights. Seawater pulled at my arms like they were in glue. Warmth spread across my body. I desperately wanted to lie on my back, look up at the sky, and sleep.

Sleep and die. Angelo's waiting.

The will came from somewhere deep. I lurched from one side to the other and clawed my way forward.

Gasping and exhausted, I *had* to rest. I rolled over and looked at the sky. Pale blue, so pretty. I closed my eyes.

No…no. Beat Richard. Beat the bastard.

I flopped over and floated on my belly. A wave pushed me toward shore. I opened my eyes underwater. Bottom, solid bottom.

My feet touched rocks. I fell backward, got my feet under me, threw my body forward. I grabbed seaweed, pulled my numb, trailing body to shallower water, crawled up onto the beach, and collapsed on my belly.

Get up. Up. Now.

On hands and knees, I panted, head down, and willed my breath to slow down. I crawled until I reached the side of the rock dome and stretched my neck so I could just see the little bay over the rock. The boat was gone.

I unfurled, shoved out a foot, tried to stand, and fell backward, shivering violently. Angry, I knelt again, planted my feet, and slowly stood. My legs and arms quivered. Trees, beach, and water swirled around.

The first steps were clumsy, zombie-like. I made it to the other end of the pebble beach, turned, and walked back faster, circling my arms like a windmill. A couple of trips up and down the beach got my blood moving. I stopped to look around and take stock of my surroundings.

The beach was small, maybe a few hundred feet long, the high-tide line littered with branches and other debris. Beyond that, higher ground was carpeted with mounds of thick green moss. I could guess why. Fresh water probably seeped through the moss before it ran into the ocean.

Fresh water to drink.

A dense forest spread back from the moss carpet.

I faced the ocean to gauge the weather. Sunset was a couple of hours away. Even so, the sky looked ominous. Black clouds raced toward me and confirmed Richard's prediction. A storm approached. I'd already had a close call with hypothermia after the fall off the *Henry George*. A long night of pelting, cold rain would kill me.

Rescuers would find my dead body sprawled out on this lonely, godforsaken beach. Angelo would be overwhelmed with grief, Harvey pale and sobbing, Ted grim and silent.

None of that was going to happen. I'd find some way to shelter in that forest—beneath the cover of overlying braches if nothing else. A rocky spine ran north-south along the whole of

Haida Gwaii. There might be a rock overhang.

The first step onto the moss carpet confirmed my guess. My foot disappeared into a hole that instantly filled with water. I dipped in a finger and tasted it. Fresh. Bending over, I cupped my hands and slurped. A little skanky, but I didn't care.

Slogging through a hummocky bog is always a challenge, but exhaustion and lack of coordination made my trek grueling. Again and again, I tripped over a hidden obstacle and fell into a puddle of waterlogged moss. My clothes were already drenched, so getting wet wasn't the problem. But getting up again was, since the glop gave no purchase.

Short of the forest, I fell again, lay back, and hooted hysterically into the sky. My situation was absurd—what did I think I was doing? There was nowhere to go. Laughter turned into tears. No question, I was losing control.

I rolled over to a stump that looked like it might hold my weight. It did. I sat on it. The puddle next to the stump had seemed warmer. I stuck my hand in the moss. Warmish water. Huh.

At the edge of the woods, I stepped up onto dried land and peered in. Dense trees and the fast-approaching storm gave the forest an unwelcoming gloom. I squeezed between two skinny trees, ducked under an inclined one, and leaned back to think.

I touched the bottom of my right pants pocket and felt a little bump. Good.

Soaked and shivering, I only wanted to lie on the forest floor and sleep. Every bit of my body ached. I closed my eyes. Dreamlike, the smell wafted in. I popped my eyes open, sniffed in all directions, and zeroed in on one. The distinct odor was to my left. The last time I'd smelled that was on Kinuk Island.

The acrid scent of hydrogen sulfide.

With renewed energy, I followed the smell, clamored over downed trees, and squeezed through standing ones. The sulfur grew more pungent and drove me on.

I pushed my way through a thicket and stepped into a grassy clearing. Twenty feet ahead lay a hill of exposed rock. I circled the base in the direction of the pungent odor. Squinting in the dimming light, I could see the rock was fine-grained— volcanic, maybe basalt. The rain was hardly noticeable at first, but as thunder boomed in the distance, the sky pelted me with cold needles. Up ahead, I could just make out what looked like an opening in the rock. I ran for it and slipped inside. Sulfur aroma greeted me.

I waited for my eyes to adjust. Light from outside dwindled a couple of yards in. Beyond that, the cave was ink black. I dropped onto hands and knees. The cave floor was smooth, hard rock. I hoped no dead animal lay in front of me. Or worse, a live one.

Blind, I slid my palms and knees across the level surface and inched forward. Twenty-odd feet in, the air became much warmer and dense with humidity. Sulfur stung the lining of my nose.

I reached my hand out. Gloriously hot water.

23

THOUGH I KNEW IT WOULD'VE BEEN SMART TO CHECK THE water for animals, dead or alive, I didn't. I slid face-forward into heated manna. The shallow pool covered my body. That was enough. I turned over and stared into the black. I might starve, but I wasn't going to freeze to death.

Outside, the storm sounded fierce. Thunder rumbled and boomed. Before I fell asleep, a flash of lightning lit the cave.

I woke up confused as to why I was hot and wet. The memory flooded in. I'd jumped off a boat into arctic seawater, clawed to shore, slogged through a bog, and discovered the cave. Outwitted Richard, so far at least. A Brothers Grimm tale.

I was terribly thirsty, but had doubts about the hot water. The alternative wasn't good. I'd have to crawl out of the cave to the bog and might not find my way back. I sat in the shallow pool, cupped my hands, slurped, lay back again, and fell into a deep sleep.

The next time I woke, it appeared to be daytime. In dim light, I could see the cave's rough roof and edges of the pool. I crawled onto the dry floor, over to the cave's opening, and blink-ed. I held out my hands and studied them. They were wrinkled like an old, old woman's. Standing in the morning light, I tried to figure out what to do, my waterlogged brain in slow mode. I shivered in the crisp morning air. Neurons kicked in.

When the sun was higher, I could spread out my clothes to dry. But that wouldn't be for several hours. My stomach rumbled. Good sign. I touched the bottom of my pocket again.

Still there. That was something I could deal with. It might even work.

In the longhouse, Ted had needed matches when the battery-operated lantern failed. I dug the emergency kit out of my duffle and tossed him the little tin of waterproof matches. When he'd finished, I'd slipped the tin into a tiny pouch in the bottom of my pants pocket and forgotten about it. Sometimes forgetfulness is a good thing. I'd seen pieces of wood mixed in with dried seaweed along the beach's high tide line. Getting there meant a slog through the bog again, but it was something I'd have to do.

Rested and with the morning light, I traversed the forest and bog quickly. Out on the beach, a cold wind gusted off the water. Shivering, I fast-walked up and down the beach to warm up, picked my way along the flotsam, and pulled up pieces of wood. The rain had drenched most of the litter but a find at the end of the beach was a blessing. A ripped piece of tarp lay across a mound of debris, its corners held down by soggy kelp and some rocks. Gingerly, I pulled the tarp aside. Amphipods jumped around in indignant confusion. I reached into the litter. For the most part, the wood was dry.

Thank you, god.

I tried to remember the rules for starting a campfire under wet conditions. It was critical to get the fledgling fire off wet ground. Crisscrossed sticks would make a good base. Also, I needed to start with little pieces of dry wood and grass. When that got going, I could add pencil-size pieces, followed by larger ones.

I built the base and made piles of tinder plus progressively larger pieces of sticks and other wood. I was about to light the first match when I remembered a few phrases from Jack London's *To Build A Fire*.

He knew there must be no failure...a man must not fail in his first attempt to build a fire...

"Stop it," I said aloud. "He was in the Yukon in a snowstorm."

Just like it said on the box, the first match burst into flames. I held it under the tinder. The dried twigs caught right away. I cupped my hands around the precious flames to protect them against the breeze and took my time adding larger pieces. Soon, the little fire was burning well. Shivering in wet clothes, I added a couple of small logs. They crackled and flamed. I stood back to let the wind reach the fire and jumped up and down to warm up. Two more logs did it. The fire radiated heat. I rotated back and front and relished the delicious warmth.

The fire was a blessing. I could sit by it at night and stay warm. There was lots of wood around. Besides that, mussels and other edible creatures lived in shallow seawater. Steamed over hot coals, they'd be delicious. When Canadian police searched for me, smoke from my fire might be visible during the day and flames bright at night.

Rescue. Harvey and Ted must be frantic, trying to figure out what happened. I hadn't shown up in the Victoria airport or called about a late plane. They would have waited for the Skidegate flight to unload in Vancouver and panicked when I wasn't among the departing passengers. They knew I'd get in touch if I could.

And Angelo. We'd talked a half hour before I was kidnapped. Harvey and Ted would call him. He'd know something was terribly wrong. I'd never miss that plane without contacting anyone. He also had a funny way of sensing my danger. I felt guilty about his angst.

I didn't know how long the Royal Canadian Mounted Police would wait before they'd begin my search. Probably twenty-four hours. Out in the swamp, a long time. No point in worrying about that now. My job was to keep myself alive until help arrived.

The place needed a name. I looked around and said it aloud. "Swampy Point."

I watched the fire until there was a good bed of coals. Time to collect more wood. Wood of all sorts littered the beach—big and small branches, pieces of dock, bark of various kinds, logs. I carted wood until the piles looked large enough to feed the fire for a good while.

Luckily, the day was clear. When the sun was higher, I took off my damp clothes and spread them out in a line along the shingle. Buck naked, I sat on a smooth log on the high-tide line next to the fire.

The first rule of survival was to find shelter. I had my shelter cave with a heat source independent of my fire. I had two sources of fresh water—the bog and sulfury water in the cave. Now I needed food.

In tennis shoes, and with a little yelp, I waded into shallow water. Mussels attached to rocks were large and abundant. I let them dry in the sun and nestled a half dozen on the coals at the base of the fire. My mouth watered with the delicate aroma of steaming mussels. With a stick, I pulled one out. The hot, soft meat was easy to dislodge from the shell. I slid it into my mouth and groaned. Delicious beyond words.

I finished the first six and cooked six more. They sizzled and smelled even better than the first batch. I tossed the shells into the water, spotted something red stuck between two rocks, waded in, and grabbed my fleece pullover. Squeezing out seawater, I added it to the row of drying clothes.

At the end the beach, movement caught my eye. I stopped dead. A hulking animal emerged from the shadow into the sunlight. The black bear moved its massive head back and forth and sniffed the air. I had to cover my mouth to stifle the scream.

The bear must have smelled the steaming mussels. My cooking had attracted a vicious predator.

Adrenaline shot through my body. I desperately wanted to run somewhere, anywhere. I whipped my head from side to side. No tree near enough to climb. The swamp and ocean were both bad choices. Nowhere to go.

My wilderness training kicked in.

"Don't run. It will chase you. Watch for aggressive behavior. Jaw snapping, huffing, ears laid back."

The bear had caught my scent. Its ears were definitely laid back, and I could hear the pants. Slowly, like a cat, it came toward me.

"They may crouch and creep in your direction, gaze laser-focused."

There was only one thing to do. Get as big as a five-foot-seven woman could and make lots of noise. I grabbed a solid piece of wood the size of a baseball bat, spread my legs, stretched out my arms, and waved them up and down. Screaming like a banshee, I prayed a naked lady would scare the bejesus out of the creature.

The bear stopped and stood on its hind feet like it was trying to figure out what this thing was. Standing, the massive animal looked ten feet tall. It dropped back onto all fours.

24

SQUEALING, THE BEAR GALLOPED AT ME. TWENTY FEET away, I could count the teeth between its orange pitchfork-sharp incisors. At fifteen, I looked into beady black eyes. Ten feet, my legs shook so hard I could barely stand. My legs trembled and arms quivered, but my god, I stood my ground.

At five, I knew this wasn't a false charge.

Both hands on the piece of wood, I reached back like I was about to hit a home run and slammed the bat into the bear's snout.

It let out a hideous scream. I was sure the beast was going to charge again. But with one look to the side, *Ursus americanus* splashed into the water and swam quickly away.

Panting, I stumbled up to the big log. I slid onto my butt, put my head down, and waited for the spinning to stop. When it did, red blotches came into focus on a rock at my feet. I ran a hand along rock's surface. My blood felt hot and sticky. Blood streamed out of three deep gashes that ran from my upper right arm nearly to my wrist. The bear had clawed me, and I hadn't even felt it.

There was no pulsing, so the claws hadn't cut an artery. Still, I had to slow the bleeding and clean the wound. I scanned the water for the bear and looked up and down the beach. Nothing. My arm began to throb. I held it away from my body, stumbled to the water, waded in to my knees, and slid the arm underwater. The salt stung. Red streams swirled away from my skin and turned the water pink. I kept the arm in as long as I could take it and pulled it out. Blood oozed from the wound but didn't flow.

William had walked into the ocean to wash his wound, too.

I stared at the slashes through my skin. They were deep, but no bone was visible.

"Nothing stitches couldn't fix," I said to my appendage. "I've only got to stay alive until someone can stitch you up."

Ooze turned into drips. I dunked my arm again and tried to figure out how to fashion a makeshift tourniquet.

Holding my arm above my head, I walked up to the row of drying clothes, grabbed my bra, twisted it into a rope, and wrapped it high and tight around the damaged limb. With both hands, I managed to tie a knot. The wounds throbbed and oozed blood, but it slowed to a trickle.

I scanned the ocean and beach for the bear. Nothing. I'd have to stay near the fire, be vigilant. In the distance, water splashed. My stomach clenched. Just a gull. To keep sane, I had to focus on essentials. Gather wood, keep the fire going, dry clothes, check the injured arm. Look for bear.

I tried to not obsess about when and if rescue would come. I'd listened for low flying planes—a sign someone might be looking for me—but heard none. There was no sound of a motorboat either. Except for gulls, crows, and my other animal neighbors, Swampy Point was maddeningly quiet.

And after being charged and attacked by a bear, I was desperate to get away from the godforsaken place.

Think about something else.

The hot pool. That was bizarre. Richard said I'd die from hypothermia, but he instructed Bart to motor far into the wetland to a spot with heated water. Since Richard seemed to know all about the swamp, where I ended up made no sense. There had to be an answer to the paradox.

It came in a flash—so obvious I felt foolish for not realizing the explanation right away.

When I first slid into Swampy Point's hot pool, the rock bottom felt smooth. Unlike Kinuk's, it was free of slime and sediment. That meant the pool had been dry until very recently. I was no geologist, but there was a likely explanation. The same tectonic event that had drained Kinuk's pool must have altered the underground plumbing here so that hot water flowed into cave's pool.

In other words, two days ago the Kinuk pool was full and Swampy Point's empty. Now it was the other way around. If that were the case, I was the luckiest woman on the planet or someone or something in another realm was watching out for me.

Even though I sometimes sent up a prayer to my dead parents, I didn't believe in guardian angels. My prayer was a gesture of remembrance, not a genuine appeal to a higher force. A week ago, I would have insisted spirits, angels, and any otherworldly creatures didn't exist. My parents couldn't intervene on my behalf. But after what had happened here, I wasn't so sure.

At the moment, this mystical dilemma felt too intense to deal with. I stared across the gray-blue bit of water in front of me. My home in Maine offered an unbroken view of the sea to a far horizon. Nearly every day, I stared into fog, a bright morning, or the setting sun and let my thoughts drift. Now, a swampy jungle blocked what I could perceive.

Huh. If a person's view of the world shaped their perception, did my automatic rejection of anything spiritual limit my self-awareness? I shook my head. A philosophical question like *that* would have to wait until my survival was more secure.

Everything but the pullover was finally dry. The blessedly warm undies and pants felt like heaven but the turtleneck was tricky. It slid it over my head and good arm but only lay shawl-like on my right side. I tossed more wood on the fire, leaned back against the log, and promptly fell asleep.

I woke confused and sore. Shoved against the log, my neck hurt. The arm throbbed. I jumped to my feet and looked around in every direction. No bear, but I'd left the fire unattended. Luckily, the bed of coals still glowed red. That fire was my lifeline. It needed my full attention, and a mistake like that couldn't happen again. I added more wood until flames curled around the crisscross of logs.

I rolled up my pants, waded into the water, soaked my arm again, and returned to the fire.

Time to experiment with smoke-making.

For smoke, there had to be wet fuel. But if I added too much, the fire might go out. To deal with that problem, I used some coals from the first fire to make another close by. A mixture of dry and nearly dry kelp plus a bundle of damp twigs did the trick. Careful not to smother the new fire, I placed handfuls of the mixture onto the new coals and fanned them until smoke billowed out the sides.

Nobody might see my attempt at smoke signals. Based on the boat trip, Haida Gwaii's swampland seemed vast, and my wood supply limited the fire's size. But I had to try.

I collected and cooked more mussels, leaned back against my log to eat, and scanned the beach and water for bear.

A glimmer of silver up high caught my attention. I strained my ears for a drone. Nothing. I cupped my hands behind my ears and closed my eyes. There it was.

I squinted up at the sly. Oh my god, my god. A plane.

I added more kelp and twigs, fanned the flames, and ran down the beach, waving my good arm. The plane looped around and headed in my direction. But it only completed the circle and flew off.

The plane was so high and far away, the pilot hadn't seen me. My chance, maybe my only chance to be rescued, was gone. What was I going to do? I dropped to my knees, looked up at the sky, and sobbed.

Spent, I got to my feet and ran my free hand down my cheeks. Crying wasn't going to solve anything. I had to think about my situation rationally.

The sun slid lower toward the horizon. At the water's edge, I splashed a little on my face. A long evening and longer night stretched in front of me. Since I left Sandspit, I'd been in survival mode and hadn't given in to fear, exhaustion, or extreme cold. But the plane forced me to face what might happen.

It was possible, maybe likely, nobody would find me. Days, a week, weeks would pass. I'd still be here. I'd lose weight, maybe get sick. The bear might come back and get me. Angelo. I'd miss years with Angelo as we both got older. Harvey. She'd become biology department chair, maybe a college president. I'd never know.

And me. Months earlier, I'd finally conquered my fear of public speaking and accepted invitations to talk about the life of oceanographers, climate change, Maine coast ecology. I'd stepped into Mom and Dad's shoes. Cutting that short would undermine their legacy.

Then there was Ted. He might become a celebrated oceanographer. And what a time we could've had. Laughing, making love, and relishing the outdoors together. I ached for him to hold and kiss me.

Feeling like the loneliest woman on earth, I walked the beach. My arm throbbed and stung, and my eyes tightened. I let myself cry, a little.

25

THE SUN FELL BEHIND SWAMPY POINT'S TREES. NINE P.M. That bit of information was comforting. I was cut off from my everyday world of computers, the Internet, and all other forms of communication and connection. Knowledge about sunset time at this latitude and time of year helped me feel a bit in control.

It was essential the fires burn all night, so I prepared for sentry duty on the beach under the Haida stars. I needed something that resembled a bed. Sand on a level spot in front of my log would be a good base. I rifled through the flotsam and found some promising items—what looked like hay, some orange netting, and clusters of dry leaves. The big find was foam, most likely lost off a passing ship. I layered all this on top of the sand and a few spruce branches. The tattered tarp served as a sheet. I stood back to study my creation. It looked like something a wood rat would make.

As the sky darkened, I tried to remember, unsuccessfully, the difference between civil, nautical, and astronomical twilight. For millennia, sailors and shepherds had looked to the night sky for guidance and inspiration. Today, many people couldn't see the stars. We'd pushed back the dark with so much artificial light, astronauts could identify cities and whole countries from space.

Issues more pressing than the nocturnal sky cluttered my thoughts. How many more nights would I be here? What if I got sick? How long could I survive on mussels and other shallow water creatures? Would I run out of fuel? What about cold weather or if the hot pool dried up? I held my hands out to the fire and tried to think about something else.

"Stop it. Do something else. Like singing." As a scientist, I liked "Inchworm."

"Two and two are four, four and four are eight, eight and eight are sixteen, sixteen and sixteen are thirty-two." But that the song was a round. Not so good with only one person.

Rogers and Hammerstein had written several great tunes for *The Sound of Music.*

"When the dog bites, when the bee stings, when I'm feeling sad. I simply remember my favorite things. And then I don't feel so bad."

If any Haida spirits hung around Swampy Point that evening, they must've smiled.

For the rest of the night, I kept myself occupied with bear sentry, walks up and down the beach, movements of constellations I could recognize, catnaps on my not-very-comfortable bed, adding wood to the fire, and any cheery ditties that came to mind.

Bizarre dreams disrupted my snatches of sleep. Doe-eyed seals carried gifts of mussels in their mouths, the bottom dropped out of a hot pool and swallowed me, Angelo piloted a plane that tipped its wings.

After the long night, dawn was a welcome sight. The eastern sky turned pink and pewter before sun poked up over trees behind me.

I crouched at the edge of the bog, a distance from the fire. Meals consisting solely of mussel meat had upset my digestive system. I was preoccupied with urgent personal matters and didn't hear the whop-whop-whop until the thing cleared the trees and blocked the morning sun.

I pulled up my pants, ran down the beach, and waved my arm. Like an enormous gaudy bee, the yellow helicopter hovered above shallow water. Wind from its blades made a circle of waves, scattered wood from my piles, and fanned the coals to flames. The sound was deafening. I covered my ears with my hands and looked at the thing open-mouthed.

A door on the side of the 'copter opened and, like a spider on its silk thread, someone in a bright red jumpsuit rocketed down on a line. I backed up as my savior swung back and forth. The pilot approached land and hovered the helicopter directly over the beach.

The jump-suited person deftly landed with both feet on the beach, unhooked the halter, signaled to the helicopter, and walked over to me.

He yelled over the sound of the 'copter. "Mara Tusconi?"

Stunned and still covering my ears, I nodded.

"Are you injured, ill, or otherwise incapacitated?"

I lifted my arm. "Just this."

"Ready to get out of here?"

"Yes!"

He handed me a helmet that came from somewhere behind his body, slipped it over my head, and fastened the strap. "Now," he hollered, "I'm going to strap you into the harness. Okay?"

"Okay," I hollered back.

"When you approach the cabin, don't try to grab the helicopter or winch operator. They will completely control your entry. Do exactly what you're told. You'll be pulled into the cabin facing out. Understand?"

"Yes."

"Repeat what I said."

I did.

"Can you lift your arm?"

I nodded.

"Good. Here we go." He put the cinch harness over my head and slipped it below my armpits and between my legs. With a firm pull of a toggle, he secured the harness tight around my body. "I'll give the signal to raise you a tad to make sure this holds."

He spoke into a microphone and waved a hand.

Slowly, I rose off the ground. He waved his hand again. I hovered inches above the beach.

"Good," he yelled. "I'm going up with you. You don't need to do anything. Just look forward at me. No twisting or turning. Understand?"

Our helmets nearly touched. With a shout that didn't hurt my throat, I indicated that I did.

He gave the "go" sign with a hand signal and voice command. With a little jump as graceful as a dancer's, he wrapped his legs around mine and placed his hands on my shoulders.

We lifted off the ground and were airborne in a half-second. Like two mating dragonflies, we zoomed up toward the helicopter. It all happened so fast, I didn't have time to be scared.

I could see below without moving my head. There was my fire, pile of wood, makeshift bed. The bog stretched lush and green. The forest was densely packed with trees. My last glimpse was of the hill. The cave entrance wasn't visible.

Suddenly, I understood that I had never truly been alone at Swampy Point. Another presence—my parents, Angelo, the spirit of the sea—something had been with me. I vowed to keep saying thank you for the generosity that blessed me.

I turned my head a tad to see "Rescue," "Sauvetage," and "Canada" on the side of the helicopter. My rescuer said something into his mouthpiece. One moment I swung in the open air on my harness, the next I was inside the machine.

The person who pulled me in was a woman in a red jump-suit with hair pulled back into a tight brown ponytail. She secured the door, took off my helmet, helped me lie on a cot, and tugged a strap over my waist. She spoke into my ear. "I'm a medic."

The medic checked my pulse, pointed to my arm, and asked if I was okay for the moment. When I nodded, she strapped herself into a seat across from me. I turned my head to see the rear of the cabin. Without regular seats, the craft looked spacious. The guy who carried me up had cinched his seat belt and mouthed into his microphone.

The helicopter rose higher into the air, banked, and sped away.

I wanted to talk to my rescuers, but noise inside the cabin was much too loud. The four other people in the 'copter—the two I'd met plus two pilots—could communicate with each other via microphones. For the moment, I was deaf and dumb.

When we were flying straight, the woman released her belt. She spoke into my ear and asked about my injury again.

I looked at my arm and shrugged.

She checked my pulse and blood pressure. "Not bad. But those are nasty cuts."

"Bear."

She nodded. "Do what I can here."

I grimaced when she swabbed the wounds with liquid that stung.

"You must be dehydrated. Your skin feels dry. I'll give you some water, but drink slowly."

"I've been drinking skanky water for two days."

She put a pillow under my back. I sat up a little and took the water bottle with my left hand. The first sip tasted pure, clean, and cool. I sipped more and vowed never again to take drinking water for granted.

I signaled the medic to come closer.

I mouthed. "What's your name?"

"Lilly."

"Can't thank you—"

She held up her hand. I took that as "not now."

"Contact?"

She spoke into my ear. "Your family?"

Close enough. I nodded.

More ear words. "That's happening."

"Where?"

She understood my question. "Vancouver hospital."

26

A S THE HELICOPTER SPED ME TO SAFETY, I LAY ON MY cot and sifted through what had just happened. One minute I battled cold, fear, hunger, and exhaustion on a beach in the middle of a swamp maze. The next, I swung beneath a deafening helicopter in the hands of a red-suited stranger. My brain had trouble making sense of it all. I fell asleep.

The helicopter landed on a tarmac and jostled me awake. Confused, I glanced around the gray cabin. The medic's hand was on her seat belt. Two pilots sat up front. By the time the din of the machine faded, I was ready. With my good arm on Lilly's, I walked to the ambulance and squeezed her hand before she stepped away. She smiled and nodded. I never had a chance to thank the guy in the red jumpsuit.

In the ambulance, I was on my back again, looking up at another attending medic. He checked my vitals—pulse, blood pressure, temperature—said I was dehydrated, inserted an IV drip, and explained it contained electrolytes. An ambulance arrival means immediate care, even at large hospitals. The ER doc and nurses checked me out and asked about my last tetanus shot. Someone else asked more questions and scribbled answers on a form. An attendant rolled my bed into a temporary space encircled by curtains on tracks.

A nurse who looked like MASH's Hot-Lips pulled back the curtain, lifted my injured arm, and tut-tutted. "How'd you do that?"

"Bear attack."

She raised her eyebrows. "You need stitches. Be right back."

She returned with a tray holding two syringes. I eyed it.

"Antibiotic and anesthesia."

The ER doctor walked in, injected the antibiotic into my good arm, picked up the other syringe, held it up to eye level, and tapped it. "This will sting a bit."

It burned like hell. When the arm was numb, I tried to count the stitches as he worked but gave up at twenty.

"You look in pretty good shape, considering what you've been through. But we'll keep you overnight just in case," the physician said.

"Sounds good. I'm real, real tired."

Sergeant Knapton showed up first. From the black smudges under his eyes and stubble on his face, I figured it'd been a long night for him. A female cop stood inside the curtain. She held her nifty cap and looked fifteen.

Knapton ran a hand across his chin. "Jesus, am I glad to see you. We've been looking everywhere." He took out a notebook and pen. "Well, Dr. Tusconi. Seems like we have a lot to talk about."

"Mara. We do, indeed. Let's start with how you found me."

"Your fire. Nobody lives in that swamp, as you can imagine. A search plane spotted the fire and radioed in your location. Helicopter crew left at dawn. We knew it was you."

"How's that?"

"Partly the location, of course. And a red pullover. Pilot could see it from a thousand feet with binocs. Called in the description. Your buddies said you had one like that."

"Harvey and Ted. Where are they?"

"Here, in a waiting room. They'll be in when we're done."

I told Knapton critical elements of what had happened—from my attempt to call him in Sandspit to the helicopter ride.

Except for a few questions to clarify a point of fact, he listened carefully and took notes. "Can I come by tomorrow? We'll need a signed statement."

"Okay."

He glanced at his pad. "There's a few things I don't get. You feel well enough to talk more?"

"Sure, go ahead."

"Tell me again why Richard wanted to kill his brother."

"He said William was weak, a Mamma's boy. Richard wanted to make millions on marine carbon credits and couldn't risk his brother voting against the project. That's basically it."

Knapton shook his head. "Same old story. Cain and Abel. Did Richard say anything about how William died?"

"No, and I didn't have time to ask."

"For now, we'll have to rely on our forensics people." He rifled through his notes. "Richard could've gotten away with William's murder. That's still going to be difficult to prove unless Bart turns state's evidence and knows the details. But Richard kidnapped you, and you're still with us, thank god. We can probably get him for your attempted murder. But I don't get why he did it."

"The man's arrogant. Sure he could pull it off. And he most likely would have if subterranean events hadn't intervened."

"He knew you suspected him?"

"Bart overheard us talking in the longhouse about who might've killed William. I said we were responsible if he died because of our visit—and that I owed it to William to find out what happened. Bart told Richard what we said. Richard knew I'd keep at it back in Maine. I'd find out he was a trader, put two and two together. Um, did you say you probably could get him?"

"Your word. His word."

"I do think Bart'll cooperate if you offer him something."

"Why?"

"The guy acts like a punk, the T-shirt with ripped-off sleeves and all. But Richard bossed him around on the boat, and Bart didn't like it. He looked furious when Richard insulted William about being Haida."

"Good to know."

Harvey and Ted walked in right after Knapton left. Side by side, they stood next to the bed. I glanced from one to the other. Both fair, trim, with an aristocratic air, in white lab coats they'd look like twin blond doctors.

"Damn, girl," Harvey said. "You gave us one hell of a scare. When we found out you never took the plane and didn't contact us, we knew something was very wrong. And then, it got later and later and we *still* didn't hear from you—Jesus, what happened to your arm?"

"Tell you about it. I'm so sorry. Have you talked to Angelo?"

"Called him the moment we knew. It sounded like he was crying."

That made me feel even worse. "Let's phone him."

"We will," Ted said. "First, give us the short version of what happened. We hardly know a thing."

I recounted the events from when we went separate ways in Sandspit to the helicopter ride.

Harvey sat on the end of the bed. "You smacked a black bear on the nose with a piece of wood?"

"Yeah. Good thing I've been working out."

"The Spruce Harbor baseball team's gonna want you," Ted said.

I pulled a face.

Harvey asked, "It was at the museum where you got the idea about Richard?"

"Right. Just a guess. I tried to call Knapton, but he was on the line and I didn't want to leave the message. I was going to call again from the airport."

Ted was still standing. "Richard would probably have gotten away with killing William if he'd left you alone. So why did he bother to, ah, try to get rid of you?"

The anesthesia was already wearing off. I flexed my arm and grimaced. "He knew I owed William and guessed I'd try to like hell to figure things out after I got back. Richard worried I'd discover who he was, what he did. It's not a huge leap from carbon trading to what happened."

Harvey put a hand on my leg. "And you really think the hot pool where you were stranded was a new one? That's incredible, Mara."

"That was very strange. I'm beginning to wonder whether the Haida have it right—ancestral spirits can take care of us."

I expected a comment from Ted but not the one he made. "Wasn't it Harvard ecologist Ed Wilson who said science and religion are the two most powerful forces in the world, and it's not productive to have them at odds?"

Once more, I'd underestimated Ted.

We called Angelo on Harvey's phone. He sounded overjoyed. "Mara, how wonderful just to hear the sound of your voice. What an awful time you must've had."

"Tell you about it later. I feel terrible you had to worry like that. But there was no way for me to reach you."

"*No fa caso*. When you get back, I'll make your favorite veal parmigiana, and we'll drink good wine. Nothing better than family and home-cooked food."

After the call, Harvey took the phone. "I heard him say *no fa caso*. What does that mean?"

"It doesn't matter."

"Mara, I hate to leave you alone after all you've been through. But I've got to fly back to Maine tonight. I can't miss my grad student's PhD defense."

"I have to leave, too. Grant proposal due in two days," Ted said.

I fell back against the pillows, disappointed and angry. I'd nearly died in a swamp, and now my best friends leave me in the hospital?

Harvey looked down. I knew she felt guilty. Both she and Ted had been through hell in the last few days. Wanting them to stay was selfish.

I reached for her hand. "I understand. Both of you have stayed too long already. I'll be fine. Besides, after two nights alone at Swampy Point, one more day in Vancouver is a piece of cake."

Harvey tipped her head. "You'll be okay?"

"Truly. I'm fine flying home on my own."

Harvey held up a bag. "Got you new clothes. Everything you'll need to travel. Fleece, cotton. Things you like. Other stuff, too."

My throat tightened. I teared up. "You're the best."

They turned to leave.

I said, "Ted, could you wait a moment?"

Harvey waved over her shoulder. "See you at home."

Ted stood at the end of the bed. He looked tired.

"Is something the matter?" I asked.

"It's been a dreadful couple of days."

"Ted, I'm so sorry."

"I am, too." He ran a hand down his face and let it drop by his side. "Take care of yourself, Mara. Have a good trip home."

He turned, walked to the door, and pulled it shut behind him.

27

I WOKE ALONE IN THE HOSPITAL ROOM, LOOKED OUT THE window, and tried to figure out the time. Nearly dark. I shifted and winced when my arm hit a bar on the side of the bed.

A nurse carrying a tray bustled in. "Good. You're awake. You need to eat."

She pressed a button. The bed whirred and pushed me to a seated position. The nurse flipped a shelf from the side of the bed and placed the tray on it. "Be back in a bit."

The tray held a plate of broiled chicken, green peas, and mashed potatoes, a glass of lemonade, a sliced apple, and a peanut butter cookie. The sight of food made me ravenous. I hadn't eaten vegetables in days. So using my left hand, I clumsily went for the peas and potatoes first. With a little butter, they tasted like sunshine. The chicken was juicy, lemonade tangy, apple crisp, and cookie sweet.

The woman returned, looked at the tray, and laughed. "Looks like you're doing well. Better get up and walk around."

She removed the tray and lowed the bars on the side of the bed. "Swing your legs over the side. Take it easy. Don't stand right away."

"Oh, I'll be fine."

I sat on the side of the bed and tried to stand. My legs shook. I fell back. "Whoa."

"Like I said. Take it easy."

"I feel so weak. It's weird."

"You've had an adventure. Want to talk about it?"

I told her some of the juicy bits—the icy water swim, discovery of the cave and hot pool, fire and mussel-roast, bear attack, and helicopter ride.

She laughed again. "And you're surprised you're a little weak?"

The nurse left. I looked through the clothes Harvey had brought and pulled out a red satin robe. It was lovely—nothing like my tattered one at home, and just the thing to cover a hospital gown.

I slept most of the day and was eating breakfast the next morning when Sergeant Knapton called on the hospital phone. "Good, you're still there."

"What's up?"

"We've got Richard Edenshaw and need you to fly over to Haida Gwaii for a hearing. We're required to prove the accused took the victim without their consent."

"What? Can't you use my statement?"

"We could, but you in person will be much more persuasive."

I sighed. "I'm flying home tonight."

"Could you change your plans? We'll pick up the cost, if that's an issue. The hearing is in Queen Charlotte City. There's a RCMP station there. Gene Edenshaw says his sister would be happy to put you up. It'll just be for one night. We'll fly you out to the islands and back. You can catch a plane to the States tomorrow."

The idea of going back to the archipelago and facing Richard made my response stick in my throat. "Um, well—"

"I've known Sarah Edenshaw for a very long time. Truly, she'll love to have you."

The afternoon flight from Vancouver to Sandspit took me over Hecate Straight on the northern end of the archipelago. It felt strange to look down on landscape I hadn't planned to see for a long time, like I wasn't supposed to be there.

I boarded the Sandspit-Queen Charlotte City ferry. Gene met me at the dock. His brown eyes looked muddy, like they'd lost their spark, and there was no hint of the lighthearted man with silly jokes.

"Didn't think we'd see each other so soon," he said.

"You got that right."

He shook his head. "This is terrible, terrible business. How Richard could—" He choked on the words and stared out at the water. "And what happened to you. Sergeant Knapton told me a little. I'm so sorry you had to go through that." He eyed the bottom few stitches on my arm. "My goodness, that looks tender."

I slipped my good arm through his. "In the last few days we've both been through a lot. Let's go see your sister. Look forward to meeting her."

Sarah greeted us from the front porch of her white painted cottage. A half-foot shorter than her brother, she had skin the color of caramel and a mass of white curls that framed her plump face. Her red skirt was covered by a red-and-white checked apron, which she used to wipe her hands before she reached for mine. From the way she spoke, I guessed she'd gone to university.

"Come in, Mara, come in. You must be tired. I've got a hot drink and cookies for you."

I followed Sarah through a tidy living room into a brightly lit kitchen that smelled of cinnamon. She gestured toward the wooden table. "Please sit. Tea, coffee?"

"Tea would be lovely."

"Milk and sugar?"

"Milk, please."

She placed a delicate white pitcher of milk on the table and poured the steaming brew into three white teacups decorated with pink flowers. Gene carried another chair from a corner and joined me. Sarah placed a plate of sugar cookies on the table and slid into her chair.

The tea was perfect—black, rich, a touch smoky. I bit into a cookie. The sugar melted in my mouth.

"This tea's excellent."

"So glad you like it, dear. There's good tea in Canada. British heritage, you know."

Gene reached for his second cookie. "I'll explain tomorrow's procedure and let Sarah take care of you." He winked at his sister. "She's very skilled at that."

Good. A little of the old Gene.

"The hearing's in the municipal building. The judge will decide if there is sufficient evidence for a trial. It'll be Sergeant Knapton, the judge, Richard, Bart. Besides you, of course."

I wondered if Richard's bravado would fade as he stood before a judge.

"I think Bart will testify against Richard to save his skin," I said. "What's with that young man?"

Sarah and Gene glanced at each other.

"I'm the grade school teacher in town," she said. "Bart's had it rough. Father died of an overdose, mother drank. Too much poverty and unemployment out here."

Gene stood. "Maybe this thing will set him right. There's good under his tough guy act. I'll come by in the morning and walk you over, Mara."

Gene kissed his sister on the cheek and left.

I sipped my last bit of tea. "Bet he's a great brother, Sarah."

"I've got three more on the mainland, but Gene's my favorite. You must be tired, dear. Your room's upstairs."

We passed through the living room. Sarah switched on a table lamp, which illuminated the only framed photograph in view—a beach scene with five people, arms around each other. A laughing Sarah stood in the middle with two men on either side.

In the guest room, I tossed my little bag of clothes onto an old cedar bureau. The double-bed quilt featured rose, slate blue, and cream squares. In the middle, five butterflies floated on a sky-blue rectangle. Sarah ran a hand across the quilt. "I don't favor the red and black Haida colors so much. Come see the Queen Charlotte Mountains."

We stood before two windows in the room that overlooked the harbor and a distant mountain range.

"What a gorgeous view. Reminds me of the Rocky Mountains," I said. "What's the tall peak in the middle?"

"Sleeping Beauty Mountain. About seven hundred meters." She patted the bed. "I think you'll be comfortable here, dear. There are pajamas in the bureau you can wear if you want. Bathroom's at the end of the hall. Come down when you're ready. I've something that will help your arm feel better, and we'll have a nice chat while I make dinner."

I went back to the window. On my next trip to Haida Gwaii—there was no doubt I'd return—I'd stay with Sarah and climb Sleeping Beauty Mountain. The idea made me smile. I'd been in her home for tea and cookies and was already planning another visit. Maybe living in all this natural beauty helped the Haida be warm and generous.

I splashed some water on my face in the bathroom. Before bed, I could rinse my nylon undies and socks. The little room was warm and I assumed both would be dry in the morning. I'd have to wear the same shirt two days in a row, but could buy something clean in the airport.

Sarah's kitchen smelled more like pine than cookies. In the middle of the table, a wooden tongue depressor poked out of an open jar of clear gel. "Arnica," Sarah said. "If you'd like to try it, swab a little on your wound. It won't hurt you, and it'll probably help. I made the preparation."

I sniffed the bottle. Sage, like desert plants. I touched a tad to the bottom of a laceration that itched.

"After I finish with this stew, we'll walk to my favorite spot and watch the sunset. Sound good?"

"Terrific. I'm a big sunset fan."

"Gene tells me you're an ocean scientist. How exciting."

I half-expected Sarah to say something about my parents but, of course, she didn't. While my hostess added onions and other vegetables to a bubbling pot on her gas stove, I told her about Spruce Harbor, Angelo, and what I did for a living.

"I can tell how much the ocean means to you, Mara."

"My blood's probably extra salty. I love being on the sea, under it, hearing and smelling it. Everything."

She dropped a lid on the pot. "Maybe there's some Haida in you. Let's go outside."

Sarah told me about the village as we walked down to the water. "We've got motels, shops, a hospital, the visitor center, even a newspaper. I teach in the school, like I said."

The rock we shared was clearly a favorite spot for Sarah. I could see why. Across a mile-wide strait, the crimson sun slid behind a purple steep-sloped mountain range thrust up out of the sea. The tide was high, and pebbles tumbled back and forth with gentle waves. Silent, we watched the red orb disappear as the earth rotated away from it. Glowing pink, the glassy bay mirrored the cloudless rose sky.

"Wow," I said. "This is spectacular."

"'Tis. I can sit here for hours."

An eagle flew less than fifty feet above—so close I could count its tail feathers. When the bird craned its neck in our direction, it seemed like the predator fixed a beady eye on me.

"Sarah, do animals ever, ah, look right at you, talk to you, anything like that?"

She answered like it was the most natural question in the world. "Once in a while. I wish it happened more often."

"It doesn't seem strange or make you nervous?"

"Oh no. Animals who make contact with us are connections to the unknown. People who animals communicate with are very lucky." She patted my knee.

"Tell me about yourself, Sarah. Do you have children?"

She sighed. "No, except for the ones I teach. It's a great sadness for me."

"Um, did something happen?"

"When I was your age, there was one special man. I knew he loved me very much. We shared a great deal—walks up these mountains, motoring around in his boat—and we laughed together. He really was a lovely man. Handsome, too."

I waited for her to say he died at sea or in some other awful way.

"Did something happen to him?"

"Gene waited and waited for the marriage announcement. Finally, he asked what was wrong. I told him I loved this man, but something held me back. A fear I couldn't explain."

"What did Gene say?"

"If I let the man go, I'd regret it the rest of my life."

I was almost afraid to ask. "And did you?"

"Oh yes. He left for the mainland. I never saw him again."

28

SARAH BUSTLED ABOUT THE KITCHEN AND WOULDN'T LET me do a thing to help. Upstairs, in the bathroom, I was amazed by the improvement in my arm. The spot where I'd rubbed arnica no longer itched and was less inflamed than before.

Sarah stood at the stove and ladled fish soup into bowls.

I held out my arm. "It looks like the arnica's helping."

She nodded toward a cupboard. "The jar's up there, dear. Use as much as you like."

I found the arnica, pulled out a chair, and sat to do an experiment. There were three long lacerations. Gently, I dabbed the gel across the slash closest to my body (number one) and repeated the procedure on number three. In the morning, I'd assess what happened.

Sarah noticed what I was doing and handed me a little plastic container. "When you see that it works, you'll have more."

She placed large bowls of steaming soup on the table. Warm rolls filled a wooden bowl. She'd even poured glasses of red wine for us both.

"This looks fantastic."

She beamed. "Ling cod stew. I made the rolls myself."

There was a smoky flavor in the rich soup I couldn't place.

"Mushrooms from Sleeping Beauty Mountain. A local specialty."

I sipped my wine. "This is my last dinner on Haida Gwaii for a while. I can't imagine a better one."

Sarah smiled. "I'm so glad you like it." Her expression darkened. "Tomorrow will be hard for you."

"It will. Do you know Richard?"

"Not like I knew William. Richard didn't go to school on Haida Gwaii. I think he wanted to get away from the traditions, all that, as fast as he could. He studied on the mainland and got rich."

That night, I lay in bed and stared up into the dark. It'd been a remarkable day because Sarah was an extraordinary woman. Kind and generous, she was also astute and willing to share her wisdom. I loved her response to my question about animals communicating with people. Of course, she'd guessed why I asked and made me feel special, not weird. Her idea that animals were a link to the unknown seemed so straightforward.

On the other hand, Sarah's story about a lost love was heartbreaking, and the lesson impossible to miss. Her experience with the unnamed man was eerily similar to mine with Ted. She deeply regretted her decision decades ago.

Her words haunted me. "Something held me back. I never saw him again."

It was obvious Ted and I were perfect for each other, but I also couldn't articulate my fear. Thirty years from now would I be alone and look back with regret and sorrow?

I sat up in bed and whispered, "*No.* That's not going to happen. Back home, I'll talk to Ted. Tell him I how very much I love him. Ask if we could take it day by day for now. He'll understand. I know he will."

My decision was easy. I couldn't imagine why it had taken me so long. I wanted to call Ted right away, but, of course, my phone was at the bottom of Swampy Point bay.

Happier than I could remember, I dropped back against the pillow and fell into a deep, dreamless sleep.

Gene picked me up right after breakfast. The morning was gray and misting. Luckily, Harvey had anticipated rain and included a waterproof camping poncho in my bag of clothes. I pulled the hood over my head and smiled. I'd find a special treat for Harvey back in Maine.

Gene noticed my maneuver. "How's the arm?"

"Not bad. I can move it around pretty well now."

We walked into the Queen Charlotte municipal building, a plain utilitarian structure you could see anywhere, down a long corridor, and into what looked like a tiny courtroom. At the head of the room, an oversized wooden chair sat empty behind a ten-foot long wood desk. Two sets of smaller chairs, separated by a couple of yards, faced the desk. A Canadian flag hung behind the desk in one corner, the Vancouver flag in the other.

"Should we sit?" I whispered.

Gene's answer sounded loud in the little room. "Let's wait for Knapton."

Sergeant Knapton swept in. Even though it was summer, he wore a mid-calf-length trench coat, a light brown suit, and a brown tie. I felt underdressed in my long-sleeved turtleneck and tatty black fleece pants.

"Good morning. We wait for the judge before we're seated."

I shifted from one foot to the other while we stood there. Richard was somewhere close by, and I wasn't sure what it would be like to see him again.

A door to the right of the desk opened. Richard walked in, accompanied by a RCMP officer. Chin up, lips pursed, he stared straight ahead and didn't acknowledge us. Bart and another officer followed. Nobody said a word.

The opposite door opened. A middle-aged man in a long black robe marched in. With high cheekbones, dark brown eyes, and copper skin, the judge looked distinctly Haida. He pointed to his right. "Knapton, you and your key witness may sit there. Other witness behind. Accused on the other side."

Chairs scraped across the floor as Knapton and the officers followed the judge's directions.

"You may sit," he said.

We did.

"Court recorder, please."

A woman with black hair severely pulled into a bun at the nape of her neck walked in and settled into a seat with a writing armrest. She opened a notebook and held a pen at the ready.

The judge cleared his throat. "I am Judge Halverson." He lifted the topmost sheet of paper from a perfect stack on the desk, pulled out a pair of half-eye reading glasses from the recesses of his robe, settled the glasses on the end of his nose, and frowned at the sheet. "Let's see. Yes. We have a case of alleged kidnapping." He looked at Knapton over the glasses.

Knapton stood. "The victim, Mara Tusconi, is here, Your Honor. She will describe how Richard Edenshaw, with Bart Benniger's help, took her against her will and left her for dead in the Moresby Swamp."

One of Halverson's eyebrows shot up. Leaving someone in the Moresby Swamp appeared to be a dangerous thing to do.

The judged turned to Richard. "Does the accused have council?"

Richard stood and spoke with a clear, unwavering voice. "I represent myself, Your Honor."

"As you wish."

Richard sat down.

Halverson gestured at Bart, seated behind us. "And who is this?"

"Witness against the accused, Your Honor."

Richard flexed a hand. I could see white knuckles.

Halverson directed a question at Gene in the back of the room. "And you, sir?"

Gene stated his name. "I'm an interested party, Your Honor. Dr. Tusconi is a visitor to Haida Gwaii. I'm a Watchman and have accompanied her on her visit."

"Mr. Edenshaw may stay. Witness may state her case."

I stood and briefly described my saga from the fake phone text to the helicopter rescue. Richard remained passive through most of my testimony. When I slid my shirt sleeve up to show Halverson the bear gouges, the judge's eyebrows shot up so high his glasses feel off. Richard glanced at the arm and flinched.

Knapton called Bart, who confirmed the kidnapping.

"Son, do you realize the seriousness of what you've done?" Halverson asked.

I glanced at Bart who stood in the space between us and Richard. He bit his lip and flushed. "Yes, Your Honor."

Richard wiped his palms on his shirt.

The judge turned to Richard. "Accused, please stand. Do you deny the charges placed against you?"

Richard lifted his chin. "I do. I'm a respected businessman in Vancouver. It's ridiculous to think I would kill my brother." He turned and pointed to Bart and me. "Both of them, they're *liars*."

Bart sucked in some air. I glared at Richard with a fury that boiled up from deep in my gut. He turned away.

Judge Halverson picked up a gavel and slammed it onto a wooden disk on his desk. "The case will go to trial. Bail is set at twenty-five thousand dollars. Witness against the accused," he glanced at his sheet, "Bart Bennniger, released to custody of a responsible adult, if we can locate such a person."

Gene's voice from the back. "I'll take that responsibility, Your Honor."

"Thank you. See my deputy. All rise."

My last view of Richard Edenshaw was from the back. He held his head high, but hunched shoulders and twitching hands gave him away.

Outside, Gene and I listened to Knapton.

"Couldn't have gone better," he said. "You made all the difference, Mara."

"It was worth it. What happens now?"

"Richard, of course, will raise the bail and hire the best lawyer. Trial won't be for a couple of months at least. You won't need to come back since the judge has your testimony. Assuming he's convicted, he'll get at least five years for the kidnapping."

"Could someone go after him in jail?" I asked. "Another Haida, I mean. Because he murdered William?"

"Maybe so." Gene said.

"And Bart?"

"Not sure. Depends on prior arrests, that kind of thing."

"What about William's death?"

"Wish that was more definitive for his parents, if nothing else. Still waiting on forensics."

"In other words, if Richard had let me fly back home, he may've gotten away with it."

Gene put a hand on my shoulder. "And if you'd died in Moresby Swamp, he would have murdered *two* people and gotten away with it."

29

I SWIVELED IN MY WINDOW SEAT FOR A FINAL LOOK BACK AT Haida Gwaii. Below, steep emerald mountains fringed by white wave-aprons thrust straight up out of the sea. A confusion of islands, inlets, bays, beaches, and river-mouths outlined the archipelago. I last glimpsed the southernmost part of the park—Rose Harbor, Augustine Island, and Kinuk.

It registered that Sergeant Knapton had spoken to me. I turned and faced him.

"Sorry, what?"

"Mara, you'd make a good detective. If you get tired of your job in Maine, you could immigrate and become a Canadian Mounty."

It felt good to laugh.

We joined the crowds in Vancouver International.

Knapton said, "When's your flight?"

"Two plus hours."

He shook my hand. "If we learn how William died, I'll let you know what I can. And Vancouver has a famous anthropology museum with a couple of exhibits right in the airport you'll enjoy."

Sergeant Knapton was right. Just beyond the security checkpoint, a sculpture that nearly touched the ceiling bore witness to the Haida's flair for humor. A panicked passenger— his glasses askew, hat falling off, suitcase in each outstretched hand—sprinted for his plane. Even someone grumpy from a long security line would have to chuckle.

Given what I now knew about the Haida, I was excited to spend time viewing "The Spirit of Haida Gwaii: the Jade Canoe," created by Bill Reid, the Haida nation's most famous artist. Surrounded by windows, the rich green sculpture dwarfed viewers. The carved canoe overflowed with paddlers and creatures. Raven hung off the stern. The bird appeared intent on steering forward but, of course, could change its mind in an instant. Beneath Raven's wing crouched an unhappy human figure with a peaked Haida hat—the grudging oarsman. The tall, proud man in the middle looked like a shaman.

A boy tugged on his father's sleeve. "Dad, where are they all going?"

The man looked at his tablet. "Here's what the carver said. 'There's certainly no lack of activity in the little boat, but is there purpose? The boat moves on, forever in one place.'"

Reid's words hit home. Plenty of people who vowed to transform their lives stayed stuck in destructive behaviors. I'd have to make sure that wasn't my personal fate, too.

Signs directed me to more artwork in a room dedicated to rotating exhibits. At one end, armchairs were placed before a sizable TV screen. I dropped into one as the video took viewers inside the entrance of the Reid amphitheater in UBC's anthropology museum.

"Holy cow."

Illuminated from above by a circular skylight thirty feet across, "The Raven and the First Men" perched on a round pedestal in the middle of a rotunda. Wings spread, the raven crouched on a clamshell and looked down at human-like creatures who peeked out from beneath the shell. Light tan, in sunlight the sculpture glowed. Photos I'd seen didn't capture the immense scale and artist's attention to detail.

The camera took viewers down cement steps that surrounded the pedestal and slowly circled the sculpture. Raven's oversized eye appeared to follow the lens.

A smiling young lady with jet-black hair cut in a cap around her head, red lipstick, and a white shirt appeared on screen. "Hello, I'm Marcia, a guide at University of British Columbia's anthropology museum. I'd like to tell you a little about this magnificent sculpture." She gestured toward the piece. "With 'The Raven and the First Men,' Bill Reid shows us the story of human creation. One day, Raven walked along the beach in Haida Gwaii. He heard noise coming from a half-buried clamshell and saw it was full of little human creatures. The Raven and the big world outside their shell terrified the people. The bird leaned his huge head close to the shell. With his smooth trickster's voice, he sweet-talked the little creatures to come out and play in his wonderful, shiny, new world."

Marcia slowly circled the sculpture, talking as she went. "Bill Reid was a master goldsmith, carver, and sculptor. In nineteen fifty-four he visited his uncle, Charles Edenshaw, in Haida Gwaii. Edenshaw's carvings changed Bill Reid's life."

A photograph of Reid carving a totem pole filled the screen. In voiceover, Marcia said, "Bill Reid's mother was Haida, his father European. The Haida call him their own. When he died in nineteen ninety-eight, they brought his remains back to his mother's ancestral village, Tanu, in Haida Gwaii."

Marcia ended with an invitation for viewers to visit the museum.

Edenshaw was such a common last name on the archipelago, like Smith or Jones in the States. And it was interesting that Reid was half-Haida, like William and Richard. Like the famous artist, the Haida called William their own while Richard had denounced his Haida ancestry.

An open case at the other end of the room displayed masks people could try on. I scanned the selection. One painted bright blue had oversized white teeth, a mean grin, and bulging black eyes. A bear with one eye circled in red bared its fangs. I'd had enough of bears. Compared to those, the raven mask looked kindly with its long black beak, fringe for a neck, and black eyes on a white background. I lifted the raven off its peg and positioned the mask over my head.

The transformation was immediate. I rose off the floor and feathers covered my body.

I yanked off the mask and shook my head. "Damn. They should put a warning sign next to this case." I carefully replaced the raven and studied its eyes. No glowing ones stared back, but I didn't need that to respect the power of Haida art and mythology. Never again would I automatically reject spiritual claims of sincere and learned people.

A display in a far corner caught my eye. "Finding Spiritual" featured quotes and images of famous people. I read the words of three again and again.

Emily Carr's photograph showed a forgettable middle-aged woman with a black cap and dog.

I am religious and always have been, but I am not a church-goer…I longed to get out of church and crisp up in the open air. God got so stuffy and squeezed out in church. Only out in the open is there room for Him. He was like a great breathing among the trees…He just was and filled all the universe.

The Dalai Lama's photo showed the gleeful monk in his younger days. He'd said:

…preservation of environment, it is related with many things. Ultimately the decision must come from the human heart, isn't that right? So I think the key point is a genuine sense of universal responsibility which is based on love, compassion, and clear awareness.

Huh. A week ago, I would have scoffed at a link between love and conservation.

Pierre Teilhard de Chardin, a Jesuit Priest, French philosopher, and paleontologist excavated caves before World War I. He looked like a serious academic in his photograph.

The day will come when, after harnessing the ether, the winds, the tides, and gravitation, we shall harness for God the energies of love. And on that day for the second time in the history of the world, man will have discovered fire.

Alone in the room, I digested the wisdom of these three people. They spoke about nature and science *together with* love, religion, and God. For them, the world they could measure and see was intimately linked to human emotion and the spiritual. The connection was undeniable to these perceptive, influential people. Why had I insisted on separating the physical and spiritual?

A question instead of an answer.

My question was akin to looking at data in a different way—when numbers I'd stared at for months suddenly formed a pattern.

Something shifted inside.

The flight was long. I skipped the Tom Hanks movie about a guy shipwrecked on an island and catnapped for most of the trip. Weird images—Gene in a raven mask and talking totem poles—interrupted my dreams.

Early in the morning, the plane approached Logan airport. From my window seat, Boston Harbor came into view, as familiar as clam chowder and baked beans. It was too early in the day for sailboats, but the ferry that steamed out could have been heading for Cape Cod or Nantucket Island.

Angelo had offered to come down to Boston to pick me up, but I insisted I'd take the bus north, since five hours one way was too long a drive. He'd relented when I reminded him about the awful Boston traffic.

With a stop in Portland, the bus took me north to Belfast, where Angelo picked me up. He jumped out of his truck as I pushed aside the bus station door. "My god, Mara, you're a sight for sore eyes."

He held out his arms.

On tiptoe, I wrapped my good arm around him His cotton shirt was soft, and he smelled mostly of salt and a little of fish.

I stepped back and patted his shirt. "Been fishin'?"

"With Connor. Blues are running now. I did wash up, though."

I stepped onto the running board and slid onto the front seat.

"Belfast's a little too busy for me," Angelo said.

I directed him back to the highway and didn't say a word. The population of Belfast was less than three thousand.

We headed north. After Haida Gwaii's ancient cedar rainforest, Maine's second-growth conifers and hardwoods along the highway looked puny in comparison.

"You too tired to come over for dinner tonight?" Angelo asked. "Thought I'd invite Connor, Harvey, and Ted. 'Course we want to hear about everything."

"For sure. Home cooking, especially your home cooking, would be terrific. I slept some on the plane and can take a nap this afternoon."

As we bounced along the mile-long dirt road down to my house, Angelo gave me the latest local news.

"Big blow-up with the Penobscot and the Gov'nor. He denies sovereignty on their land."

"That's not surprising." Maine's governor was one of my least favorite people in the world.

"And The Neap Tide's serving crab cakes now."

"Fantastic." I spent a lot of time in the Spruce Harbor café.

It was strange to walk into my kitchen after a trip without a suitcase trailing behind me or a duffle on my shoulder. I opened the cottage's windows and stepped outside to enjoy the view from the edge of my tiny lawn. In the chilly afternoon breeze off the water, it felt good to sit on a granite outcrop warmed by the August sun.

I'd tasted death, and was very glad to be *home*. I drank in the coast of Maine and watched naked waves turn into whitecaps, gulls fight over fish, and an eagle land on a pine tree. When I stood to head inside for a quick nap, I took the screech of an osprey as a welcome-back.

There were four trucks in Angelo's driveway—Harvey's, Ted's, Connor's, and Angelo's. At least they were different colors. Harvey's bright red Ford with shiny black wheels and a black bumper-winch combo outclassed the others.

I ran up the stone steps and pulled open the oak door. Everyone was in Angelo's big kitchen. My godfather stood at the old-fashioned slate sink rinsing fish fillets. Beside him, Ted scraped cucumbers onto an oversized cutting board. Heads close together, Harvey and Connor sat at the kitchen table. They hadn't seen each other for over a week. From Connor's nods, it looked like she was describing highlights of the trip.

Not that long ago, Harvey had claimed she was lonely, but local men were too rough for her. She and Connor clicked when they teamed up to help me investigate our colleague's death. It was pretty clear Connor adored Harvey, and the admiration was mutual.

With bright blue eyes and black curls going to gray, Connor looked like an aging Irish altar boy. A striking blond with high cheekbones and large gray eyes, Harvey was an inch taller and eight years younger. I was proud of Harvey. She put aside her silver spoon and private-school upbringing, and fell for a local Mainer and former cop. They did have a lot in common. Both loved the outdoors and hunted deer, moose, and bear.

Connor was teaching Harvey how to fish. She'd introduced him to jazz, and they'd driven down to Portland for a couple of concerts. Because she was willing to change, Harvey found a terrific soul mate.

I was excited to talk with Ted, and turned toward him. He stared into space. A couple of cucumber scrapings lay at his feet. I guessed he hadn't caught up on his sleep.

I walked over to him. "How're you doing?"

Ted shrugged. "Okay. How was your trip?"

"Fine. I texted you about why I needed to stay longer."

He grabbed another cucumber. "You did. You'll have to tell us about it."

"I'll pick some salad greens," I said. "Be right back."

The kitchen garden was next to the house. I closed the door behind me. Why was Ted so distant? His grant proposal had probably kept him up all night. I wished he'd followed me out so I could ask.

I squatted to pinch off arugula and leafy lettuce, and looked up at Angelo's so-called cottage. On the end of Seal Point, the rambling cedar-shingled house commanded a sweeping view of Spruce Harbor. Growing up, I learned every room, closet, and bookcase. I'd sat on the stairs with a book while Angelo and my parents talked about exotic-sounding things like "deep sea vents," "whale bubble feeding," and "cod collapse." I wanted to grow up fast so I could do what my parents did.

We ate outside on the patio. Over a dinner of barbequed fish and salad, Angelo and Connor learned about the iron project,

Ninstints and the totem poles, our scuba dive, the hot pools, and William's death. I described the miracle of hot water in Swampy Point, my close call with hypothermia, and the unexpected trip back to the archipelago. I wanted to skip over the bear attack but figured it'd be better to own up to it. I slid the sleeve up on my injured arm. After a couple of days and Sarah's arnica salve, it didn't look too bad.

Angelo thought otherwise. "My god, Mara! Something big mauled you in that swamp. Must've been a bear. Christ almighty."

Connor let out a low whistle. "Obviously, it charged. What'd you do?"

"Swung a piece of cedar at its snout as hard as I possibly could. The bear veered off into the water. Never saw it again."

I glanced at Ted. In the hospital, he'd teased me about joining a baseball team, but he didn't repeat the joke.

"Sarah—she's who I stayed with—gave me arnica for the wounds." I pointed to the ones I'd treated. "I only applied her salve to those two lacerations. Looks like the stuff works."

Connor laughed. "Mara, leave it you to experiment on your own arm."

Harvey changed the subject. "How did Richard behave at the hearing?"

"He said Bart and I were liars. But the judge didn't buy it. Based on my testimony and Bart's, he called for a trial."

"So justice may win in the end."

I shrugged. "Sure hope so, but Richard has the money to hire top lawyers."

Connor, a former cop, wanted to know more. "Speakin' of justice, if you, ah, disappeared in that swamp, would he have gotten away with murdering his brother?"

With Connor's Maine accent, "disappeared" sounded like "disappeahed."

"Could be. Sergeant Knapton said they didn't have a strong case against him. So, if Richard hadn't kidnapped me, he'd be thinking about trades instead of jail."

"Some crooks," he said, "think they're masterminds and too smart to get caught."

"Excuse me," Angelo said. He marched to the cliff's edge.

I followed him. "What's the matter?"

My godfather frowned at the darkening seascape. In the bay, buoys flashed red and green to mark the channel.

He turned to face me. "Hearing you and Connor talk about you disappearing in that swamp brought it all back. Not knowing where you were, what happened. That was horrible. Mara, I don't think you appreciate the toll all this takes on those of us who care about you."

Tears in my eyes, I took both his calloused hands in mine.

Behind us, the threesome on the patio were mum.

Angelo and I were silent as well, the only sound crashing waves on the rocks below.

Finally, Harvey rubbed her arms. "Hey, it's getting chilly out here."

Connor leaned over and draped his fleece jacket across her shoulders.

We carried everything inside. Harvey and Connor murmured a few words to each other as they dished out ice cream and wild blueberries. Angelo made coffee. We pulled chairs around Angelo's old pine table in the kitchen to eat dessert.

Connor broke the gloomy mood. He savored a spoonful of ice cream smothered in blueberries. "Nothin' better than wild Maine berries."

Harvey smiled, I guessed because "better" came out "bettah."

Across from me, Ted announced he was bushed. Hair

disheveled, ashen smudges beneath his eyes, he certainly looked it.

Desperately wanting to reconnect with the old Ted, I walked him out to the front steps. "You okay?"

"Just tired." He walked down the stairs, toward his truck.

I called out, "Good night, Ted."

"Good night," he said over his shoulder.

The chill wind scattered dead leaves on the driveway. I hugged myself and stared into the gloom until last the bits of red rear lights died out.

Harvey left a few minutes later. In the kitchen, Connor pulled his jacket off Harvey's chair.

"Looks like things are good with you two," I said.

"Well, you know the Irish sayin' about men."

"Bet you're going to tell me."

"Women like men like they want their coffee. Hot, strong, and Irish."

I rolled my eyes.

Connor and Angelo set a time for the next day's fishing trip. Angelo and I quickly cleaned up.

"Would you like some decaf?"

"Only if you have biscotti."

It was supposed to be a joke. Angelo didn't laugh.

My godfather poured hot water into the coffee press. He carried the press to the table, slowly pushed the top down, and poured black, steaming brew into little white cups.

I placed a plate of biscotti between us. "Thanks for dinner. It's great to be home."

He sipped his coffee.

"I really am sorry it all happened, but it wasn't my fault."

He sighed and slowly slid the cup onto its saucer. "Trouble seems to follow you around, Mara."

"Can we talk about something else?"

He tapped his cup with his finger. "Our phone call?"

"From Sandspit?"

"That one."

"Strange, we talked so soon before I was kidnapped." I regretted the words as soon as they were out of my mouth. My disappearance was still too painful to talk about.

"You seemed awfully tense about the, um, unusual things that happened, Mara."

"I feel calmer about all that now. Like I was worrying about something not so important." I described the exhibit at the airport.

"Teilhard de Chardin. There's a name I haven't heard in a very long time. Your mother read a lot of his books and essays."

"Really? I didn't know that." Any new tidbit about my mother was a treat.

"It was back in the sixties, when Catholicism went through big changes. Folk music and all. As I recall, she saw him as a radical thinker and respected how he talked about science and religion."

"Who'd ever think there'd be a connection between Bridget Tusconi and Teilhard de Cardin via a British Columbia museum?" I said.

"Sometimes it's as if coincidences like that are meant to happen. The right thing comes along if you open your heart to it."

During the drive home, I considered Angelo's proclamation about coincidences. He had returned to his usual thoughtful self and, for the second time that night, I blinked back tears. This time, though, they were tears of gratitude.

Early the next morning, I pulled into the Maine Oceanographic Institute. It was Saturday, and I easily found a parking spot behind my building. The day promised to be warm and muggy. I took advantage of the cool breeze and strolled over to the water. It felt like I'd been gone a month, but Spruce Harbor was exactly as I'd left it. MOI's research vessel *Intrepid* was tied to the institute's pier. Most of the moorings in the harbor were empty because lobstermen had left at dawn, as usual, and a couple of gulls picked at dried fish skeletons stuck to the tarmac.

I walked into my office and groaned. My "to-do" list on the whiteboard reminded me of all the work I'd left behind. There were grad students' research papers to read, two of my own to revise, a grant proposal to review, and people I needed to e-mail or call. Most pressing was the Haida Gwaii UN report.

I'd only managed to go through half my e-mails before Harvey knocked on my door. Given the backlog she was trying to catch up on, it wasn't surprising Harvey was at work on the weekend. "Hey. You free to meet with Ted and me this afternoon at two? We can put together the report from the drafts we've written and add the sonde data. If you have a chance to look at the satellite photos, that would be great."

"I'll add it to my list."

"Know what you mean."

At one fifty-five, Harvey and Ted had already commandeered the easy chairs in our tiny third floor lounge. The view of the harbor and relative quiet made it a popular place for scientists to meet.

I fell into the empty chair. "How you doin'?"

"Not too bad," Harvey said. "Ted and I had a couple of days on you."

"How'd the thesis defense go?"

"Kathy's a star. She's got two post-doc offers already. I imagine she'll take the Scripps one. Maybe she'll end up back here to take my place if Seymour steps down in a couple of years, and I'm Chair."

I looked over my shoulder. "Better not say that too loud."

I looked at Ted. "And the grant proposal?"

"Got it in."

Harvey glanced at both of us. "Right. Mara, did you have time to look at the satellite data?"

"That NASA ocean color data archive is terrific," I said. "We might need to look at more images, but there was a pretty obvious phytoplankton bloom in the fertilized area right after the iron was added. We were lucky to have such clear skies."

"Something happened in that eddy," Ted said. "But we can't jump to conclusions. How long did the iron effect last and how large an area was impacted?"

The comment irritated me. I knew that.

Harvey nodded. "Good. We agree the satellite images indicate iron-stimulated phytoplankton growth. I did look at the eddy's time and spatial scales. The area is quite small and bloom-lifetime short—less than a week. It appears that only a fraction of the iron was taken up by algae in the eddy."

"How about the sonde data?" I asked.

"I don't see any fertilization effect in that transect," Ted said.

I thought he'd offer to e-mail the file so I could see this for myself, but he didn't.

"If the effect was that short-lived, maybe we missed it," Harvey said. "Mara, when will you have a chance to look at the phytoplankton? I've got the samples in my lab."

"Monday."

She stood. "Good. Looks like we've got a report that gives everyone something. The Haida will be pleased the iron had an impact, however little. The UN will be able to point to the small spatial and time scales and waste of all that iron. It's up to them to take it from there."

Harvey left to check on an errant machine. Ted and I walked down the stairs to the second floor.

I asked, "Think there's a future in geo-engineering?"

"I wouldn't buy any stock."

30

BETTY BUTTZ MET US AT THE BOTTOM OF THE STAIRS. Even in August, the retired oceanographer wore her usual plaid flannel shirt and army boots.

Ted offered his hand. "Dr. Buttz. Ted McKnight. So happy to finally meet you."

Five-foot-two Betty stepped back to look up at six-foot Ted. She shook his hand and stammered, "Young man, yes, thank you. Good you've come to MOI." Her wind-weathered face turned beet red.

Grumpy, brilliant, infamous Betty was blushing. I studied my feet so she wouldn't see my grin.

"You two see yesterday's *Gazette*?"

"We just got back. Still catching up," I said

"There's a photo of both of you and Harvey on the *Intrepid*. Caption says, 'Three MOI Scientists Investigate Iron Controversy in British Columbia Islands.'" Sounds like an interesting trip, the Haida and all."

"And challenging."

"I bet. You going to the meeting tonight? Penobscot River pollution and the Indians?"

"I am," Ted said.

Betty looked at me.

"Ah, actually, I've got a ton of work to do."

Betty's scowl would've scared a barracuda. "So you fly to the Pacific Ocean and work on ecology problems with Indians in Canada but don't do that here? What would your mother think?"

Betty didn't wait for an answer. She marched down the hall to her tiny office and slammed the door.

I paced around my office like a trapped lobster. While Betty's decree pissed me off, the comment about my mother stung. Betty and my parents were among Maine Oceanographic's founding scientists, and she knew them well. My mother was an avid environmentalist who gave talks about whales, overfishing, and the astonishing diversity of ocean life. Before 3-D movies, she helped people experience ninety-seven percent of the world's water in ways they never forgot.

There was a sharp knock on my door. Only one person announced his presence like that. I pulled the door open and stepped aside for Seymour Hull, MOI Biology Chair.

Seymour held up the *Spruce Harbor Gazette* and pointed his long finger at a photo. "At it again, Mara? A little publicity? How many times do I have to tell you to focus on your research and not distractions like this that get you nowhere? You could've written a grant proposal in the time you spent in British Columbia."

There was no point in reminding Seymour that the MOI Director, his boss, had recommended the three of us for the UN team. A two-bit scientist, Seymour was hired because he knew how to raise money. The professorship he held as chair honored my parents, and people regularly told him stories about the legendary Tusconis. That, plus his innate nastiness, made him resent me bitterly.

I'd been trying to not let Seymour goad me, so I pasted on a blank face. He threw the paper on the floor and marched out.

I picked up the *Gazette*. In the photo, Harvey, Ted, and I were on the aft deck of *Intrepid* the day before the fatal research trip. The MOI photographer caught us checking buoys we'd deploy to track increasing temperature in Maine's coastal waters.

Of course, we had no way to know that one of them would crush our friend and colleague the next afternoon.

I dropped the paper on my desk and locked my office door. With Betty's and Seymour's dressing-downs, I needed to talk with Homer.

As usual, the cavernous basement was loud and empty. MOI sold marine animals for research and teaching, and seawater pumped from the harbor raced through tanks that held squid, fish, crabs, and the like. The roar of the cascading water was deafening, air saturated with salt water, and floor covered with brine crust. I loved the place.

Homer nestled in his bottle at the bottom of his solo fifty-gallon tank. I lightly tapped on the window.

Homarus americanus, the American lobster, is mainly interested in preying on animals, including other lobster, and protecting themselves from the same. They don't give a damn about people, except when they're caught.

Homer was different. He wiggled out of the bottle, glided up to the window, and touched it with an antenna. I put my finger on the other side. He waved his swimmerets.

"Hungry, baby?"

Homer rotated his eyes toward the tank surface.

I dropped a piece of mussel into the tank. Homer snatched it in a microsecond. After three more large pieces, he appeared sated.

"I've got a problem I need to work out."

Homer settled on the bottom, walking legs splayed out, for a good sit.

I paced back and forth in front of Homer's tank. "On my trip, I worked with people called Haida. It's the first time I've done anything like that. It was hard, but really interesting. Now I'm back and have a ton of work to do. But there are native people in Maine who have difficult environmental issues to deal with, like the Haida. If I care about the environment and these communities, I should apply what I learned in Canada here. But that's going to take a lot of time. Seymour was just in my office telling me, as usual, that I should focus on my research. He's a jerk, but not all wrong on that. You remember how hard it was for me to get grant money in the spring."

I paused and peered into the tank. Homer was all eyes.

"Right before Seymour, Betty said my mother would be ashamed of me if I didn't get involved locally. You see the problem. Not sure what I should do."

Homer rotated his eyes up and toward the door.

"Yeah. Ted's going. I could ride with him. Won't hurt to see what this is."

Homer spun around. He liked Ted.

I went back upstairs, tapped on Ted's door, and stuck my head in. "Can you pick me up tonight for the meeting?"

The response was clipped. "I'm going with someone else, Mara. Sorry."

Back in my office, I fell into my chair. Ted had been standoffish at Angelo's house, cool when we talked about the satellite data, and cold just now. Come to think of it, he wasn't overly warm at the hospital. I'd assumed he was tired, but something was obviously wrong. I felt uneasy, but pushed that aside. Ted loved me. I'd explain how Swampy Point changed my feelings toward him. Then he'd be happy. We'd be happy together.

The meeting about the future of the Penobscot River took place in Spruce Harbor's town hall. The Penobscot was a big deal in Maine since it drained over a third of the state. I'd read a little about the meeting before I left. A tribal chief would debate someone from the Benoit administration. An attention-grabbing format. Governor Benoit's people weren't exactly known for their congeniality.

By the time I arrived, three-quarters of the metal foldup chairs in the first-floor meeting room were already occupied. Two podiums stood in the front. Nearby, clusters of people were already engaged in heated discussions. You could tell who was who. State officials wore suits and ties, and I didn't spot a single female. People from the Penobscot Nation and their supporters were more casually dressed, along the line of jeans and short-sleeved shirts. There were several women among them.

I found a seat in the back. In the third row, Ted chatted with a woman seated next to him. She didn't look familiar, but I could only see her from behind. Heads close together and gesturing toward the podiums, they seemed to know each other well. The woman apparently said something funny because Ted threw back his head and laughed. Unease pricked at me. I wanted to march down and find out who she was.

A man walked up to the front of the room.

"It's terrific to see such a good turnout on a Saturday evening for this critical discussion. I'm Bill Grimm from WGMB Maine, moderator of tonight's debate." Grimm outlined the debate's schedule—opening remarks followed by questions from the audience.

Everyone settled down. Behind one podium, the governor's representative was dressed in a black suit, white shirt, and red tie. He ran a forefinger under the neck of his collar and rotated his head back and forth. The speaker for the Penobscot Nation was thirtyish, athletic, and tall with black wavy hair. His wore a light-blue short-sleeved oxford shirt and a blue tie, and scanned the audience with a smile.

Ted's female friend whispered something to him. I'd always found people who talked during presentations extremely irritating.

Red-tie was named Fred Baxter. Fred jumped right in. "You need to understand that the issue in this federal case *isn't* just water quality of the Penobscot River." He swept a meaty hand across the room. "If the Indian Nation wins, hardly any of you'll have access to the river. Tribal victory means nothing less than exclusion of non-tribal people. As you know, the Penobscot is beloved by fishermen, canoeists, and kayakers. I'll bet some of you boat and fish. Think about losing access to that magnificent river."

As Grimm introduced Peter Miller, I watched Baxter. Grinning, he looked pleased with himself. I bet he'd never boated the Penobscot, never mind fished it.

Miller thanked the audience for attending the debate. He said, "The Penobscot River was named by native peoples who've lived in its valley for over five thousand years. We don't want to restrict access to this river. That is not our way. Our goal is to protect traditional fishing rights. For more than a century, our river has been contaminated by waste from pulp and paper plants and domestic wastewater. Since the mid-eighties, water quality has been so bad tribal members can only eat small amounts of fish. Maine must adapt tighter standards to protect sustenance fishing rights of the Penobscot Nation Indian tribe."

When Grimm asked for questions from the floor, people lined up behind the microphones.

"Why should the EPA have control over the river?"

"Who is going to pay for the cleanup?"

"You said sustenance fishing. What fish are you talking about?"

At the end of the meeting, Bill Grimm thanked the speakers and the audience. I walked toward the exit and glanced back. Ted's companion was young and very pretty. Her blond hair was cut in a cute pixie that complemented a pert nose, blue eyes, and petite figure she showed off with tight white pants and a crimson camisole.

Outside, Ted and the young lady were so engaged in conversation, they walked right by me. I was about to run up from behind when he placed a hand on her shoulder.

31

I PULLED UP TO MY HOUSE, SHUT OFF THE CAR, AND RESTED my head against the steering wheel. On the way home, my emotions had run back and forth between anger, self-blame, and worry. I hardly remembered driving.

It was hard to believe Ted would claim he wanted to marry me, and go out on a date a couple of days later. Of course, I knew nothing about the pert blond. Maybe she was just a friend. Maybe I was blowing what I saw way out of proportion.

Maybe, maybe. Only one way to find out. Talk to Ted. Tomorrow was Sunday. I'd show up on his doorstep. Tell him what happened at Swampy Point. How I'd changed. That I wanted to be with him. How great it would be.

The Neap Tide restaurant at eight on a Sunday morning was busier than I expected. Like a lineup of rowdy gulls, half a dozen fishermen at the counter squawked about quotas and poor catches. Scientists I recognized leaned over Sunday papers spread out before them, oblivious of shipmates who peered at checkers and dominos at adjacent tables. People who looked like tourists sipped coffee and took in the scene. There was an empty table in the back corner. I plopped into the chair and ran my fingers through tangled hair.

Sally slid an oversized mug across the table and filled it with steaming coffee. She stood back and put a hand on her ample hip. "Mornin', Mara. Have to say you look like crap."

I grabbed the cup. "Bad night. How 'bout some toast and a fried egg?"

"Over easy?"

"That'd be good. Thanks."

I drank the coffee quickly and walked up to the counter for a refill. On the way back, I passed a couple leaning so close to each other their foreheads touched. From my corner, I tortured myself and watched them. She reached over and caressed his cheek, and he kissed her hand. Unaware of anyone else in the noisy room, they were in their own perfect world. Ted and I could've been like that if I'd let it happen. If I could only explain how I'd changed, we still could be.

Ted lived ten miles inland in a charming old cottage. I'd visited often for dinner and overnights. The drive west from the coast took me through open farmland, dense forests, lakes, and ponds. Usually, I was on the lookout for wildflowers in bloom, eagle nests on ponds, loons on the big lakes. Today, I practiced what I would say, and worried about Ted's response.

If a moose had crossed the road, I probably would have missed it.

I parked at the bottom of Ted's driveway and walked up the hill. An unfamiliar station wagon was parked near the house.

Ted stepped out the front door, closed it behind him, and met me halfway. Barefoot, he wore faded three-button fly jeans and a white T-shirt that showed off a flat belly and toned muscles. I wanted to run up to him, be wrapped in a bear hug, and know his early morning scent.

He crossed his arms. "Did I miss something?"

"What do you mean?"

"I didn't know you were coming."

"Didn't know I needed an invitation. I wanted to, um, talk with you."

He gestured toward a picnic table on the back lawn. We'd last sat there on a warm July day, drinking beer and laughing at antics of grad students playing volleyball.

We slid onto opposite benches. I glanced at the car and raised an eyebrow.

"It's Diana's."

"Who is—?"

"Daughter of my parents' closest friends."

I tipped my head.

"She's thinking of transferring to UMaine, Orono, and has an appointment there tomorrow. I invited her to stay for a few days."

I must have looked skeptical because he added, "For god's sake, Mara. I'm fifteen years older than she is."

"Ted, what's going on?"

"You mean with us?"

"With us. Yes, of course."

He studied his hands and looked up at me, eyes blue as Maine waters on a calm spring day. "When we were waiting in the hospital, I had lots of time to think. I realized it then."

"What? Realized what?"

"The drama. What it does to me."

"Drama?"

"Everything that happened in Haida Gwaii. You nearly got swept into the open ocean in your kayak and fell off a ship's stern. Then you were kidnapped and attacked by a bear. We didn't know what happened to you for days. It was horrible."

I slid my hand across the table in his direction. He glanced at it.

"I'm really sorry, Ted. Most of that wasn't my fault, though."

Ted's face was pale. I hadn't noticed the dark circles under his eyes.

"I'm not saying it's all your fault. The drama follows you around."

Angelo had said the same the previous day. "Guess I get that."

"It's not the only thing, though."

My stomach clenched.

Elbows on the table, he rested his chin on his fists. "You say you love me, but it sure doesn't seem like it. I try to be close. You push me away. That really hurts, and I've had it."

My eyes tightened. I blinked back tears and pulled back my hand. "So you want to end, um, what we have?"

"Before it gets worse. You're a terrific colleague, Mara. I don't want anything to get in the way of that."

I grabbed the bench, sat tall, and tipped up my chin. "Me neither." Swinging my legs over the seat, I pushed myself to standing.

Ted cleared his throat and stood. "Mara, was there something you wanted to tell me?"

"What? Um, just something I realized back in Haida Gwaii. I'd like to talk about it sometime, but not now.

"That's it, then. See you at work tomorrow."

Marching down the hill, I waved a hand over my head. "See you tomorrow."

I drove down the road a ways, and pulled over. Gripping the steering wheel, I shook it so hard the car rocked, cradled the wheel, and sobbed. Spent, I took a slug from my water bottle and stumbled into the August heat. A path on the other side of the road cut through a forest. I stepped into the gentle shade of maples and beeches and followed the path. With only a chattering squirrel for company, I was alone and felt it.

On my way to Ted's house, I'd pretended my fears about his distant behavior were misplaced. When Ted understood I'd changed, he'd be elated. Amazing how I'd refused to acknowledge the obvious. Ted was distant in the hospital, more so at

Angelo's house, and curt when we discussed the satellite data. Clear signs that something was very wrong.

I headed back to the car, unsure where to go or what to do. Six months ago, I would've driven to my office, buried myself in work, and told myself to suck it up. That was before I understood that people closest to me wanted to help—and I needed it.

I called Angelo. He asked me to come right over.

I found him on the patio with the Sunday paper. A breeze off the water ruffled his hair, snow-white in the morning sun. I tousled the curls and kissed his cheek.

"Good morning, dear. What can I get you? Coffee? Something cold?"

"A cold drink would be terrific."

I leaned over the newspaper and scanned the headlines of the *Portland Times* while he was gone. Fishermen were complaining that record catches had forced prices down. International news remained bad. Angelo returned with a frosty glass tinkling with ice.

"Italian soda. Lemon."

"Perfect." I took a sip and nodded at the paper. "There's a piece about a mass grave in Africa. Compared to that, my worries are pretty trivial."

"We're very lucky to live in our country, this town. But that doesn't mean we don't hurt."

A couple of tears rolled down my cheeks. I fell into a deck chair.

He handed me a white handkerchief. "Take your time and tell me about it."

I dabbed my cheek and blew my nose. "It's Ted. He, um, just wants to be colleagues."

Angelo put a hand to his heart. "I am sorry to hear that. He's a fine young man."

I sniffed and dabbed my nose. "The irony is I'd just realized how much I cared. That I wanted to, ah, commit."

Angelo tipped his head and held up his palms. "Explain."

"Before we went to Haida Gwaii I was hesitant. Like I'd be trapped. I wanted to talk to Ted about it. You know, explain, when we were there. With all that happened, I never did."

He smiled.

"What?"

"You sound like your mother."

"But she and Dad—they were so close."

"That was later. When they first met, Bridget was hot and cold. Nervous about commitment. Drove Carlos crazy. I worried I'd made a mistake introducing them."

My mother anxious about being with my father? Impossible to imagine.

"But Mom and Dad were perfect for each other."

"Bridget Shea was fiercely independent. She was afraid of losing that. You're a lot like her, Mara."

"So what happened? Why did she change?"

"It took a shock. Carlos was in a train accident, but he wasn't hurt. Bridget realized how much she loved your dad when she almost lost him."

Not so different from my own jolt about Ted.

"I didn't know any of that."

"It happened years before you were born."

I sipped my drink. "I'm at loose ends. Not sure what to do."

"Something that makes you happy. Try to not dwell on what's happened. At work, be yourself. You never know, Ted might change his mind."

An hour later, I launched my kayak from the beach in front of my house. Water temperature in the sixties, wind light, sky cloudless. A perfect day to paddle. I took quick, short strokes until my arms screamed, and didn't think about my destination until I was halfway there. The boat pointed right at Cove Island, Ted's favorite.

To change direction, I swept the paddle in a half circle, pulled back, glided to a stop. I didn't need to avoid Cove because Ted liked it. A paddle sweep on the opposite side returned the kayak to my original heading. I waited for an approaching motorboat to pass before moving forward.

Connor waved his Boston Red Sox cap, cut the motor on his wooden fishing dory, and slid alongside. As usual, *Irish Wake's* green hull looked newly painted and cream interior spotless.

"Why're you out here alone? Where's Ted?"

I pushed off the hull and looked up at him. "We've, ah, split up."

Connor pressed his lips together and shook his head. "Really sorry ta hear that."

I ran a hand through the water and watched the ripples as they faded. "Yeah."

"Mara, you've got the Irish's green eyes 'n chestnut hair 'n Gina Lola what's-it Italian good looks. The man's a fool."

"Gina Lollobrigida."

"She's the one."

I gave Connor a half-hearted grin. He was studying me intently. "What?" I asked.

"I get the idea something happened to you back at that Haida Gwaii place. Something important about you here." He placed his hand over his heart.

This wasn't the first time Connor had peeked into my soul. "You're right. I'm still trying to work it out, but it has to do with being grateful for love and friendship. I'm so lucky to have Harvey, you, Angelo, even Ted, in my life. Maybe I need to worry less about work and pay more attention to each of you.

He handed me his baseball cap. "Here."

I pulled it on. "Isn't this your favorite cap?"

"The best ship's friendship, Mara. The cap'll remind you how much we love you."

He started his motor and backed up. I waved the hat and with quick, fast strokes, flew toward Cove Island.

ACKNOWLEDGMENTS

Special thanks go to Connie Berry, Lynn Denley-Bussard, Judy Copek, and Mary Woodbury, whose comments fundamentally changed this book. Kirsten Allen and my agent Dawn Dowdle edited an early version. President of Hampshire College Jonathan Lash proposed Haida Gwaii as the setting for this story. The Wilfrid Laurier University Press granted permission to use quotes from *This Woman in Particular: Contexts for the Biographical Image of Emily Carr* by Stephanie Kirkwood Walker. "A Buddhist Concept of Nature" by the Dalai Lama can be seen at www.dalailama.com, and quotes for Teilhard de Chardin at the American Teilhard Association site (www.teilharddechardin.org/index.php/biography). Sarah Blair helped with the book cover and map design and Nicolle Hirschfeld with the scuba scene. I am delighted to be working with the good folks at Maine Authors Publishing, who recommended the excellent editor Katherine Mayfield. Finally, I thank my husband, John Briggs, for his ongoing patience and support.

Stay tuned for the next
Mara Tusconi Mystery *expected June 2018*

HONOR THE LOBSTERS' SEA

NATURE FAVORS LOOPS, TWISTS, AND TURNS. ALL CORners and straight lines, Gordy's mussel aquaculture raft looked like an oversized soggy matchbox floating out there off Spruce Harbor.

From my office window at the Maine Oceanographic Institute I eyed the thing through binoculars. Yup, there it was, bobbing up and down like it'd been for weeks. Damn. Back-to-back fall research cruises had left me zero free time. Still, I should've checked out my cousin's pet project.

Gordy had saved my life when a madman tried to dump me into icy Maine waters last spring. I owed him big time.

I powered off my computer, refused to look at the to-do list on my whiteboard, and pulled the office door shut behind me. Harvey Allison, brilliant marine chemist and my best friend, stopped me halfway down the science building's stairs. Her layered blonde bob kissed the collar of a lab coat that would've made Mr. Clean proud.

As usual, my ponytail had transformed itself into an unruly mess. I tucked wayward locks of auburn hair behind my ear. "What's up, Harve?"

Harvey rolled her shoulders. "Ugh, that's sore. I'm back up to the lab for another bout with the auto-analyzer." She tipped her head to the side. "Mara, you look happier than I've seen you in weeks."

We blinked at each other for a few awkward seconds. Harvey's half-brother Ted, also an MOI scientist, had broken off our relationship a month earlier. She didn't want to pry back then—or now.

I squeezed Harvey's hand. "I'm practicing gratitude—and going for a paddle."

"Kayaking always puts you in a good mood. But gratitude practice? Sounds way too touchy-feely for you," she said.

"Invite me for dinner. I'll explain. Surviving being left for dead in that B.C. rainforest taught me something."

"Now I'm really curious," she said. "You're on."

I slid into my sea kayak, pushed off from the public boat launch, and glided by the stern of MOI's research vessel *Intrepid*. Two days earlier and dozens of miles offshore, I'd watched our half-ton temperature buoys dangle from the ship's massive A-frame off the rear deck. Now the hinged metal frame was pulled toward the bow like a mighty mousetrap ready to spring. I hurried by.

Humming, I paddled quickly as my seventeen-foot-long, twenty-inch-wide sea kayak sliced through the water like an arrow. Not bad for a thirty-one-year-old who spent way too much time in front of her computer. My spirits always soar when I'm on the water, but today they skyrocketed. September is my favorite month on the Maine coast. The water's plenty warm for paddling and days perfect for a hike. Along the roads and on the hills, maple and oak leaves tipped with red and gold foretell a fall riot of color.

I wondered what Harvey thought about a revelation so out of character for get-up-and-go me. I hadn't told her—or even Angelo, my godfather and only family—that I'd been meditating on the word "gratitude" as I picked my way along the beach in front of my house or leaned against the granite boulder on top of Spruce Harbor hill to take in the sunset. The practice grew out of a harrowing event. A month earlier, I'd been kidnapped and left for dead in an archipelago called Haida Gwaii way out in the Pacific Ocean off Vancouver. After I'd figured out how to make a fire, keep warm, and cook mussels, my panic subsided.

I felt instead that I was not alone. Something or someone was watching over me.

As a scientist who believes every so-called mystical experience has a physical explanation, the Haida Gwaii experience was unnerving. So I'd translated what happened into something I could understand. National Institute of Health research shows that gratitude fostered feelings of wellbeing and connectedness. I had put aside my anger and hurt toward Ted and focused instead on my good fortune—Angelo, Harvey, Gordy, a career I was passionate about.

The tactic was succeeding. My ire toward Ted for dumping me had made working on our shared research projects awkward, to say the least. When I admitted to myself that I, not Ted, was to blame because commitment scared the crap out of me, the anger turned inward. Finally, I let that go as well and took each day as it came. A few days earlier, I'd even dropped by Ted's office to go over some water temperature data. The exchange had gone well.

Thank goodness angst was a thing of the past.

Gordy had anchored his raft between two islands where fast-flowing current carried an abundance of microscopic plankton to the filter-feeding mussels. The kayak slid to a stop just as the tide turned slack. Up close, Gordy's contraption was pretty impressive. Fifty-odd-foot square with a steel I-beam frame, wooden cross-members, and oversized polyethylene floats, the thing could easily weather a major blow.

I circled the raft a few times, looking for a way to explore beneath the platform. That's where the excitement was—for a marine ecologist, that is. I had all sorts of questions. What were the mussels attached to? Were they big or small? How many were there?

One place looked as good as another to begin my investigation. So I maneuvered my boat parallel with the raft and secured the paddle under my deck bungee. Still in the kayak, I leaned over and peered into the gloom below the platform. Slits of light from above danced across row after row of swaying rope that looked creepily alive. The rope was attached to the underside of the platform, and I could just make out a foot of exposed line before it plunged down into the water out of sight. Seawater sloshed over mussels the size of my fist that encased the exposed rope. Hand over hand, I traveled down one side of the raft, stopped at intervals, flattened myself across my deck, and peered into the gloom for a better look. Water slapped against the platform—and my face.

At the corner I straightened up, ran a hand across my eyes, patted the raft, and said aloud, "Gotta give it to you, Gordy, this is one wicked piece of engineering."

I really, really wanted to examine the mussels. Maybe they were bigger on the outside edge because they grew more quickly there with better access to seawater. Or maybe the inner ones were fouled with barnacles or invasive sea squirts—not so good for an aquaculture business. I blinked at the sky. There'd be more light on the opposite western side. I tried the same flatten, crank my neck, squint routine over there but still could see squat.

I pushed back from the raft to consider a different maneuver. "Time for a frontal attack," I announced to gulls overhead. A couple of quick strokes sent me bow first under the platform. The skinny boat slipped between two rows of drop lines. Leaning over the front of my vessel, I plowed further in. Surrounded by a tapestry of dangling, dancing mussel-rope, I closed my eyes and let over senses take over. Pop, slosh, and gurgle enhanced the slap-slap-slap melody. Sharp, briny perfume tickled my nose, sea life exhaling.

I reached out to gauge the thickness of mussel growth. Stacked atop one another, they completely surrounded the lines, so many that my two encircled hands didn't come close to touching. Hardly any barnacles or other encrusting critter disfigured the mussel monopoly.

Just beyond the tip of my bow, something out of place bobbed in the water. Squinting, I tried to make out what it was. An errant lobster buoy? Cast-off bucket? The bulky object didn't belong in the middle of a mussel farm, that was for sure. Gordy would want it out of there. I released the paddle from its bungee hold, reached out, and tapped the object. It felt bulky, big. I pushed harder. The thing submerged out of sight. Peering into the murk, I scanned the spot where it'd been. Where was the goddamn thing?

Suddenly, like a sea monster from the depths, the sunken mystery bobbed straight up out of the water. Its eyes held mine for a moment before the head slipped back down into the black.

My scream ricocheted off the platform into an uncaring sea.